**"Did the**

"Is that wh _____ _____ about your past?"
Ginny's voice broke.

"No, they did not. I could have stayed. I just didn't
think it would be fair to the kids. The gossip
would have ruined my attempt to teach
them anything."

"How noble. Apparently it was all right to take a
job caring for my child. Was it also all right to
make love to me without telling me anything?"

"Ginny, I did nothing wrong." Mitch moved
toward her.

"Don't touch me."

His eyes became dull and his shoulders drooped.
"You want me to leave?"

"Yes." Her voice was almost inaudible. But Mitch
had no difficulty hearing her.

"I'll be out in an hour," he said sadly.

## ABOUT THE AUTHOR

Arizona author Vicki Lewis Thompson makes no bones about the fact that she completely sympathizes with the heroine of *Critical Moves*. "I know exactly how Ginny feels watching her son being pummeled on the wrestling mat. I remember watching my own son being tackled by an enormous guy on the football field. It was awful." Vicki lives in Tucson with her husband, Larry. The couple's two children are now in their early twenties.

## Books by Vicki Lewis Thompson

### HARLEQUIN SUPERROMANCE
211–BUTTERFLIES IN THE SUN
269–GOLDEN GIRL
326–SPARKS
389–CONNECTIONS

### HARLEQUIN TEMPTATION
240–BE MINE, VALENTINE
256–FULL COVERAGE
278–'TIS THE SEASON
288–FOREVER MINE, VALENTINE
344–YOUR PLACE OR MINE

Don't miss any of our special offers. Write to us at the following address for information on our newest releases.

Harlequin Reader Service
P.O. Box 1397, Buffalo, NY  14240
Canadian address: P.O. Box 603,
Fort Erie, Ont.  L2A 5X3

# Critical Moves

## VICKI LEWIS THOMPSON

# Harlequin Books

TORONTO • NEW YORK • LONDON
AMSTERDAM • PARIS • SYDNEY • HAMBURG
STOCKHOLM • ATHENS • TOKYO • MILAN
MADRID • WARSAW • BUDAPEST • AUCKLAND

Published April 1992

ISBN 0-373-70497-6

CRITICAL MOVES

For Robyn Carr, friend and catalyst

# CHAPTER ONE

"UGH." Ginny winced as Arnold's opponent threw him to the mat with a solid thud. Thank God for protective helmets. The boys squirmed, arms and legs braided together, as the encouragement of the sparse crowd echoed in the cavernous gym. A child bounded up the bleachers, shaking Ginny's seat, but her attention remained on the struggle below.

The other kid pressed Arnold's face against the blue mat and Ginny's hand went to her mouth. His braces! She imagined the metal grinding into Arnold's lip. A blond man in gym shorts and a tank top leaped to his feet, shouting something, and Arnold twisted away from the hold. Ginny strained to see if the boy was bleeding, but nothing showed. The grappling continued, punctuated with blasts from the referee's whistle. Arnold hit the mat again and Ginny groaned.

A tightly permed, overweight woman sitting one level below her on the bleachers turned around. "First time?"

Ginny nodded without taking her gaze from the yellow-banded circle where the boys writhed, their bodies slick with sweat. Arnold was panting desperately. Ginny didn't understand wrestling, but she did understand that her son was losing. No wonder. The boys weighed about the same, but so might an Afghan hound and a bulldog.

She hated this, hated watching Arnold being humiliated in an arena where he did not belong. Nobody here cared that he'd played first-chair clarinet in the eighth grade concert band this past year or that he'd written poems that had made her cry. All that mattered in this gym were toned muscles, coordination, aggression—all qualities Arnold had formerly disdained.

No more. Not since Billy Herman—middle-school jock, trumpet player and ex-best friend—had lured him into a fight after the eighth grade awards ceremonies. Billy had expected the plaque for top band student in addition to his football award. Instead, Arnold had won the band's top honor. Their consequent grappling in the cafeteria had cost Arnold his plaque and Billy his football award.

Arnold was embarrassed, not because a teacher had caught him fighting, but because half the school saw him losing. Afterward, the last week of school had been hell, Ginny knew, and she suspected that Billy had taunted Arnold mercilessly. Soon after eighth grade graduation, Arnold had shown her a Seattle parks and recreation pamphlet and announced he was signing up for the summer wrestling program offered at a high school halfway across town. He'd vowed that someday he'd get even with Billy Herman, and he intended to prepare himself.

Ginny had argued against the use of physical force, labeling it barbaric. She'd pointed out that Arnold was too intelligent to need to prove himself with some macho sport. But nothing she'd said had changed his mind. His latest obsession had derailed her whole image of him. She'd assumed that her careful mothering had produced an artistic, sensitive boy who would skip the crass posturing of most teenagers and move directly into confident adulthood.

Arnold crashed to the mat for the third time, and Ginny covered her face with both hands.

"He'll get better," the woman in front of her said.

Ginny uncovered her face and leaned toward the woman. "It's so rough. Don't you worry about injuries?"

The woman made a half turn on the bleachers. "I'm a mother. Sure I do. But I'm impressed with this coach. He really cares a lot about the boys, and my David's learned so much already."

"That's good," Ginny said, dividing her attention as best she could between the informative woman and Arnold's predicament on the mat.

"Of course he's a teacher, a little older than some of the college kids they usually hire for the summer," the woman continued. "He's in the science department here at Westwood, I think. I can't imagine why he's not coaching at school, too, as good as he is at it. I'll bet you'll see a big improvement in your son by the end of the season."

Ginny had no idea how to respond, so she nodded vaguely and dropped eye contact with the woman, who seemed satisfied with the exchange and turned around. Ginny didn't want Arnold to get any better. She wanted him to quit. She hated sitting here in agony while some kid with pushier hormones squashed her son to the mat.

Arnold didn't escape from the final assault, and the match ended. As the referee held up the stocky kid's arm to signify his victory, Ginny forced herself to look straight at Arnold and give him an I-love-you-anyway smile. He wasn't paying any attention to her.

Instead, he was focusing on the man who had shouted instructions to him during the match. The man balanced a clipboard on one knee and had a whistle around his neck. The coach, Ginny guessed. Mitch. Arnold had mentioned his name several times in the past two weeks. The coach said something Ginny couldn't hear, and Arnold grinned, his braces shining. *Grinned*. Ginny couldn't believe it. Arnold had given up smiling since the braces went on last fall. And he'd never taken defeat gracefully in his life.

Both boys left for the locker room and Ginny watched them walk away, Mutt and Jeff. The short kid's bare back undulated with honest-to-goodness muscle, and his wrestling trunks stretched tight across his behind. Arnold's shoulder blades jutted out like sprouting angel wings and his trunks hung loosely from his narrow hips. She'd never thought much about his build before, but then she'd never imagined him in a place like this, displaying his gangly frame, his thin arms and bony knees to the world.

Shame on me, she thought. She was uncomfortable because her kid hadn't performed well and didn't look like the others on the team. Judging from his cheerful expression as he'd left the floor, Arnold had taken this far better than she. This coach, Mitch whoever-he-was, must be pretty good.

Ginny glanced at the coach. The next wrestler on the team crouched in front of him and listened intently as the coach gave him last minute instructions and a quick clasp of hands for good luck. As the match began, Ginny observed the coach's reactions to gauge if he did, in fact, care about these boys. Arnold had been showing signs of impending hero worship, and Ginny needed to know what sort of hero her son worshipped.

Fortunately for her, the guy was an open book. Any fool would know from the intensity of his expression and the forward tilt of his body that he loved his work. He was not still for a moment. He scribbled on his clipboard, jumped to his feet to argue a referee's call and shouted encouragement to the boy on the mat. He wrestled every second of the match along with the kids. She supposed that if boys had to do this sort of thing, they were lucky to have a coach who devoted himself both to them and the sport. But she didn't want Arnold to love wrestling, at least not for more than a summer. She was counting on this being a passing phase.

Arnold returned, dressed in jeans and a T-shirt, his dark, curly hair still wet from the shower. He carried the prized gym bag he'd begged her to buy, denying her accusation that he was falling for slick marketing techniques. He'd asked her to quit worrying about marketing for five minutes, which had aroused her guilt about how her career cheated Arnold of valuable time with her. She'd bought the bag.

Arnold climbed the bleachers to sit next to her and plopped down the gym bag with studied nonchalance. "What'd you think?" he asked.

She looked into his eyes, fringed with long, dark lashes that girls his age would kill for. "I, um, think you did great for your first time, and everything."

"Mitch said I was excellent." He flashed the compliment the way he used to flash A's on his report card. Then he turned his attention to the action below, as if Mitch's evaluation ended the discussion.

"Well, you *were* excellent," Ginny amended, upping the quality of her praise to match the coach's. "That kid had a tough time with you. He knew he was in a match, all right."

"I think so, too," Arnold said, concentrating on the pair of wrestlers below. "Just wait'll next time. I'll cream the guy. Hey, that's some hammerlock," he said, leaning forward in perfect imitation of the blond man below them. "He'll never get out of—damn, he did! I gotta have Mitch show me how to do that."

Ginny noticed the "damn" but let it slide. This was exactly what she was afraid of—this degeneration into locker-room talk and undue emphasis on the importance of physical prowess.

"When is the next meet?" she asked.

"Next Monday," he mumbled. "Wow, check it out! He's pinned the S.O.B."

"Arnold, I'd rather you didn't use—"

"Sorry, Mom," Arnold said absently without taking his eyes off the mat. "It's over! What technique. Did you see that?" he asked, turning to her with an eagerness that made her heart sink. "Pretty impressive, huh?"

She didn't have the heart to burst his balloon by admitting that she found the whole experience awful. "Yes, pretty impressive. Listen, can we get a schedule of the meets or something? I'll need to know, so I don't have conflicts. Fortunately I don't have any appointments Monday night."

"Yeah, Mitch said he'd hand out schedules. There's only one more match tonight. I'll ask him after that."

"Could you ask him now? I was thinking we might leave."

"Leave? Aw, Mom. The last weight division's the most exciting. These guys are tanks. You'll love it. Besides, I have to support my teammates. Mitch said we gotta do that, so I can't leave now."

Ginny knew enough to tread carefully. "Supporting your teammates *is* important. Your coach is certainly right about that, but we have some business to take care of. I have to make those calls, Arnold, before it's too late at night. We must have another housekeeper by next week, and I—"

"Don't remind me," Arnold said, grimacing. "Some moose-faced battle-ax I'll bet, like old lady Widdle-Waddle."

"Mrs. *Waddell* wasn't so bad. You didn't give her a chance."

Arnold tensed. "I don't want to talk about her. You docked my allowance, so let's drop it, okay?"

"Just so we don't have a repeat of your performance with Mrs. Waddell."

"Don't worry. I can't afford it. Anyway, why can't we try another college girl? Bambi was cool."

"Let's not discuss Bambi, either," Ginny said as her stomach tightened.

"Hey, Bambi only thought, since I'll be in high school this year, that I ought to at least *taste* some beer. She didn't want me to be some inexperienced nerd who doesn't know anything. Which I'm gonna be if you keep hiring those old ladies who treat me like a kid, like I need a baby-sitter or something."

Ginny sighed. They'd been arguing about this since spring. Every summer she'd hired a live-in housekeeper. During the school year she could always piece together an arrangement that didn't require live-in help, but summers demanded that someone be there to drive Arnold to his activities and generally supervise his days. And when Ginny had to be out of town on business, the sitter was already in place.

Arnold hadn't bucked the system until this spring, when he'd complained about the type of women Ginny usually hired—older women, often widows, whose own children were grown and who wanted to earn some extra money. Ginny had brushed aside his complaints and hired Mrs. Waddell. After a week Mrs. Waddell had turned in her notice along with a lecture about the rude boy Ginny was raising.

Ginny had disciplined Arnold for his behavior, but privately she'd understood that at thirteen he probably had trouble relating to the Mrs. Waddells of the world. As an experiment, she'd hired Bambi, a cheerful honor student who came highly recommended. The beer incident had happened on Bambi's third day.

Even without the beer issue, Ginny probably would have let Bambi go. Arnold had seemed far too interested in Bambi's brisk little figure. Ginny had caught him lurking more than once by the bathroom door when Bambi was showering, his plan to accidentally bump into her towel-clad body painfully obvious.

"No more college girls," Ginny said more to herself than to Arnold.

"A college guy, then."

"I don't think so. We've got to have someone more mature, Arnold. When I'm away on business, I have to know that a seasoned hand is on the tiller."

"Oh, man, when you start talking like that I can smell another Mrs. Widdle-Waddle coming along. Why don't you just let me stay by myself? I know how to dial 911."

"Arnold, you're a good kid. A responsible kid."
*For your age, which is still only thirteen,* she added to
herself. "But I can't leave you alone when I'm out of
town. Apart from anything else, it's against the law."

"This is a depressing subject, Mom. Let's just watch
the match. Mitch says when I fill out, I'll be right up
with these guys. That one there's bigger than Billy
Herman."

"I never paid much attention to Billy's size," Ginny
said. *And I wish you hadn't, either.*

"Aw, come on, Mom. Billy was the biggest guy on
the eighth-grade football team. Everybody knows
that."

"So what?" Ginny challenged. "You're smarter,
and a better musician."

"Nobody cares about that, Mom."

"I do."

He regarded her with disdain. "You're my mother."
*Which makes me nobody,* she concluded silently.

"Mitch says I might want to start lifting weights,"
Arnold commented as he returned to watching the
match.

"Weights?" Ginny couldn't fathom it. A few
months ago she'd had a shy clarinet player for a son.
Now she apparently was the mother of a junior Hulk
Hogan in training. She gazed at the giants who had
locked arms and were circling the mat. Neither of
them stood much taller than Arnold, and perhaps
weren't much older, but there the resemblance ended.
These two weren't really boys anymore, she thought.
They were men, and they did remind her of Billy Herman. She glanced sideways at Arnold, almost fearing
that his transformation was taking place, time-lapse

photography style, as they spoke. But Arnold still looked like a boy.

And he still needed a mature person to watch after him this summer, and for the next two. Maybe, when he turned sixteen and could drive... Ginny hated to even think about that. Arnold driving. Arnold filling out. Arnold growing up. Tears pricked her eyes and she concentrated on the wrestlers until the moment of emotion passed. Arnold would disown her if she cried in public and embarrassed him.

She glanced at her watch. Not much chance she'd be able to make her calls tonight. Her leads weren't all that hot anyway. It was three weeks into the summer vacation and everybody registered with an agency had been snapped up by now. She'd pumped all the people she knew for names and had three unpromising possibilities to call. She couldn't really blame Arnold for driving away Mrs. Waddell; she hadn't been wild about the woman, either. She'd ignored her instincts and hired the old biddy just to get the job done. Now she'd have to go through the process all over again.

"Come on, Mom, let's go. I thought you were in a big hurry."

"Oh." She glanced up at Arnold standing beside her. "It's over?"

Arnold shook his head in disgust. "I can't believe you weren't even watching. I hope you at least pay attention when I'm out there."

"I most certainly do. With my heart in my mouth," she added as she gathered her purse and stood. "I'm just waiting for you to get smashed in the teeth, which would bash in your braces and possibly end your career on the clarinet, in case you hadn't thought of that."

Arnold flushed and glanced around. "Mom, don't talk about that now, okay?"

"Arnold, for heaven's sake. For the last time, there's nothing wimpy about playing the—"

"Mom!"

She held his gaze. So this was what the parenting books talked about: the pain when your kid clearly wishes he weren't your kid, at least for the moment. She'd imagined the bond between her and Arnold had rendered them immune to such breakdowns in communication. Even when Arnold had conspired to get rid of Mrs. Waddell, Ginny had agreed with him in spirit. "You'd better go get your schedule," she said.

He galloped down the bleachers, obviously eager to leave her. She watched him draw near his new idol with equal eagerness, and she felt cruelly displaced. Before she quite realized what she was doing, she'd negotiated the trip down the bleachers in her high heels and business suit and walked over to where Arnold was talking with his coach. "Excuse me," she said, sticking out her hand. "It's Mitch, isn't it? I'm Ginny Westerfelt, Arnold's mother. He talks about you all the time."

Beside her she felt Arnold cringe. No doubt he expected his mother to embarrass him, but Ginny merely wanted to know her enemy. "I think you're doing a fine job with the team," she continued, giving his hand a firm shake.

"You're a wrestling fan, I take it." His smile was open and uncomplicated. She returned it without thinking.

Arnold laughed. "My Mom? Are you kidding?"

Ginny shot him a warning look and he sobered immediately. She'd already established that she could be lethal to his reputation. "I don't know much about wrestling," she said, "but I like the way you handle the boys. You seem to really care about them," she added, borrowing the phrase she'd heard from the mother who had spoken to her during Arnold's match.

"Yeah, well, it's easy. They're great guys."

Ginny was impressed. This man knew how to field a compliment and return it while still managing to sound like one of the boys. She also realized he was quite good-looking, if you liked the jock type, which normally she didn't. Sun-bleached hair and a tan usually indicated to her that a man didn't spend much time on intellectual pursuits. A person would have to really work at maintaining a tan in Seattle. No matter, she needed to align herself with this coach and close the gap widening between her and Arnold.

"I wonder if I could ask you a favor," she said, and almost laughed as she imagined Arnold's inner frenzy.

"Sure."

She fingered the double rope of pearls around her neck. "It occurred to me that you may have contacts that I don't. I'm looking for someone, preferably over twenty-five and under forty, who could be my housekeeper for the summer. I thought you might know someone who's free to do that, maybe a person in the parks and recreation department. I pay well."

Arnold groaned. "Mom, this isn't—"

"A housekeeper?" The coach looked puzzled. "You mean like a maid or something?"

"No. I guess that's a misleading term. I really need someone for Arnold, to drive him to his activities and be there when I'm out of town on business. Of course,

I can also use help with the housework, but that's not my main concern.''

"I see. I take it you mean a live-in person.''

"Just for the summer,'' Ginny hastened to explain. "We usually manage fine once school starts. This isn't a long-term commitment or anything.''

"Hmm.'' The coach tapped his clipboard against his thigh.

"Nobody, right, Coach?'' Arnold said. "Good try, Mom. We'd better go.'' He started off across the floor.

"Arnold,'' Ginny called. "Wait a—''

"How about me?'' the coach asked.

Arnold halted in midstride and Ginny's gaze swung back to the coach. "You?'' She hadn't expected this. The prospect brought a quickening of her pulse. This jock in her house? "Well, I hadn't meant you, really,'' she fumbled. "I just thought you might know someone.'' *Not someone like you, someone less tan, less blond, less . . . less male.*

"This job for parks and recreation is only part-time, and I get a little bored when I'm not working, to tell the truth,'' the coach said. "I like Arnold and furthermore I fit your criteria. I'm thirty-two years old, single, and I could sublet my apartment for the summer.''

Arnold returned, his face glowing. "You could do it? Really?''

"Don't see why not.''

"Well . . .'' Ginny thought quickly. Arnold's new hero living under the same roof could go one of two ways. Either Arnold would become a complete muscle-brain or he'd be overexposed to the jock's life and tire of it. Maybe she should take that gamble.

Arnold displayed no reservations. "Hey, that would be cool, Mom! Mitch could show me some of those special wrestling moves we've talked about, and we could start weight training, and—"

"Excuse me," Ginny interrupted. "But before we settle this one way or the other, there are a few things I need to know."

"Shoot."

"Your last name, for one thing."

He smiled. "Adamson. Mitch Adamson."

"And you're a high school science teacher?"

"Right. At Westwood."

"Look, Mitch, I don't mean this in any derogatory way, but I'll need references before I can make a final decision."

"Mom!" Arnold flushed. "The guy's my coach!"

"No, your mom's right," Mitch said. "She shouldn't hire somebody for a job like this without checking them out first." Mitch consulted his watch, the face of which was turned to the inside of his wrist. "Give me twenty minutes to get home, and I'll call you with a list of people you can contact. Anything else?"

"I—I guess not." She tried to think of other possible roadblocks. "Except that I'd need you by this weekend, and you may not be prepared to move that fast."

Mitch nodded. "No problem. I travel light."

"Okay," she said slowly, aware that beside her Arnold was holding his breath. "Then I'll talk to you shortly," she said, and Arnold sighed.

"And thanks for the offer," Ginny added. She shook hands with Mitch again and looked into his eyes. They were gray, she noted, and...interested. For the first time she acknowledged an awareness that had been present ever since Mitch had suggested himself for the job. He might want to alleviate boredom, and he seemed to like Arnold, but he had another reason. Ginny was that other reason.

The realization made her alert, but not displeased. Nothing would come of it, of course, because they wouldn't see that much of each other. Whenever she was home on summer nights, she encouraged her housekeepers to take the evening off. That way she could ask that they not socialize when she was out of town and they were in sole charge of Arnold. With those good looks and obvious supply of energy, Mitch probably maintained an active social life. Once he discovered the strictness of her personal code of conduct, he'd probably lose that gleam of interest that now flickered in his eyes.

"I think this will work out well for everyone," Mitch said, releasing her hand.

Ginny refused to commit herself until she had checked his references. If anyone said the slightest thing that made her nervous about his taking care of Mitch, she would cancel her offer. "Perhaps it will," she said with a smile.

Once she and Arnold had moved out of earshot, Arnold let her have it. "I can't believe you gave him the third degree. Talk about major embarrassment. He tries to do us a favor and you act like he's some criminal or something."

"I can't expect you to understand," she said as they stepped into the cool night air. "I don't know Mitch Adamson at all, and we're proposing to bring him into our home. I have to be sure he checks out."

"Mom, the guy's a teacher, and during the summer he works for the parks and recreation department. How much more do you need?"

"More, Arnold." She unlocked the passenger door of their cream-colored Volvo. "I'm sure your Mr. Adamson is of sterling character, but I want somebody else, somebody he's worked for, to tell me that."

"If he takes the job, are you gonna, like, order him around and stuff? Because if you are, I don't want any part of this."

She paused and gazed at her son. Her beloved, and at the moment thoroughly exasperating son. "Do you think I order people around?" she asked.

"Some people. Like Bambi."

Ginny sighed. "Bambi lacked judgment. If Mitch Adamson is as wonderful as you seem to think, we won't have the same sort of problems with him as we had with Bambi, and I won't need to 'order people around' as you put it."

"I hope not."

"Arnold, all I care about in this world is keeping you safe."

His expression softened. "I know that, Mom. But sometimes . . ."

"I want you safe because I love you, Arnold."

"Yeah," he said softly. "I know." He got into the car. "We'd better go home or we'll miss his call."

MITCH HADN'T ACTED on impulse in a long time, three years to be exact, and he hoped he wouldn't regret it now. He paged through his address book and made some notes before calling Ginny Westerfelt. He was doing this mainly for the kid, he told himself, who seemed to be facing the journey into manhood without a map or a compass. Arnold didn't seem to have the first idea of what being a man was all about.

But to be honest, and Mitch was usually pretty honest with himself, Ginny Westerfelt had figured into his impulse, too. Arnold had told him that she owned her own marketing research company, that she'd built it from scratch after Arnold's father died five years ago. With that information and knowing how competitive the marketing research field could be, he'd somehow expected a different sort of woman. Taller, maybe, and harder around the edges. Instead, she was diminutive, with the appealing physique of a gymnast. Even her short, blond hair, feathery and touchable, belied her career-woman image. Only her clothes fit the picture—a silk suit in business beige, black patent heels and a string of pearls.

Dressed more casually, Ginny would have been the type he'd have gravitated to at parties, back in the days when he'd attended parties. Something about her, a sweetness and vulnerability, brought out every protective instinct he possessed. Ginny and her son made a touching pair—Ginny with her struggle to be both mother and father to this boy, and Arnold with his struggle to become a man. They might not realize it yet, but they needed Mitch.

Maybe he needed them, too. Maybe he'd been a loner long enough. He looked over the list of references he'd compiled—his current principal at Westwood, the foreman at the canning factory, and Jack Granger, his principal in Cedarville. Good old Jack had been churning out excellent references for three years now. If he had chosen to do otherwise . . . but he hadn't. Someday Mitch would go back to Idaho and thank Jack, maybe take him and Elaine out to dinner. Not yet, though. Three years wasn't long enough for people to forget.

Mitch picked up his clipboard and flipped to the page listing the phone numbers for his wrestling team. The boys had filled in the information themselves, and most of it was nearly unreadable. But not Arnold's. Mitch dialed the carefully written number. "Well, Arnold," he muttered as the phone began to ring, "maybe by the end of the summer you'll learn it's okay to scribble once in a while."

## CHAPTER TWO

AT MIDMORNING the following day, Ginny cradled the telephone receiver against her shoulder and twisted the cord around her index finger as she listened to Jack Granger, principal of Cedarville High, extol the virtues of his former teacher and wrestling coach. She tried to ignore the blinking buttons on the telephone; the receptionist was routing all calls to Maggie until Ginny had finished checking Mitch's references. Granger was the last and most long-winded of the three.

"All that's good to hear, Mr. Granger," she said during a space in the principal's monologue. Granger plunged on, and Ginny swiveled her desk chair to face the window.

Her fifteenth-floor view afforded little of interest this morning. Fog clung like lint in the crevices between the neighboring office buildings of downtown Seattle, obscuring Ginny's view of Puget Sound, a view for which she paid an exorbitant rent.

"He sounds like the perfect candidate, all right," Ginny said when Granger paused for a breath. "There's no need for you to put it in writing, though. The verbal recommendation is fine." As Granger slapped on another layer of praise for Mitch, she swiveled her chair back to face the room.

She'd chosen the decor with days like this in mind. Damp weather outpaced sunny skies in western Washington, so Ginny had counteracted the gloom with daffodil-colored walls and light-hued woods. Her sleek Scandinavian desk and the wall units housing her video equipment were oak. A large abstract tapestry in shades of yellow and blue hung over an ivory sofa in glove-soft leather. "Well, that's terrific, and thank you so much for your time, Mr. Granger," she said, edging her voice with polite finality. "I'll certainly give Mitch your best wishes. Goodbye."

Ginny hung up the phone. Mitch Adamson was almost too good to be true. She picked up the receiver again and buzzed the receptionist. "I'm through, Claudia, but I need a short conference with Maggie. Hold all calls for both of us, except emergencies, okay?"

"Sure thing," Claudia said. "There's a call on another line now. Excuse me."

Ginny replaced the receiver with a sigh. Considering next week's trip, she should be concentrating on her business, not child care. On this trip she'd explore what average Americans in five selected cities thought about cat litter. She'd advertised for cat owner volunteers in each city to take part in a videotaped round table discussion in front of a one-way mirror. Ginny's client, owner of a company that made the product, would observe the group interview from behind the mirror.

This focus-group approach to market research had served Ginny and her clients well over the years. The details were in place, but details could quickly change, and at this critical stage Ginny didn't like being preoccupied with having to find a housekeeper. Yet she had no alternative.

Ginny left her office and walked the short distance down the hall to Maggie's. She rapped on the partially open door and went in. Maggie signaled that she'd be off the phone in a minute, and Ginny sat down to wait in one of two chintz-covered wingback chairs in front of Maggie's desk.

Maggie Quebedeux's office neatly delineated the differences in their personalities. Maggie's antique desk, a massive expanse of carved cherry, squatted in the middle of the room. Dark wooden shutters provided a slatted glimpse of the misty Seattle morning, and the light from two standing lamps reflected against wood-paneled walls covered with a collection of nostalgic prints—children with dogs, old men playing checkers, young girls in ribbons and lace. A visitor to both offices would have pegged Maggie as the working mother and Ginny as the unencumbered career woman, when in fact Maggie, older than Ginny by ten years, had no children and no plans to have any.

"Yes, the deposit's in the mail," Maggie said into the phone. She took off her reading glasses and winked at Ginny. Maggie's reading glasses were the only visibly no-nonsense thing about her. Her clouds of dark hair, elaborate makeup and layers of jewelry suggested pleasure, not business.

Skeptical of Maggie's style at first, Ginny had come to respect her colleague's gift for putting clients at ease, in person or on the telephone, before hammering home some terrific deals for Virginia Westerfelt and Associates, Inc. After five years of partnership, Ginny realized how much she'd needed an aggressive saleswoman like Maggie. The business would not have flourished without her.

"Call me if you don't receive it by tomorrow," Maggie said. "Yes. Fine. Goodbye and thanks for everything." She hung up with a chuckle. "That was Indianapolis. I guess the deposit for the conference room hasn't arrived and they're getting antsy."

"Thanks for fielding everything for me this morning," Ginny said.

"No problem." Maggie laced her multiringed fingers together. "What about your wrestling coach?"

*Her wrestling coach.* The phrase unsettled Ginny, who was working to keep all her thoughts about Mitch strictly businesslike. "All the references checked out fine," Ginny began. "Although one thing's a little strange. His current principal said he's a good science teacher, but a bit of a loner. None of the faculty knows him very well. He doesn't socialize, at least not with them. But Mitch's principal back in Idaho described him as very outgoing, besides being a talented teacher. According to Jack Granger, I couldn't find a better companion for Arnold unless we were treated to the Second Coming."

"What's the mystery? This coach is probably a shy young man who felt more secure in a small town like . . . what was it again?"

"Cedarville," Ginny supplied.

"Right. Maybe Seattle intimidates him a little and he's not making friends very fast. That happens."

"Then why did he leave Cedarville?"

Maggie laughed. "You're asking me? Unless you've forgotten all your interview skills, I'm the wrong person to answer that question. You should have snagged that information for your long-distance nickel."

"I did ask Granger that, early in the conversation, and he said Mitch left for personal reasons."

"Hmm. Sounds like a ruined love affair or something. But you're the lady doing the hiring. If you need to know why he left a boss who thinks he hung the moon, ask him."

"I will," Ginny said, "but depending on his answer, I need to make this decision today."

"You're telling me. It's a zoo around here." As if on cue, the phone rang in the outer office.

"There's one thing, Maggie. He didn't get a teaching job here right away after he left Idaho. He spent two years in a canning factory."

"So?" Maggie shrugged. "Teaching's a rough job. Maybe he became disillusioned with the system. I say ask the guy why he left Cedarville, and if you're satisfied with his answer, you should probably hire him. After all, Arnold likes him, and that's a plus these days."

"You think I'm seeing bogeymen in the closet, don't you?"

Maggie leaned forward. "I think you're a mother, and one who is solely responsible for her kid, at that. One of the job requirements is raging paranoia. I looked it up."

"Oh, Maggie, I wish I had someone like you to stay with Arnold. This business of hiring a total stranger is unnerving."

"You know he's welcome to spend the night with Phil and me any time. I adore Arnold. He's the most polite kid in the world."

"Tell that to Mrs. Waddell. Anyway, I appreciate the offer, but I can't impose on my friends any more than I already have over the years. I'm sure Mitch

Adamson is my solution for this summer, at least. I just..."

"Just what? Is something else bothering you?"

Ginny's face grew warm.

"Virginia Westerfelt, you're blushing! Come on, out with it."

"He's very attractive. He—well, I think he might be taking the job because he thinks that I—you know." She traced the flowered pattern on the arm of the chair.

"And would you?" Maggie asked with a grin.

Ginny's skin tingled. "Of course not. You know how I feel about that, especially now, when Arnold is old enough to know exactly what's going on."

"So he's a hunk, is that right?"

*Yes.* "I suppose you could say that," Ginny admitted. "In a fitness-center sort of way."

"Muscles?"

A picture of Mitch in his tank top and shorts flashed into Ginny's mind. Definitely muscles.

"You have a dreamy look on your face," Maggie commented.

Ginny sat erect. "Nonsense. I'm only trying to decide if he's the right caretaker for Arnold. I'm afraid he'll put funny ideas in Arnold's head. For example, he wants him to start lifting weights."

Maggie gasped and covered her mouth. "No. Not *weights.* How shocking."

"Go ahead. Make fun of me."

"Sorry, sweetie. But you said that as if Arnold would be performing rituals with poisonous snakes. Most boys get into weight lifting sooner or later. And Arnold had that horrible incident with Billy what's-his-name last spring. I'm sure that's motivating him."

"I'm sure it is, too. I could strangle that kid for embarrassing Arnold."

"I know, but..."

"What?"

Maggie hesitated. "Arnold could use a little physical training. Not to be a real jock or anything, but you can't expect a boy his age to spend all his time playing the clarinet."

Ginny eyed her suspiciously. "Do you and Arnold have some conspiracy going? I feel decidedly outnumbered on the whole issue of which direction Arnold's future development should take."

"I haven't talked to Arnold," Maggie said, laughing. "I've been too busy coddling our client the cat litter king." The phone continued to ring in the outer office. "That's probably him trying to get through. If you want my opinion, I think you'd better quit diddling around and hire this guy before he changes his mind and you have to cancel next week's trip. Six weeks of work would go down the drain. I'm not qualified to handle the focus groups, and we both know it."

Ginny gazed at Maggie. "I only need someone for two and a half months," she said, reminding herself of that as much as Maggie. "Mitch will probably work out fine for two and a half months."

"I say do it." Maggie glanced up as Claudia appeared in the doorway.

"I can't hold people off much longer, guys," she said. "Meerstahl's secretary has called three times."

"And I have to go," Ginny said, standing. "I have to pick up Arnold at the gym. Practice is over."

"I'll take Meerstahl," Maggie said, and Claudia returned to the outer office as the phone rang again.

"I'll be back as quickly as I can," Ginny assured her, heading for the door.

"And that's another point." Maggie's phone buzzed and she reached for the receiver. "You know we can't afford to have you running around town chauffeuring Arnold, when you could be here dreaming up cogent questions about cat litter."

"Point taken." Ginny waved and left Maggie's office. As she went out the door she heard Maggie launch into one of her famous sweet-talk routines with Alan Meerstahl.

Moments later Ginny maneuvered the Volvo through misty rain and for the first time appreciated Arnold's wisdom in having chosen an indoor sport, if he'd had to choose a competitive sport at all. Kids who preferred baseball or soccer simply played in the rain in Seattle or they wouldn't play at all.

The wet climate grew flowers and grass like crazy— dandelions as big as chrysanthemums, grass that poked through cracks in asphalt and concrete. But kids didn't react as well to the constant moisture. Arnold had snuffled his way through his childhood and had finally, in adolescence, begun to enjoy weeks at a time without a head cold. A season of baseball could have changed that; it would also have forced Ginny to sit on cold metal bleachers, much of the time clutching an umbrella and a thermos of coffee. Suddenly wrestling didn't seem all that bad.

She parked in the lot next to the gym and hurried through the double doors into an echo chamber of shouts, thuds and whistle blasts. Practice was running overtime. Ginny caught the acrid smell of pubescent boy-sweat and the tang of warm, rubber mats.

Boys in pairs grappled on mats spaced around the polished, wooden floor. Ginny sat on the lowest rung of the bleachers. Someone had scraped Tiffany Loves Jared into the varnished pine with a ballpoint pen. Probably Tiffany, Ginny thought, and wondered if Arnold's name would ever be scratched on a desk or locker wall. Or if it already had been. She picked him out among the wrestlers, his head locked between another boy's thighs.

"Watch him," Mitch said, sitting beside her and obscuring the message about Tiffany's preference for Jared. "He's going to escape from that scissors."

Ginny watched, but her concentration was shot. She hadn't sat thigh to thigh with a man in gym shorts in years. The scent of after-shave, deodorant and male sweat kindled memories she'd deliberately repressed ever since she'd found herself the single parent of a growing boy. She'd decided then that if nuns could practice celibacy, so could she. Better to deal with a little frustration than with the guilt of setting a dubious example for her son. Her decision had rested easier on her with each passing year. Until now. Until Arnold, ironically, had propelled this man into Ginny's life.

She considered not going through with the arrangement. But Maggie would never forgive her, and neither would Arnold. Furthermore, if she didn't find a housekeeper soon, her business would suffer, and if she alienated her son over this matter, she might not retrieve his goodwill for a long, long time. So, if Mitch came up with a satisfactory response to her question about why he'd left Cedarville, she'd hire him. And she'd stay the hell away from him, and the temptations of that virile body.

"There! Fantastic, Arnold!" Mitch called out. "Couldn't have done better myself." He turned to Ginny. "Pretty impressive, huh?"

Ginny remembered Arnold using the same phrase the night before. Now she knew where he'd picked it up. "Pretty impressive," she echoed. "Mitch, I called the people on your list this morning."

"Yeah? Excuse me a minute." He faced away from her and cupped his hands to his mouth. "That's it, guys. Put away the mats and grab a shower. You're all looking terrific." He turned back to Ginny. "And?"

"Not a blotch on your record."

"No kidding." He smiled.

"I had to check."

"Sure you did, and I didn't mean to poke fun at you for that. I love cautious parents. It's the other kind that worry me."

"But I do have a question."

"Oh?"

Was that wariness she saw in his expression? Or was she supersensitized to the possibility? "Your first principal, Jack Granger, said such wonderful things about you, that I finally asked why you'd left. He said the reasons were personal. I don't mean to pry, but could you elaborate a little on those reasons?"

He hesitated a fraction of a second, but he held her gaze. "There was a question about my ability to do the job. An incident got blown out of proportion. I don't know if you're familiar with the way small towns magnify minor issues, but I decided it would be in the students' best interest if I moved on."

It was an answer, but not quite enough for Ginny. Normally she tried to be tactful, but she was running out of time. "Why would they question your abilities?'' she asked, deciding not to pussyfoot. ''Granger said you were a wonderful teacher and coach.''

Mitch looked at her. His eyes didn't flicker. ''Ever hear of envy? How it can affect people?''

''I—I suppose so.'' The question made her uncomfortable. Just the night before, envy had propelled her off the bleachers to break up the cozy chat that her son had been having with his coach. And she prided herself on being conscious of her motivations. A parent or group of parents jealous of their children's relationship with this man might try to knock him down a peg or two, and in a small arena, the repercussions could be deep. ''Yes, I do understand,'' she said more firmly. ''And I'd like you to supervise Arnold for the summer, if you still want the job.''

''I still want the job.''

Ginny's heart somersaulted at the look in his eyes. He wanted more than the job. If she had any choice, she'd be wise to end this dangerous business before it started, but she had no choice. From Arnold's point of view, Mitch was perfect, and Ginny was going out of town the following Tuesday. With luck, she'd spend most of the summer traveling and not have to deal with this attraction. ''You're hired, then,'' she said. ''Assuming the salary is satisfactory.'' She named a weekly figure and he nodded. ''You'll have the guest bedroom and share a bathroom with Arnold.''

''Sounds fine. Is there space in the bedroom for a weight bench?''

Ginny stared at him. *A weight bench?*

''Arnold said he'd like to start a weight-lifting program, and unless you already have a bench . . .''

''No.'' Ginny tried to picture a weight bench in her guest room. ''That's fine.'' She realized she didn't have the first idea of how this plan would impact upon her life. "I suppose if you'd like to come over tonight we can work out any other details, like having a key made, and deciding on how we'll handle meals."

"Tonight's okay, but I can start moving in this afternoon, to save time."

"So soon?" Ginny had figured on a day or so to get used to the idea of Mitch living in her house. She wondered if she'd left panty hose dangling in the bathroom. The reality of sharing space with this very virile man began to sink in. "What about subletting your apartment?"

"I've decided not to worry about that. I'll notify the landlord in case somebody shows up who needs a place short-term, but the more I think about it, the more I wonder if the hassle's worth the money made. Nothing's wrong with leaving it empty for a couple of months, and I won't have to think about making the apartment ready for a tenant."

"I suppose."

"So going to your place will be more like leaving on an extended vacation." He smiled.

"Only in that particular respect, however," Ginny warned him, wishing her heart would behave and beat normally. "Arnold will keep you hopping, believe me."

"I plan to enjoy it. In case you haven't been able to tell, I have a soft spot for Arnold."

Her mother's pride bloomed. "That's nice to hear." She realized it was perhaps the most important thing to hear. "But he's been on his best behavior for you. Friction is inevitable when you're together all the time."

Mitch regarded her with amusement. "I have some idea of what I'm getting into. I was raised in a large family."

"Oh. Well, good. I'm an only child, myself, and of course, so's Arnold, so we—let's just say I'm not fond of conflict."

"I'll try to remember that. But I can't promise everything will run perfectly smooth."

"I wouldn't expect you to make such a claim. I—" She turned, sensing someone standing behind her. "Why, hello, Arnold. I didn't hear you come up."

Arnold's grin dominated his face. "Mitch is gonna do it, isn't he, Mom? I heard what you said. You're talking about his staying with us, aren't you?"

"Yes, we are. Mitch said he could start moving in this afternoon."

"All right! Can I help? I can show you where everything is."

Mitch glanced up at Arnold. "Sounds like a plan. Want to ride over to my apartment with me right now?"

"You bet." Arnold thrust back his shoulders. "We'll have you moved in no time."

Ginny felt disoriented. She'd planned to take Arnold home and make sure he had lunch before she ran a few errands and returned to the office. "But you haven't eaten," she said to Arnold.

"I'll see that he gets fed," Mitch said.

"And your library books are due, and we need milk."

"We'll take care of both things in conjunction with our trips back and forth," Mitch offered. "Do you have a key, Arnold?"

"Sure do. We'll take care of everything," Arnold said with a newly acquired swagger. "Don't worry, Mom."

Ginny stood and glanced around uncertainly. "Then I . . . I'll just go back to work, I guess."

"Sounds good." Mitch stood and glanced at Arnold. "You about ready, Arnold?"

Ginny started to caution Arnold about eating something nutritious for lunch, but the glow of independence on his face stopped her.

"Ready when you are, Mitch," Arnold said.

"I'll see you both at home tonight, then," Ginny said. The statement came across sounding more intimate than she'd intended it to. This wasn't going to be easy.

Warmth flickered briefly in Mitch's eyes. "See you then."

She tried to think of something to say that would prevent that flicker of warmth from erupting again, but she couldn't come up with anything that wouldn't sound unpleasant. Breaking contact with Mitch's soft gaze, she turned and walked away, her high heels clicking a retreat across the wooden floor.

AFTER WORK, Ginny drove up the hilly street to her townhouse. The homes were two-story, built in pairs, each unit having an attached single-car garage. The houses at the top of the hill had a view of Lake Washington, but Ginny's was too far down the street to afford such a view. Still, it was an expensive neighborhood, and she felt proud every time she drove home. Except on this particular evening when anxiety won out over pride of ownership.

Daylight saving time gave her plenty of light to inspect the brown, dented Toyota that sat at the curb like an oversize russet potato on wheels. She didn't care that it was ugly, but she wished it weren't a light compact. Collision statistics weren't wonderful for small cars like this; it might crumple like paper in a wreck.

She hadn't thought to ask Mitch what kind of car he drove, but it probably wouldn't have made much difference. She'd been backed into a corner on this deal and she'd have to accept the Toyota along with everything else. As she activated the automatic door opener and pulled the Volvo inside the single-car garage, Ginny wondered if he'd put the dents in his car and if she had to worry about his driving habits. Usually she asked her prospective housekeepers about their traffic records, but she'd forgotten to ask in Mitch's case. With luck she hadn't forgotten anything else of importance.

Her attaché case strapped over one shoulder, her keys in one hand and a bucket of chicken from a fast-food restaurant in the other, Ginny opened the kitchen door. She smelled spaghetti sauce simmering, the aroma a shade different from that of her own recipe. Dropping her keys and attaché case on the built-in oak desk by the door, she noticed Mitch's worn wallet and a set of keys already there in the center of the desk. Next to that was the mail stacked by size, as Arnold loved to arrange it. At least Mitch hadn't appropriated Arnold's favorite job.

Ginny moved Mitch's wallet and keys to one side of the desk and put her keys and case in their place. Then she set the warm bucket of chicken on the yellow-and-white tiled counter beside a loaf of french bread that lay ready to be sliced.

She heard their voices in the living room. As she walked through the dining room, a heavy thump was followed by laughter and another thump. She reached the archway into the living room and stood there, speechless and unobserved, as Arnold pinned Mitch down in the center of her ivory-and-rose Oriental rug. They'd moved all the furniture back against the wall—the rose damask sofa and love seat, the gray velvet wing chairs, the marble coffee and end tables, the Waterford lamps.

Ginny cleared her throat.

# CHAPTER THREE

"HI, MOM." Arnold glanced up at Ginny with a sheepish smile. "Mitch is showing me some new holds."

"So I see," Ginny said, folding her arms. "And interior design, too, I take it."

"We didn't want to break anything," Arnold said, unwinding himself from the wrestling hold and sitting up. "We moved it real careful. We—"

Mitch got to his feet in one fluid motion and stepped toward Ginny. "I'll take the responsibility." He gazed at her with a faint smile. "I suspect from your expression you don't approve of our having moved the furniture."

She swallowed. Against the backdrop of the gym's echoing expanse he hadn't seemed so overwhelming a presence. Even on the floor pinned beneath Arnold he'd appeared manageable. But standing erect in her modest-sized living room he dominated the space. His green neon tank top stretched over the broad shoulders and muscled chest of a well-conditioned athlete. One of his thighs probably measured the same as her waist. Her dainty little townhouse didn't seem big enough to hold him.

"We'll put it back," he said quietly when she didn't respond to his comment. He extended a hand to Arnold to help the boy up. "Come on, let's get to work."

Ginny came to her senses. "Just a minute."

Mitch turned back to her, his gaze questioning.

"I appreciate your wanting to take the blame for this, but as much as you'd like to, you can't. Arnold is the one who knows the rules, and roughhousing in the living room isn't allowed. He should have told you that instead of helping you move the furniture out of the way."

"But Mom," Arnold complained. "This isn't roughhousing. It's *wrestling*. And besides, there's no place else to practice the holds." His thin body stiffened in defiance. "I thought the idea was for Mitch to coach me on the holds. How can he if we can't even try stuff out?"

Ginny clenched her fists in an effort to control her temper. She'd had a long day with much to think about and she'd probably made a terrible mistake in bringing Mitch Adamson into her house. Now her kid was getting mouthy, no doubt trying to dazzle his coach with his ability to stand up to his mother. "We have a backyard, Arnold," she said evenly. "It may not be huge, but it's bigger than this Oriental rug, and grass is a lot more easily replaced."

"But Mom, it's sopping wet outside! It rained today, in case you forgot."

"That's enough, Arnold."

Mitch held up both hands. "Time out. Look, we're all hungry and tired. How about if Arnold and I put everything back the way we found it, and then we'll have a nice spaghetti dinner, and talk about this afterward?"

Ginny wanted to slap him. How dare he be so damned reasonable, so calm and collected, while she felt as if she were turning on a spit over a slow fire? "I brought home chicken," she said.

"Oh." He shrugged and grinned. "Then we can have chicken and spaghetti. A smorgasbord."

Frustration and exhaustion hit Ginny with a combination punch that knocked the fight right out of her. "Fine," she said, moving toward the stairs that led to the second floor and the bedrooms. "Arnold knows where everything is—plates and silverware. I'm taking a shower."

Arnold turned to Mitch after she'd topped the stairs, and disappeared down the hallway. "It's my fault. She really doesn't let me do anything but watch television and read in here. One time she got real mad when this guy Billy and I brought our hamburgers and fries in to eat while we watched TV. Billy couldn't believe it. His family eats in front of the television all the time."

"Well, eating in front of the tube isn't such a great thing, really," Mitch said. He reached over and tousled Arnold's hair, wanting to erase the boy's cowed expression. "But don't be too hard on yourself. I was the one who suggested moving the stuff and trying out the holds, not you. As for your mom, she's probably tired from work, and coming home to a rearranged living room wasn't the best ending for a hard day. Let's put the furniture back, fix up the table for supper, and everything will be fine after we've all had a good meal."

"Yeah." Some of Arnold's bravado returned. "Women are touchy, huh?"

Mitch smiled. "No more than men, buddy. Depends on timing, and whether you push their hot button or not."

Arnold gazed at Mitch. "You got any hot buttons? You never get real mad, not even at the refs."

"Oh, I've got hot buttons," Mitch replied, thinking briefly of Cedarville. "Everybody does." He punched Arnold playfully on the shoulder. "Enough discussion. Let's get this stuff back where it belongs. And watch out for those lamps. They look expensive."

"Six hundred dollars apiece," Arnold said, picking up his end of the sofa. "Waterford crystal."

Mitch almost dropped his end. "What? Why the hell—excuse me—didn't you say so?"

"Does it matter? We're not gonna break them."

"You've got that right." Mitch wondered why a woman with a teenage son would put twelve hundred dollars worth of crystal lamps in the living room. Then he answered his own question. Because there would be no roughhousing in there, that's why. But Arnold was right. There wasn't much place to let loose in these stylish surroundings. Apparently nobody had ever told Ginny Westerfelt that kids need a place where they can goof around. Perhaps, when he knew her a little better, he would tell her.

THE MEAL WENT BETTER than Ginny had expected. Mitch had cooked a darned good spaghetti sauce and she'd had the good grace to tell him so. Dinner conversation flowed smoothly, too. Ginny discovered that Mitch knew quite a lot about current events; obviously he read more than the sports page of the daily paper. Maybe he wouldn't be the ruin of Arnold, after all.

"By the way, Mitch," she said, laying her fork on her empty plate, "Arnold and I have tickets for the symphony on Saturday night, so if you'd like to make plans to be with friends or do something on your own, that's fine. In fact, your weekends will be basically to do with as you wish, because I'm usually here."

His eyebrows lifted. "You don't go out?"

"Seldom." Her glance was designed to bring that particular topic to an end. She'd explain to him later, when Arnold wasn't around, why she'd curtailed her social life. "Work keeps me so busy that what little time I have left over I like to spend with Arnold," she added, taking her napkin from her lap and touching it to her lips.

Arnold shifted in his seat. "I'm not sure I can make it on Saturday, Mom."

"Not make it?" Ginny put down her napkin and stared at him. "But we've planned this for weeks. You love the symphony."

Arnold colored, but he bravely met her gaze. "People change, you know."

All Ginny's mellow thoughts about Mitch disappeared as she gradually comprehended why Arnold was refusing the symphony. In his quest to be manly in front of Mitch, he perceived going to the symphony with his mother as a sissy thing to do. Dammit! Arnold had also made her look like a fool in front of Mitch. She'd just delivered a speech about liking to spend her free time with Arnold, and he'd promptly indicated that an evening with his mother didn't thrill him at all. She tossed down the napkin. "Then I suppose I'll go alone," she said, gathering every dish within reach and arranging them in a pile in front of her. "If you two will excuse me, I'll get a start on the dishes. I brought home some work and I need to get at it soon."

She noticed their exchange of glances as she left the table with her stack of dishes, and her fury mounted. Two against one. In the past, she and Arnold had been the two. Fickle kid. Some guy flashed a few muscles and wrestling holds and Arnold switched allegiance without so much as a backward glance.

Clanging the dishes in the stainless steel sink, she flung open the dishwasher with a loud thunk. Spaghetti made such a mess, she thought, scouring the plates with a vengeance. Mitch probably never thought of the mess when he decided to make his world-famous spaghetti, which Arnold had praised to the skies, as if he'd never had homemade spaghetti sauce before in his life.

Come to think of it, the sauce hadn't been as damned wonderful as she'd told him it was, and the noodles were overcooked. Arnold probably would have been excited about spaghetti from a can if his wonderful Mitch had heated it up for him. Mitch. What a coarse, typical name for a jock. To think that she'd even felt the slightest bit interested in such an inappropriate, uncultured—

"You're liable to scrub the flowers right off those plates if you keep that up."

Ginny glanced up to find him standing inside the kitchen door holding the rest of the dirty dishes. "I always rinse everything before I put it in the dishwasher," she said, sounding even to herself like a prim dowager. "If you don't get the food off, it bakes on in the dishwasher and then it's even more work," she added, and looked down at the sparkling plate in her hand. She had no idea how long she'd been cleaning it. She put it into the dishwasher and reached for another. "Just leave those on the counter, please," she instructed.

"I thought you could use some help."

"I work best alone."

"I have a suggestion about the symphony."

She looked at him again. "Where's Arnold?"

"Watching TV. I told him you and I would handle the dishes tonight, and he could have a turn another night."

Ginny pressed her lips together. Mitch had only been in the household a few hours and already he was driving her crazy. "Arnold and I have a schedule for dishes, so you needn't have worried about setting something up. Tonight's my night, tomorrow night's his, and so on. I know you find this difficult to believe, but Arnold and I muddled along somehow, in our misguided fashion, before you came along."

A muscle in his jaw tightened and he placed his load of dishes on the counter so carefully they made only a soft click. "Would you like to call this off?" he said in a deceptively mild tone. His eyes were like granite. "No money has exchanged hands, so we can forget the whole thing. I'll have my stuff out in two hours."

Ginny stared at him while water from the faucet ran over her hands. The smiling, congenial helper of boys had vanished, to be replaced by a man whose quiet anger evoked her grudging respect. And something else, something more erotic than respect. She turned off the faucet and wiped her hands on a kitchen towel. "We need to talk," she said, facing him.

"Agreed."

"This is a difficult adjustment for me."

"I can see that."

Ginny groped for the words, not sure how much to say. "Gerry, my husband...Arnold's father, died five years ago."

"I know. Arnold told me."

Ginny twisted the terry cloth towel in her hands. "Poor little guy. He was only eight, but he was so brave. And ever since then, Arnold and I have been...a unit." She glanced at him. "No one's ever challenged that before."

"I'm not challenging anything."

"Maybe not consciously," she acknowledged, "but your very presence here—"

"But you've had other housekeepers."

"All women. And all—" she rubbed her finger along the grouting between the counter tiles "—this is hard to admit, but maybe I picked dull, uninteresting types on purpose. I didn't want them to be Arnold's best buddy." She met his gaze once more. "You said something about envy today. I understood that immediately. Arnold's all I have, and now suddenly here you are, some sort of god to him."

"I repeat. I can leave."

"But don't you see? I can't win. If you leave, Arnold will hate me for sending you away. But if you stay, I have to watch Arnold turn his back on all the little pleasures we used to share, because he doesn't want to appear to be a mama's boy in front of you." Ginny felt tears gather behind her eyes and she clenched her jaw. She would not cry.

"I don't want to be your enemy." Mitch's gaze gentled. "Maybe I don't understand what you're going through. I don't have any kids. But I've seen a lot of them suffer through this stage Arnold's in. They're trying to find out who they are, and they seesaw between being a child and wanting to be a grown-up. Keeping up with it can give you whiplash.''

Ginny's tension eased a fraction. "Yeah," she said with a weak laugh.

"But it's been my experience that—" he hesitated and glanced at the ceiling "—I'm so afraid of saying the wrong thing."

His hesitancy spurred her guilt. She couldn't really blame him for all this, as she'd been trying to. "That's my fault. I've really been prickly."

"You have." He smiled at her. "But you don't look so prickly now."

Awareness of him, the same quickening she'd felt from the first time they'd met, made her rush back into conversation. "What were you going to say about your experience?"

He looked blank for a second, as if he'd totally forgotten, as if his mind had been wandering, too. "Um, just that you can't hold these kids too tight, I guess."

"Which you think I've been doing."

"Lots of parents do. And you're raising Arnold by yourself, taking that whole responsibility, so of course you'd tend to be more concerned."

Ginny sighed. "I thought I knew Arnold, knew what to expect. But now—"

"Now he's going through puberty, but he's still a lot the same underneath, and he'll probably keep many of the characteristics you cherish."

"I'd like to believe that."

"You can." Mitch leaned against the counter. "And as for this symphony business, I think he still wants to go, but he's really working on his macho image, and he's leery of anything that doesn't fit in with it."

"So what do I do?"

"Could you get a third ticket? I'd pay for it, or you could take it out of my salary."

Ginny thought about the offer. The symphony had always been a special night out for her and Arnold as they shared their love of music and debated the playing abilities of the musicians. Ginny secretly hoped that Arnold would play for the Seattle Symphony one day, that he'd rise to first-chair clarinet and she'd attend every performance. But at the moment, that dream seemed far away. It galled her that she had to lure Arnold to sit in the audience by baiting the trap with Mitch.

"I do own a suit and tie," Mitch said, "if you're worried that I'll show up in gym shorts and embarrass you."

Ginny flushed. "I'm sure you wouldn't embarrass me. Do you like the symphony?"

"Not much. I prefer songs with words."

"But you'd sit there and pretend, for Arnold's sake."

"Why not? Who knows, maybe I'll learn something."

"What a waste of a good ticket," Ginny said, shaking her head. "But I suppose it's the best solution, and I do appreciate your willingness to try this. Since you don't like symphony music, I'll pay for the ticket."

"If you insist."

*He's so darned secure, he doesn't have to battle me over who's going to pay,* she thought with reluctant admiration. "All this is assuming Arnold agrees to go if you're going."

"Right. Want me to propose the idea to him?"

Ginny felt envy prick her again. She wanted to be the one to convince Arnold, but no doubt Mitch would have greater success. "Yes, I'd appreciate that," she said, swallowing the bitter taste of wounded pride. "Let's hope this works."

It did. Arnold changed his entire attitude about the symphony performance once he knew Mitch wanted to go. Mitch didn't pretend to have any great knowledge of classical music, but he said he'd love the chance to hear more in the company of two people who knew something about it. Arnold was thrilled. Now he had something he could give Mitch. And Ginny, chiding herself the whole time, spent many of her free moments in the following days trying to decide what to wear on this occasion, which was beginning to seem very much like a date.

MITCH SAT in the dark auditorium and loosened the knot of his tie while violins and flutes carried on like gossips on a Minnesota party line. He'd hoped for at least some stirring trumpet and French horn parts, but so far the music had been high-pitched and without much of a beat.

From the corner of his eye he watched Arnold, and next to Arnold, Ginny. Both of them looked rapt. They really ate this stuff up. He slowly pushed back the sleeve of his suit jacket and turned his wrist to peer at his watch. Only fifteen minutes had elapsed. This was going to be a long evening.

His discomfort had been somewhat mollified already, however. He wondered if Ginny had worn the black dress to impress him. If so, he was mightily impressed. He'd only seen her in business clothes, which included jackets that draped her in such a way that he hadn't seen much of her shape and could only guess at her proportions.

The black dress eliminated the guesswork. In the dictionary next to the definition for ''hourglass figure'' should be a picture of Ginny. Her breasts were surprisingly voluptuous, or perhaps it was her tiny waist that made them seem that way. The dress she wore tonight had a high neck and long sleeves of see-through black lace. The opaque portion of the dress cupped her breasts and sculpted her waist and hips so beautifully that he'd had to fold his arms to keep from reaching for her when she'd first come down the stairs tonight. Arnold had whistled, stating Mitch's opinion exactly, and she'd laughed and tossed her head, causing her earrings to sparkle like sun-coated rain.

On the drive over, and here in the auditorium, Mitch had been intensely aware of her. Occasionally, even in the dark, he caught a flash of her rhinestone earrings. Or maybe they were diamonds. After the crystal lamps he couldn't be sure. At any rate, Ginny was well-off financially. She'd probably received a hefty insurance settlement after her husband's death, and she ran a profitable business, so of course she had money. She also had wide blue eyes, soft blond hair that he longed to comb with his fingers, and a body that mesmerized him with its beauty. He'd gladly sit through a dozen symphonies if it meant that afterward he could hold her in his arms.

He congratulated himself for having come up with this solution to Arnold's balky behavior. Everybody had won. Ginny was able to enjoy the symphony with her son; Arnold could indulge his love of music without fear of adverse labeling, and Mitch got points for being a nice guy. After the rocky beginning of this association with Ginny, he could use the points. Although his primary goal in this whole endeavor had been to help Arnold through a crucial summer, his secondary goal had been to get to know Ginny Westerfelt better. After living with her less than a week, the gap between his primary and secondary goal was narrowing.

Arnold leaned toward his mother and whispered something to her. In the shadowy half-light Mitch saw the curve of her smile and the sway of her sparkly earrings when she nodded her head. He longed to switch places with Arnold, but had known from the beginning this would have to be the configuration, with Arnold between them. He just hoped the arrangement wouldn't cement itself permanently in the next few weeks.

"I was telling Mom that the flutes seem to be a little ahead of the conductor in this movement," Arnold whispered to Mitch. "Do you think so?"

"Could be," Mitch whispered back, not having a clue. The flutes could get so far ahead that the flute players had to leave early as far as he was concerned. He wanted to hear some brass, or maybe a few clashes on the cymbals and a roll on the drums. At last he got his wish, and the piece ended in a more satisfying way for Mitch. Then followed a shorter number, which still seemed interminable, and finally intermission arrived. The houselights came up, and Mitch straightened his tie.

Ginny leaned across Arnold and gave Mitch a smile that almost compensated for the whole ordeal. "How're you doing?" she asked.

"Fine." *Now.*

"Shall we stretch our legs?"

"By all means." Mitch was on the aisle, so he got to his feet and stemmed the tide of people to let Arnold and Ginny out. That move also positioned him right behind Ginny on the way out to the lobby, and the crush of the crowd gave him an excuse to be close and put his hand protectively at her waist.

"What a mob," she said over her shoulder.

"Mmm." He couldn't think of a clever rejoinder, not with her floral perfume filling his senses and his fingertips brushing the soft velvet of her dress. The top of her head came to his chin, and once he was so close that a wayward wisp of blond curl tickled him there.

He tried to rechannel his straying thoughts. She didn't date, and had explained to him that it had been a conscious decision on her part because she didn't want her son subjected to a string of boyfriends. Mitch admired that sort of self-restraint enough not to want to sabotage it. They reached the lobby and Mitch was about to suggest they have a drink when he saw the Taylors. The Taylors of Cedarville. Oh, God. They were probably on vacation. Cedarville was about five hundred miles away—a day's drive at most. Mitch vaguely remembered they loved classical music. Of all the damned luck.

He didn't think they'd seen him, but that could change any minute. Mitch would have to act quickly. "If you two will excuse me," he said, gesturing vaguely to the men's room.

"Sure," Ginny said. "Arnold, do you—"

"Nope." Arnold shook his head.

"Be right back," Mitch said, and plunged into the crowd. He stayed in the rest room as long as he dared. When he ventured back out, he scanned the lobby and saw Ginny and Arnold on the far side talking to a man who seemed to be alone. From the guy's well-groomed, distinguished appearance, Mitch pegged him as someone who could talk about the flutes galloping on ahead of the conductor and know what the hell that meant, the sort of man Mitch would expect Ginny to date, if she dated anyone. The Taylors were closer to him now, and he'd have to do some fancy shuffling to avoid them.

Maybe he shouldn't try, he thought. Maybe he'd be better off talking with them now and getting it over with, thereby possibly avoiding a chance meeting after the concert when Ginny and Arnold would be with him. He didn't like leaving Ginny with the Brooks Brothers suit guy too long, but he didn't want to end up introducing the Taylors to Ginny, either. He made up his mind and headed straight for the Cedarville couple.

"Hey, Bob and Ruby, great to see familiar faces," he said in his most jovial tone.

"Mitch Adamson!" Bob said, with only the slightest hesitation as he held out his hand. "Fancy seeing you at one of these. Don't tell me you're into classical music these days?" He clapped Mitch on the back.

"I came as a favor to a friend," Mitch said.

"How is everything, Mitch?" Ruby asked, her dark eyes bright with interest. "We've been so concerned, not knowing what happened to you."

"I'm teaching here in Seattle."

"That's *wonderful*," Ruby gushed, sounding far too pleased to be sincere.

"Uh, how about coaching?" Bob asked, with only the flutter of his eyelids giving any indication that he was uncomfortable.

"Just some parks and recreation stuff this summer," Mitch said, keeping his gaze steadily on Bob. He'd always suspected Bob and Ruby of having sided against him in Cedarville. "How's Jason?"

"Great, great," Bob said. "Got a wrestling scholarship to Michigan State. If he can keep his grades up, he may even graduate some day." Bob's laugh invited Mitch to join in. He didn't. "You know, that was a hell of a thing that happened to you," Bob said, clapping Mitch on the shoulder again. "Ruby and I know you just couldn't possibly have done anything like that."

"I was found innocent," Mitch said quietly.

"Which of course you were," Ruby said.

"That's right. I was." Mitch felt the bitterness overwhelming him again. He'd thought maybe he'd passed the stage when the bile would rise in his throat at the thought of his unjust treatment in Cedarville. Apparently time and counseling hadn't quite worked the miracle yet.

"Yeah, but a charge like that," Bob said, lowering his voice. "Once somebody points a finger at you for that, it's pretty hard to go on doing the job, know what I mean?"

"That's why I left, Bob." Mitch stood on the balls of his feet, as if poised for a fight. But there was no fight. There never had been. He'd never truly been able to thrash this one out in a way that would cleanse his soul. Seeing the Taylors, he knew he still wanted to, still had the fantasy of slaying the dragon and emerging the hero.

"Well, Mitch," Ruby said, putting her hand on his sleeve and bending her head close to his. "No matter what anybody in Cedarville says, we know you could never molest a student.''

The phrase ripped into him, destroying all the optimism and faith in people he'd been trying to rebuild the past three years. He wanted to throw up.

Ruby squeezed his arm. ''We'd better be going. Good luck to you, Mitch.''

# CHAPTER FOUR

DURING THE RIDE HOME from the symphony Arnold kept up a steady commentary on the performance, and Ginny praised him for his insights. She couldn't remember the last time she'd felt so alive, and she had Mitch to thank for that. He'd sacrificed his own preferences to gift her with a night at the symphony with her son. Her formerly sharp envy of Mitch dulled against his display of generosity.

Yet gratitude only partly explained her jubilation. Grudgingly she admitted to herself that a man's admiration, particularly this man's, felt wonderful. She'd soaked up his appreciation when she'd appeared in her black dress, and throughout the performance she'd been aware of Mitch's covert glances her way. Buffered by the presence of Arnold sitting between them, she'd indulged in some harmless flirting and had basked in the heady knowledge that Mitch found her desirable.

Now that the evening was nearly over, she'd spirit herself away like Cinderella, because she couldn't afford to linger at the ball. She'd properly express her thanks to Mitch for enduring the symphony, though. The poor man had suffered, apparently more so during the second half of the concert than the first. As they rode home, he'd said practically nothing, but she couldn't question him in front of Arnold, who still believed his hero had enjoyed himself.

Arnold seemed to have exhausted his monologue by the time they walked into the kitchen, lit only by a fluorescent light over the stove, and he climbed the stairs to his bedroom with a cheerful good-night to both of them.

When Arnold was out of earshot, Ginny turned to Mitch. "You were wonderful to do this. You look thoroughly wrung out, but I appreciate your gesture. You can see how much Arnold loved being there to-night."

Mitch's reply was listless. "Yeah," he said, pulling off his tie. "He seemed to like it." He walked over to the refrigerator and opened the door. "Think I'll have a beer, if you don't mind."

"No, I don't mind." The cold air from the open refrigerator was no chillier than Mitch's manner. Ginny felt rebuked. She'd expected perhaps a weary smile, a warm agreement about Arnold's enthusiasm, a kidding comment about the length of the concert. She hadn't expected rejection. "You don't have to ask before you eat or drink anything, Mitch," she added. "I thought we'd discussed that the other night."

He closed the refrigerator door and popped the top of the can of beer. "I don't think we discussed alcohol." He leaned against the counter and took a sip. "I don't think we discussed a lot of things, as a matter of fact." Instead of looking at her, he studied the label of the blue-and-silver can. "I sort of rode to the rescue like the cavalry, without really considering all the ramifications. Now it seems pretty stupid of me to have rushed into this arrangement."

"Mitch, what are you saying?"

He gazed at her. "Maybe we should forget this arrangement."

"Forget it?" she repeated, hurt and confused. "Was sitting through the symphony that tough? You won't have to go again, if that's what this is all about."

"The symphony was fine." He took another swig of the beer. "Listen, do you want something to drink? I didn't even ask."

"No, I want some answers. What's with the sudden about-face? You offered your services to me, and almost aggressively pursued this job. Now, when you're entrenched here, you're ready to quit?"

Mitch glanced upward. "Better keep your voice down."

She clenched her jaw. He was right, but damned if she liked being told to keep her voice down in her own home. "All right," she said more quietly. "Will you explain yourself, then?"

He was studying the label on the beer can so intently he might have been debating going into the brewery business.

"Well?"

"I guess sitting in the auditorium tonight gave me time to think. This is a loaded situation, me staying here with you and Arnold. Until now I didn't realize how loaded."

Ginny let out her breath. She understood. The gleam in his eyes when she'd come downstairs in her sexy dress. The light yet electric touch of his hand at the small of her back when they'd left the auditorium during intermission. Mitch doubted his ability to control himself around her, and although that presented a problem, it gratified her, too.

"So I've been wondering," Mitch continued, "if we should cut our losses and I'll leave now. Maybe I can even help you find a replacement."

Ginny shook her head, feeling responsible for this unpleasant turn of events. She shouldn't have worn the black dress, shouldn't have flirted, even a little. "Please don't talk like that," she begged. "You know Arnold would be heartbroken if you left."

"Yes, but—"

"And there's the practical consideration of my trip next week," she continued, determined to convince him for Arnold's sake. "I wouldn't dare leave with someone brand-new in charge around here, and canceling that trip would be disastrous for my business."

"How about your relatives?" he asked. "Isn't there a grandmother somewhere who could fill in?"

"I'm afraid not. My mother died ten years ago and my father couldn't leave his own work in South Carolina to come here. As for Gerry's parents—they live in Arizona and neither of them is well." Ginny knew that in a pinch she could call on Maggie, but she didn't want to give Mitch any way out. Arnold needed him. As for Mitch's attraction to her, she'd make certain that never got out of hand. She'd been foolish to think she could play with fire.

Mitch gazed at her. "Looks like I'm stuck, at least for the time being."

"Only until the end of the summer. That's not very long."

"Depends."

Ginny didn't ask on what it depended. She knew. She would assume the responsibility of maintaining a platonic relationship between them, for everyone's sake. "If that's settled, I think I'll go to—" she paused and edited what she'd been about to say "—up-stairs," she finished. Even using the word *bed* at this moment seemed inappropriate. "Good night."

"Good night," he said softly. Then, as she left the room, he called after her and she turned. "You looked wonderful tonight," he said.

Warmth rushed through her and nearly washed away her resolutions of only moments ago. She stood transfixed by the appeal of him, his dress shirt unbuttoned at the throat, his blond hair tousled and his gray eyes sparkling in open admiration. Slowly she retrieved her willpower and quelled the urge to return to the kitchen. "Thank you," she managed, and hurried out of the range of his powerful spell.

ON MONDAY MORNING, Maggie appeared in Ginny's office carrying a folder. "Plane and hotel confirmations," she announced, placing the folder on Ginny's desk. "Meerstahl's flight from L.A. should connect with yours out of Seattle-Tacoma, so you'll head out together in the morning, as planned."

"Good." Ginny gave the word more emphasis than she'd intended.

"Anxious to be off, are you?"

"Sort of."

Maggie studied her. "And how are things on the home front? Did Arnold enjoy his concert Saturday night?"

"Oh, he loved the concert. Had a ball."

Maggie settled herself in one of the Scandinavian-design chairs opposite Ginny's desk. "And?"

"And yesterday he and Mitch went jogging, watched sports on TV and lifted weights. Arnold's overjoyed."

"And Mommy's nose is out of joint," Maggie guessed.

Ginny stood up and began pacing in front of the window. Sun streamed in this morning, signaling that perhaps the summer dry spell had begun. "I've never felt so...so *extraneous* before," Ginny explained. "Not that I want to join in their activities. That would present problems of a different sort." Ginny instantly regretted her last statement.

Maggie pounced on it. "What sort of problems, pray tell?"

"The obvious."

"You don't say?"

"You don't have to sound so delighted, Maggie."

"Sorry, but you know I've never approved of your nunlike behavior. By the way, can I come to Arnold's wrestling match tonight?"

Ginny stopped pacing and looked at her in exasperation.

"Well, it's not as if I've never taken an interest in Arnold's activities," Maggie said defensively. "Didn't Phil and I go to his band concert this past spring? And his eighth grade commencement, come to think of it? I'll bet Arnold *expects* me to come and watch him compete."

Ginny put both hands on the back of her desk chair and leaned forward. "That's not why you want to come to the wrestling match, and we both know it."

Maggie abandoned her pose and laughed. "The question is, why don't you want me to come?"

"Because once you see Mitch, you'll tease me unmercifully for the rest of the summer. I have enough to deal with as it is. He nearly quit Saturday night because he's afraid of this attraction between us."

"He admitted that?"

"Not in so many words, but I got the message."

Maggie placed her hand over her heart. "I can't stand it. A hunk with a conscience. Ginny, I'm coming to that wrestling match. You can't deny me my entertainment. After all, they took *Beauty and the Beast* off the air, so where am I going to get my fix of romance, if not from your most interesting life?"

"Maggie, so help me—"

"Aw, sweetie, I was only teasing. I won't come if you'd rather I didn't. I realize this is a serious problem for you, and I don't mean to make light of it. But really, hundreds of women would love to be in your place, with a gorgeous guy hanging around who likes your kid and likes you even more. Maybe you should relax and enjoy it."

Ginny sighed and sat down behind her desk. "Forgive me, Maggie, but you don't have any kids, or you'd know how inappropriate that would be. Arnold's thirteen. One of these days he'll discover girls. The last thing he needs is to be confronted with his mother's sexuality. Besides that, he'd probably be jealous if he thought Mitch had an interest in me. He'd feel shut out."

"I'm sure you're right." Maggie reached across the desk and patted Ginny's arm with her ring-bedecked hand. "I'll try to keep my mouth closed on the subject."

Ginny chuckled. "Might as well try turning off Old Faithful."

"I beg your pardon," Maggie said with a renewed show of indignation.

"But I love you for caring, Maggie. You're welcome to come to the wrestling match tonight, if you like."

"I'll be there," Maggie said immediately, and Ginny laughed. "Incidentally," she added, "do you still need a ride to the airport in the morning?"

"Actually, no. Mitch offered to take me."

Maggie brightened. She opened her mouth to say something but immediately closed it again.

"What?"

"I'm trying to control myself."

"For heaven's sake, Maggie. Say whatever you like. We've muddled through together this long by being frank with each other—let's not stop now."

"Okay. It's just that this is exactly what you need, and I hope you don't throw away a chance for happiness because you're afraid of some psychological damage to Arnold. You may be overstating the dangers."

"As I typically do, right?"

"Right, but it's natural, I'm sure. Just remember that Arnold will be grown-up and gone someday," Maggie said. Ginny's phone buzzed and Maggie rose from the chair and smoothed her skirt.

"And until then, his mental health is my responsibility," Ginny said, reaching for the phone.

"I only hope Arnold appreciates what a good mother he has," Maggie said, and with a wave, left the office.


"GINNY, HE'S DARLING," Maggie whispered as they sat together on the wooden bleachers that night.

"I wish you wouldn't talk like that. I'm trying to keep my attitude toward him perfectly businesslike."

"Good luck. When I met him a few moments ago he still had his jacket on. Now that he's stripped down to that tank top and shorts . . . well, let's say the only other place I've seen muscles like that is on my Chippendale calendar," Maggie said, keeping her voice low.

Ginny stared at her. "Where do you have a Chippendale calendar? I've been in your office and in your house, and I don't remember ever seeing such a thing. And believe me, I would have remembered."

"It's in the bottom of my desk drawer. Lower left. You're welcome to peruse it any time."

"Maggie, you fraud. All those cute pictures on your wall of children and old people, and a calendar full of sexy guys hidden in your desk. Does Phil know about this?"

Maggie smiled. "Wouldn't want to intimidate the poor guy, now, would I? Especially considering he's French and imagines himself a fantastic lover."

"Maggie, for goodness sake." Ginny glanced around to see if anyone was listening.

"Well, Phil's a sweetheart, but nobody would ever ask him to pose for a calendar," Maggie continued. "Your wrestling coach, however, is a different story."

"He's not *my* wrestling coach."

"Excuse me. *Arnold's* wrestling coach. *Your* live-in child supervisor, part-time cook, occasional escort—"

"Once!" Ginny insisted, and then noticing a couple of people turning to look at her, she lowered her voice. "Let's drop this fascinating topic, shall we? People are staring."

"Okay. Let's concentrate on that gorgeous young man down there with the whistle and clipboard. Incidentally, aside from his awesome shoulders and cute buns, he seems like a nice guy. The kids obviously adore him, and that's a good sign.''

"Arnold thinks Mitch is some sort of superman.''

Maggie nudged her. "Maybe he is.''

"Stop that, Maggie.''

"Okay. Speaking of Arnold, when does my favorite thirteen-year-old do his stuff?''

"We have two more weight classes to go. If you're bored . . .''

"Absolutely not. I enjoy watching Mitch in action." Maggie winked. "And watching you watching Mitch.''

"Excuse me?" Ginny said, flushing.

"You may have yourself fooled, but you can't fool me. You're aware of him all the time. Even while we've been talking, you've kept him in sight almost constantly. You're falling for him, Ginny.''

"No, I'm not. I just—''

"Listen, who could blame you? He's handsome, sexy and nice to kids. I'll bet most of the mothers sitting here have a crush on him, but you hold the advantage. He's living with you.''

"Maggie," Ginny said, blushing furiously, "I should never have let you come here tonight. You've assumed all the wrong things.''

"Know what I think?" Maggie put her arm around Ginny's shoulders and peered into her face. "I think you secretly wanted me to check him out. And I give my wholehearted approval.''

"You're impossible. You asked to come, remember? And I don't need your approval, because I'm not doing anything.''

"Yet.''

"Maggie, please!"

Maggie merely smiled and squeezed Ginny's shoulder before releasing her to watch the wrestling. Ginny watched, too, and found the combination of Maggie's comments and Mitch's presence on the floor below a very potent mixture.

Ginny reminded herself that Maggie, childless, couldn't appreciate her position as the mother of a teenager. Suppose, for example, that Ginny had given in to her attraction on Saturday night, returned to the kitchen and allowed events to progress? Mitch had said she looked "wonderful." Instinct had told her that a kiss might have followed if she'd stayed in the kitchen after that remark, a kiss that would have been partly her fault. Perhaps Arnold would have remained upstairs and never known, but perhaps he would have come down for a glass of milk, right when she and Mitch—no, that was unthinkable.

Even if a stolen Saturday-night kiss had gone undetected by her son, Ginny knew that a kiss from Mitch would only be the beginning. He didn't strike her as the kind of man who'd be satisfied with a few stolen kisses. He would want more. A sweet ache centered in Ginny as she imagined Mitch driven by passion. She couldn't allow the tumult of such an emotion to jeopardize this crucial summer of Arnold's. Ginny conceded that Maggie understood some of the situation, the part involving Mitch and Ginny, but the part involving Arnold, only a mother could understand.

"Wake up. It's Arnold's turn," Maggie said, nudging her.

"I'm awake. I can see that it is," she protested, though in fact she hadn't realized her son was on the mat. Arnold and another boy, not quite as muscular as last week's opponent, circled each other within the yellow boundary.

"Go get him, *Ar*-nold!" The voice cracked, revealing it had come from another adolescent. Jeering laughter followed.

Heart pounding, Ginny scanned the crowd. Sure enough, Billy Herman lounged at the top of the bleachers, surrounded by three of his recently acquired jock friends. All of them wore rock band T-shirts with the sleeves torn off and dark glasses. Ginny knew the boys were Arnold's age, but they looked much older than thirteen.

Maggie turned to follow the direction of Ginny's gaze. "And who are those juvenile delinquents?"

"The kid with his initials shaved into his head is Billy, the boy who turned on Arnold this past year. I guess the other three are his friends, probably football players, too. They must have found out Arnold joined the wrestling program." Ginny returned her attention to Arnold. He had to have heard Billy's taunt. Ginny thought he looked tense, but then he'd looked tense the previous week during the match.

"Haven't they got anything better to do?" Maggie asked.

"Apparently not."

"Hey, Westerfelt! Studman!" called another boy from the quartet above Ginny.

This time Ginny saw Arnold flinch and glance upward. His opponent picked that moment of inattention to lunge, and Arnold went down.

"Dammit, I won't have this," Ginny muttered, getting to her feet. She wished now she'd changed clothes after work, but there hadn't been much time.

"What are you going to do?" Maggie asked, looking worried.

"Go up there and stop them."

"Should I go with you?" Maggie, in higher heels and a tighter skirt than Ginny, didn't appear eager to follow her friend up the bleachers.

"That's okay. They're just a bunch of obnoxious kids. Guard my purse. I'll be right back." Ginny climbed the bleachers with as much dignity as possible considering the limited movement allowed by the narrow hem of her skirt.

"You got him now, Arnie-smarmy. Keep holding him on top of you like that. Good move," Billy called out, and the other boys laughed raucously. "Hey, Arnie! Pencil-neck! Who ever told you you could wres—" Billy stopped when he noticed Ginny coming up the bleachers.

She continued climbing until she was standing next to the boys, who still sprawled across the wooden seat with exaggerated ease. She glared at them. "I want this behavior stopped now," she said.

Billy glanced at her. At least she supposed he did. His mirrored sunglasses hid his eyes. "What behavior, Mrs. W.?" he asked, and smirked at his buddies.

"You know very well what behavior, Billy Herman."

"We're just supporting our good friend Arnie," Billy said with an air of injured pride. One of his friends stifled a laugh.

Ginny's hand itched to whack Billy across his supercilious face. No wonder Arnold had been so miserable the last week of school, if tonight was any example of what he'd endured from this bullying creep and his gang. "You're not Arnold's friends," she said.

"And you will either behave like gentlemen here or leave." Ginny had no idea how she'd enforce such a threat, but she'd find a way.

"Oh, yeah?" Billy said, challenging her.

"Yes," Ginny said. "I—"

"On your feet, all four of you. You're speaking to a lady."

Ginny turned to find Mitch right behind her, his gray eyes like flint.

The boys obeyed, and Billy started to speak. "We didn't—"

"Right," Mitch interrupted, his tone steely. "You sure didn't. Didn't show any manners, didn't show any class, didn't show any sportsmanship. If I hear anything more out of you, you'll all be gone. Is that clear?"

"Yeah," Billy said, glancing down.

"What?" Mitch demanded. "And take off those shades when you speak to me."

Billy removed his sunglasses, revealing a troubled gaze. "Yes, it's clear," he said.

"Good." Mitch turned to Ginny. "Are you satisfied?"

"For now," Ginny said.

"Then I think we've spent enough time on this." Mitch took her elbow and helped her down the bleachers.

"Thanks," she said, made nervous by his touch. "I was wondering how I'd make my ultimatum stick."

"You were doing fine. I just got ticked off when I saw those lugs up there acting like they owned the gym, and I had to get in my two cents worth. You could have handled them without me."

"Maybe, but all the same, I'm suitably impressed. I've wondered if Arnold would get away with murder while I'm gone, but I'm not worried anymore."

Mitch chuckled. "Thought I was a pushover, huh?"

"Well, I'd noticed the boys all liked you, and sometimes that means the object of their affection doesn't impose much discipline. I'm glad I was wrong. And thanks again."

"You're welcome. Maybe sometime soon you can tell me who those goons are and how they know Arnold."

"Sure." As they neared the spot where Maggie waited, smiling up at them, Ginny glanced past her at the empty mat on the gym floor. "Is Arnold's match over?"

"Yep. He was pinned almost immediately, so I asked the ref to hold up the next match until I could take care of those jokesters. Then I turned around and saw you were already dealing with them."

"And needing help," Ginny said.

"Just a little backup," he said with a grin. "You looked pretty tough."

Ginny felt herself blushing. "You'd better get back down there, then. I'm fine."

He squeezed her elbow and smiled. "That's for darn sure. See you after the last match." Then he bounded down the bleachers and signaled to the referee to call the next weight class.

"Yum," Maggie said as Ginny rejoined her on the bleachers. "And a knight in shining armor, to boot."

Ginny still felt the warmth of his touch at her elbow. Dazed, she sat beside Maggie. He'd taken the chance of paying her another compliment and used the excuse of helping her down the bleachers in order to touch her. Yet this was the same man who'd been on the verge of quitting Saturday night because he feared the temptation of living in such proximity to her. Nothing made sense.

"Yo, Ginny. You in there?" Maggie shook her by the arm.

"Um, what?" Ginny blinked and turned to gaze at her friend. "Were you saying something?"

"Obviously nothing as important as what's on your mind. What was that you said about keeping this alliance purely business?"

"That's how it has to stay," Ginny said, striving to remind herself, as well.

"From the look on your face, I'd say it's already gone past that stage."

Ginny swallowed. "I'm leaving tomorrow. I'll be gone a lot this summer. We have another focus group tour coming up soon."

"Not that soon, sweetie. Remember, we deliberately schedule fewer trips in the summer, so you can be available when Arnold's not in school. So I'm afraid that once you come home from this one, you'll be around for a while." Maggie presented the information with obvious delight.

Ginny groaned and put her face in her hands. "Maggie, I don't deserve this."

"I happen to think you do," Maggie said with a laugh.

# CHAPTER FIVE

THAT EVENING Ginny was too busy packing and organizing for her trip to fill Mitch in on the history behind Billy Herman's behavior at the gym. At least, she gave herself that reason for not spending time alone with him. Deep down she knew that his rescue of her at the wrestling match and his subsequent gentle touch as he helped her back to her seat had created a yearning that she dared not acknowledge. Worse yet, she no longer wanted to leave the following day.

Mitch drove the Volvo when they left for the Seattle-Tacoma International Airport at six the next morning. He'd offered and she'd accepted. Amazing, she thought, how quickly she'd grown fond of being taken care of. The trend was a threat to her hard-won independence, but she hadn't felt like fighting it. And she was glad she hadn't, especially when Mitch appeared downstairs in a lettuce-green sportshirt and white slacks, looking like every woman's dream.

As they pulled out of the driveway, Ginny gazed lovingly at the townhouse and experienced an unexpected wave of homesickness. She'd imagined herself long past such emotions. She'd always missed Arnold on her business trips, but seldom had she missed the comfort of being home. This morning, however, seemed drenched in Technicolor detail she'd never appreciated before.

In the well-kept yards of her neighborhood, dew-soaked flower beds sparkled, transforming red geraniums into clumps of rubies, marigolds into topaz, petunias into amethyst. Sunlight this early meant a brilliant day ahead—cobalt skies, zesty breezes whipping up whitecaps on Lake Washington, the heady fragrance of lush growth at the height of the season. Summer days like this caused even the most rain-weary Seattle residents to pledge their hearts to the city forever, or at least until another winter season dulled their enthusiasm for the climate.

Ginny thought of Mitch and Arnold enjoying the day, perhaps playing a game of catch in the yard and barbecuing their dinner outside, all without her. Then they might set up Arnold's telescope and look at the stars. Mitch was, after all, a science teacher, and he'd already told Arnold he'd love to spend the next clear summer night stargazing. Ginny felt very sorry for herself.

"Pretty quiet over there," Mitch remarked.

"Guess I'm not quite awake yet," she fibbed.

"Don't worry about Arnold. We'll be fine while you're gone."

"Oh, it's not that," she said, thinking that she didn't like the idea that they'd get along fine without her.

"I'm pretty sure we covered everything."

"Me, too," she agreed, but now she doubted that they had. The farther away from the townhouse Mitch drove, the more uneasy she became. "Did I show you where I keep the orthodontist's number?" she asked.

"No, but I'd guess in the Rolodex by the phone."

"Yes, but you need to know his name. Dr. Augat. *A-U-G-A-T.*"

"Got it."

"Here, I'll write the name down for you," she said, rummaging in her attaché case for a pen and notepad.

"Not necessary. Besides, I imagine Arnold could tell me his name if I happened to forget."

She found the notepad and pen. "But Arnold might not be able to tell you. He might be—I don't know—unconscious or something."

"If Arnold's unconscious, the orthodontist would hardly be the first person I'd call," Mitch said, glancing at her with a wry smile.

"Oh. I guess you're right." She tapped the notepad with her pen. "You remember when the garbage is picked up?"

Mitch nodded.

"And Arnold said he'd water my indoor plants, but sometimes he forgets and—"

"I'll supervise the watering."

"Let's see." She pressed the end of the pen against her lower lip as she thought. "Emergency numbers are taped right by the phone, so that's no problem. If Arnold gets suddenly sick, or he hurts himself, try to get Dr. James. The others in the office are okay, but James is the best, and Arnold likes him the most."

"Okay."

"And I showed you where the fuse box is, and the water shut-off valve. I have the feeling I've forgotten something, though."

"You have," Mitch said with a chuckle.

"I knew it. What?"

"You've forgotten that I'm a grown man of thirty-two who's managed to stumble through life with some measure of success so far. I can handle things while you're gone, Ginny. That's why you hired me, so the best thing for you to do is relax, do your job and let me do mine."

"I didn't mean to imply that—"

"I know," he said gently. "And trust isn't built overnight. I realize that. But you can trust me, Ginny. With Arnold...or with anything that's important to you."

Her heart lurched. That was a loaded statement, if she'd ever heard one. She hoped he hadn't guessed the growing attraction she felt toward him. His statement might indicate that he had. Perhaps he was subtly encouraging her to allow those feelings to deepen. As his employer, she'd have to make the first move if they were to— But no, she'd been over that with herself a hundred times and always came to the same conclusion. A romance with Mitch could jeopardize Arnold's well-being. She couldn't risk it.

She glanced at Mitch, who seemed to be engrossed in his driving. With a start she realized she hadn't thought about his competence in that area since the first day he'd moved in, when she'd noticed the dents in his Toyota. She'd blithely allowed him to drive Arnold around and take them both to the symphony. This morning she'd relinquished herself to his control without a second thought. That wasn't like her.

Yet she couldn't find fault with the way he maneuvered on the increasingly busy thoroughfares as they headed for the airport. He drove with the same assurance he brought to whatever he tackled. He would probably demonstrate the same assurance when he made love to a woman.... As a warm flush spread through her, Ginny admitted to herself that she was in trouble. No matter how she tried, she couldn't suppress these sensual thoughts about Mitch. *You can trust me,* he'd said, *with anything that's important to you.* Powerfully seductive, a vow like that, especially to someone who hadn't allowed herself to surrender to a man in a long, long time.

"Apparently I've convinced you that Arnold and I will be okay," Mitch said, breaking the silence. "Or else you're over there thinking up another long list of concerns."

"No, I was just thinking about—" Ginny flailed around in her mind for a reasonable explanation "—about Billy Herman," she finished, remembering that she'd promised to discuss Billy with Mitch.

"Oh, yeah. Our nasty little friends from last night. What is the story?"

"Billy and Arnold used to be good friends, back in grade school. In fact, they've played in the band together since fifth grade, Billy on trumpet and Arnold on clarinet. In junior high they started drifting apart when Billy became first string on the football team, but they still had band together. According to Arnold, Billy got an overblown idea of himself, thought he should be best at everything, including band. When Arnold got an award this year for best band student, Billy taunted Arnold into a fight in the cafeteria."

"Sounds like a boy with some big problems."

"His father's pretty overbearing, too," Ginny said. "I'm not surprised Billy's turning out this way."

"So how did the fight end?"

"A teacher broke it up. They stripped Billy of his sports awards and Arnold of his band award."

Mitch shook his head. "And it wasn't really Arnold's fault. I'll bet he hated losing that award."

"Actually, that didn't seem to bother him. What he hated was that he was losing the fight, and half the school was watching. If the teacher hadn't stopped it, Billy would have beaten him up." Ginny paused. "I hate to say this, but I think Arnold wants revenge."

Mitch stretched his arms against the steering wheel. "So he decided to become a wrestler."

"Yes. I don't think Billy's tried wrestling, just football and basketball. Arnold probably imagines himself pinning Billy in a wrestling match, or some such fantasy."

"That's not such a fantasy."

"Oh, Mitch, yes it is. Arnold's not an athlete. He's a musician and a poet. He has no business out there competing, trying to be something he's not."

Mitch glanced at her. "Is that what you think?"

Taken aback by his tone, she hesitated. "Well, yes."

"How do you know all of Arnold's potential?" Mitch shot back, sounding impatient with her. "He's only thirteen."

"But he's never shown the slightest interest in sports before," she said, her pitch rising. "Doesn't that say something?"

"It might say that he hasn't had very many sports-minded people in his life."

"Is that so terrible? All Arnold needs to learn is to avoid types like Billy. Not everyone should become some muscle-bound, aggressive—"

"Are you trying to say that not everyone has to be like me?" Mitch finished mildly.

She blushed. "I'm not talking about you."

"Sounded like you were."

"You have a reason to be fit. You coach kids. But Arnold's destined to become an artist, not a wrestling coach. He doesn't need muscles."

"What he needs is self-respect."

"Agreed! But not based on his ability to throw somebody else down and sit on him. That's primitive."

Mitch grinned. "Thirteen-year-olds are pretty primitive."

Ginny absorbed the beauty of his smile and wished all the emotions generated in her by that smile weren't so inappropriate. "Maybe most thirteen-year-olds are primitive, but Arnold's always been different. Surely you can see that."

"Of course I can. And Arnold's a neat kid, just as he is. Still, it won't hurt him to prepare physically as well as mentally for the challenges he'll face in life. Don't you want him to have confidence in what his body can do, as well as in what his mind is capable of?"

She didn't answer. He'd made a point, but it wasn't one she felt ready to acknowledge.

"He does have a body, Ginny. I'm not advocating that he train that body just so he can go gunning for Billy Herman, although Arnold may need to take him on some day, to prove something to himself. But aside from that, he'll want to improve his physical coordination for all sorts of reasons. As an adult he'll need it for dancing, for taking walks in the park, for balancing sacks of groceries...for being with a woman," he finished more quietly.

Ginny swallowed. "I, um, hadn't thought of it that way."

"Usually mothers don't." He paused, as if wondering how much further he should pursue the topic. "Take it from a guy who's been there. It's tough enough being a teenager faced with understanding your own sexuality, without the added burden of thinking you're scrawny and uncoordinated, and that no girl would want to snuggle up to you because you're all skin and bones."

"Are you saying that you were once skin and bones?" Looking at the way he filled out his knit shirt, she couldn't believe his physique had ever resembled Arnold's.

"You're riding with the official seventh grade weakling and supernerd of Lanier Junior High, Minneapolis, Minnesota."

"No kidding." Ginny sat in silence for a moment, digesting the information. She was also touched by his candor. "That's really amazing, Mitch. Next you'll tell me you also played the clarinet."

"No, I'm definitely not a musician. But I was on the chess team."

"So was Arnold. League champion, two years running."

Mitch groaned. "I might have guessed. Poor kid. Ginny, you have to loosen up on this wrestling thing. Right now he needs success in that area far more than in chess championships. Winning a few wrestling matches will give Arnold the courage to look people like Billy in the eye, to run for class office, maybe even to kiss a girl."

"For heaven's sake, don't rush the last part. He's only thirteen."

"And how old were you when you were first kissed?"

Ginny considered his question. "A kissing game or a real kiss?"

"A real one. Hearts pounding, palms sweating, the works."

Ginny squirmed a little at the direction of the conversation, but she answered the question. "I was fourteen. We both were. A whole year older than Arnold," she added pointedly.

"Life moves faster now," Mitch said. "We have cable TV, for one thing. Another question. Was the guy you kissed a skinny, ninety-pound weakling?"

She was very aware of the ripple of his biceps as he turned the wheel at the highway exit leading to the airport. "So what if he wasn't skinny? That doesn't prove anything."

"Ginny, be honest. You can't tell me that you don't care about a guy's build."

*I care about yours far more than I should,* she thought, as the secret ache began. "Physical beauty is secondary to a wonderful personality," she maintained, but the words sounded pretty clichéd as she uttered them.

"But if you had a choice," he persisted, "between a scrawny guy with a great personality and a well-developed guy with a great personality, wouldn't you take the person who felt good in your arms?"

*Oh, yes. Yes, I certainly would.* "Men are fixated on the physical side of things, not women," she said.

"I think you're kidding yourself."

"I think we need to find a new topic of conversation. Besides, we're almost at the airport."

Mitch smiled. "Coward," he murmured.

She didn't respond, and the silence throbbed with almost the same intensity as had the previous discussion. But she didn't know how to break it; she was completely out of small talk. As they arrived, she suggested Mitch drop her off without parking, but he ignored the suggestion, parked the Volvo and carried her luggage into the terminal while she walked beside him and tried to concentrate on the trip ahead instead of the man she was leaving behind.

They'd made excellent time on the freeway and her plane wasn't scheduled to leave for another fifty minutes. Meerstahl and his assistant weren't due in for another half hour. She explained this to Mitch after they checked her bags and she urged him to go home.

"I'll walk you to the gate and stay until Meerstahl arrives," he said. His tone preempted further discussion. "Want some coffee?"

"No, but if you—"

"No. We'll just go to the gate, then," he said, cupping her elbow and guiding her toward the concourse.

She tried to ignore his touch and pretend that it wasn't affecting her. She didn't succeed. She glanced up at him, and he immediately met her gaze. He was obviously as aware of her as she was of him, and the knowledge of their mutual attraction made her heart pound. At the scanning station he released her elbow, and on the other side of the passage Ginny switched the strap of her attaché case to the shoulder nearest Mitch, thereby creating an obstacle between them. He raised an eyebrow, but said nothing.

To add to Ginny's distress, the waiting area near the gate seemed filled with couples bidding passionate farewells. Everywhere Ginny looked she encountered men and women hugging, kissing, holding hands and gazing adoringly at each other. "I never realized

Seattle was so romantic," she said, trying to make a joke of it.

Mitch didn't reply. He stood watching her.

"Well, as you can see, we have all sorts of time and Meerstahl's not here," she said. "This must be boring for you. Why don't you drive on home?"

"Trying to get rid of me?" he said with a faint smile.

"Maybe."

"Why?" His gray eyes challenged her.

She hesitated. "I think you know," she said at last.

"You're right. I do." His gaze softened as it roamed over her. Then he sighed. "I also wish you weren't leaving this morning."

Her mouth went dry. "It's for the best," she managed. "We probably both need some distance."

"I suppose."

"Arnold's welfare is the top priority. Our... concerns are secondary."

"You're right." He gazed toward a man in a business suit locked in an embrace with a woman in jeans and T-shirt.

"This is a terrible place to be having this discussion," Ginny said. "With all these people—" She broke off the sentence abruptly.

"Yeah." Mitch glanced at her. "Sort of like standing outside the candy store when it's closed."

"Mitch, I didn't mean for us to be in such an awkward position."

A twinkle appeared in his eyes and he began to chuckle.

"What?"

"Nothing."

"Tell me," she insisted.

"I just wondered what sort of position you'd prefer."

Warmth rushed to her cheeks. "Mitch, that's exactly the sort of remark to avoid. We—"

"You asked," he reminded her. Then he sighed again and shook his head. "Well, Ginny, I'm grateful for one thing. At least I know we're both struggling with this. That boosts my ego."

"Somehow I didn't imagine your ego needed boosting."

"Then you have a lot to learn about me."

Ginny gazed into his eyes and for the first time allowed herself to recognize the vulnerability lurking there. Or perhaps Mitch was revealing it for the first time. In any case, she admitted to herself that Arnold might not be the only person in danger of being hurt in this crazy situation. "Perhaps, when I get back, we should reconsider the wisdom of continuing our arrangement," she said softly.

"Maybe."

"Give it some thought while I'm gone, okay?"

He gave a short laugh. "I probably won't think of much else."

"Mitch, I'm sorry." She gazed down at the carpet.

"Hey, don't be sorry." He tilted her chin up with one finger. "There are worse problems than being attracted to someone who's off-limits. We just have to figure out what to do about it, that's all."

The gentle compassion in his eyes nearly undid her. She stared, transfixed, and her breathing grew shallow.

"I'd give five years of my life to kiss you right now," he whispered.

Her resolve wavered. Perhaps just once. Here would be the perfect spot, where a kiss could go no farther. Yes, they could chance one kiss. They could—her inner debate ended as an impatient male voice called her name. She whirled in embarrassment to find Meerstahl and his associate striding toward her. His flight had arrived early.

DRIVING BACK from the airport, Mitch couldn't decide which he regretted more, embarrassing Ginny in front of her client or missing out on the kiss her eyes had promised him. She might never allow herself to be so susceptible again. If he had any sense, he wouldn't allow himself to be, either.

He ought to get out of the situation now, before anyone got hurt. The chance meeting with Bob and Ruby Taylor at the symphony had pointed out a truth he'd been avoiding for three years, namely that his past could catch up with him at any time. Foolishly he'd imagined his only worry was how to rebuild his own self-confidence.

He thought about Monday night's phone conversation with his psychologist, Jan Weiderman. He'd attended counseling sessions with her once every two weeks for the past year, and he'd wanted her advice on moving in with Ginny and Arnold. She'd hesitated, reluctant as always to tell him what to do, but finally she'd suggested that he needed to reestablish meaningful connections with people. That had been Jan's way of telling him to go for it.

And boy, had he connected, especially with Ginny. The excitement of living with her had lulled him into forgetting that the time bomb still ticked away. It

could go off at any time, destroying everything he'd
worked so hard to create.

He could defuse the bomb, of course. All he had to
do was tell Ginny about the incident in Cedarville, and
that he'd been found innocent. While he was at it, he
could tell his principal, too, the guy who'd been so
eager to renew his contract at Westwood for next fall.
And Arnold. He'd need to tell Arnold. Strangely
enough, Mitch thought Arnold might be the only one
who'd understand.

Ginny, superprotective mother that she was,
wouldn't want to take the risk of having him around
Arnold, not with a blot like that on his record. She
might even wonder, just a little, if the jury had been
mistaken. His principal, supportive though he'd been,
was a conservative when it came to scandal. Mitch had
decided that several weeks into the school year and
had dismissed the notion of confiding in the man as
self-destructive. If Jack Granger hadn't seen fit to
mention the incident in Mitch's letters of reference,
then Mitch would be dumb to fall on his sword by revealing everything.

He'd probably been crazy to think he could eventually resume the profession he'd trained for. If he left
teaching forever, and put more geography between
himself and Cedarville, Idaho, the whole thing might
go away forever. Maybe, by the time Ginny returned,
he'd have decided to do exactly that. Arnold would be
upset, but that was better than having the bomb go off
in everyone's faces.

Trouble was, if he left, he'd close the door on
Ginny, too, and that wouldn't be easy. He'd often
wondered as he'd bungled through the usual infatua-
tion and disillusionment cycles of young adulthood if

he'd recognize the right woman when she appeared. He didn't wonder anymore. His feelings for Ginny deepened each day, along with the urge to take her in his arms and tell her so. He'd fought his inclinations successfully so far, restricting himself to the slight contact that masqueraded as social courtesy.

The thought of tossing away the potential joy he and Ginny could find together made his heart ache. Damn the circumstances that had brought him to this point! And damn the immaturity of a young kid who'd had no idea that his accusations could affect another's life so completely.

Whatever Mitch decided to do, however, he couldn't act on it until Ginny came back on Sunday. Even then, she might choose to let him go for her own reasons; she didn't want to become involved in a love affair right under Arnold's nose, and Mitch understood that. If she came home convinced that the temptation was too great, then he'd be packed and out of there by Sunday night. Between now and then, though, he'd do one hell of a job taking care of her kid for her.

With that resolution firmly in place, Mitch arrived at the townhouse to find Arnold dressed for wrestling practice. Arnold greeted him with a big smile of welcome, confirming for Mitch that for these few days, at least, he was in the right place. He remembered the special activities he'd planned as surprises for Arnold, beginning with a Mariners baseball game that night. If he only had six days to work with, he'd make them six memorable ones for Arnold.

THE MARINERS LOST to the Boston Red Sox in extra innings, but Arnold insisted it didn't matter that the home team had been defeated. "Are you kidding?" he said, his braces flashing in the gleam from oncoming headlights as they drove back to the townhouse. "Just to *be* at the game was great. I've only been once before."

"When was that?" Mitch asked.

"This guy from school asked me to go along when his dad took him. His family's into sports and stuff. Mom isn't much for that, you know."

"True, but she's given you some other terrific opportunities, like encouraging you to play an instrument. I understand you're pretty good on the clarinet." Mitch suspected that Arnold's "guy from school" was Billy Herman.

"I guess." Arnold didn't sound particularly proud of the fact.

"Not many people have musical talent. I don't."

Arnold glanced at him. "You don't need it," he said. Then, before Mitch could respond, Arnold pointed out the window. "Wow, that's a neat '57. Did you see it?"

"Yep. Good restoration job." Mitch realized that the switch of topics to restored '57 Chevies had been no accident. Arnold didn't want to talk about his talent for the clarinet, let alone his feud with Billy Herman. Mitch began to wonder if six days was long enough to be of much help to Arnold, after all.

"When I'm sixteen, I'm gonna get an old car and fix it up, like that. Maybe I'll take auto mechanics in high school."

Mitch could just imagine what Ginny would think of that as an academic choice. Still, if discussing cars forged a conversational link with Arnold at the moment, he'd cultivate the topic. "Maybe tomorrow you'd like to help me change the oil in this buggy,'' he said.

"Hey, yeah! I'll have to learn how to do that, if I'm gonna work on my own car.'' He sighed. "Some kids already know about stuff like that. Some of them even have a chance to drive, like on a private road, or something. I hear them talking about it, and I don't say anything, because I've never done it. Sometimes I feel like such a geek.''

Mitch passed an abandoned discount store fronted by a large, empty parking lot. On an impulse he made a U-turn at the next light and came back to it.

"Where're we going?'' Arnold asked. "This place has been closed for a couple of months.''

"I thought you might like to try driving.''

Arnold turned to him in astonishment, and his dark eyes sparkled with the lure of forbidden delights. "You mean it?''

Mitch shrugged and turned off the ignition and headlights. "Why not? This is private property, so we're not breaking the law, and the Toyota's used to it. Back in my other teaching job I taught drivers' education, too. Sometimes on Saturdays kids would want some extra practice, and their parents weren't available, so I'd take them in this.''

"Is that where it got all the dents?''

"Mostly.''

"I wouldn't dent it,'' Arnold said solemnly.

"I'm sure you wouldn't. So, you want to try?''

"You bet!'' Arnold unsnapped his seat belt and flipped open the passenger door. "This'll be cool!''

"Remember it's a stick shift, Arnold. That's a little trickier than an automatic, like your mom's Volvo.''

"That's even better. When I get my car, I'm putting in four-on-the-floor. I *need* to learn on a stick."

When Mitch settled Arnold in the driver's seat with the boy's left foot on the clutch and his right on the brake, Arnold was so excited his legs shook. "Just relax," Mitch said gently.

"I'm relaxed. Can I turn the key?"

"In a minute." Mitch carefully explained the workings of the clutch and the gas pedal. The parking lot was empty of cars, but it still contained several unlit lampposts, and a car out of control could easily ram one of them.

"I think I've got the idea," Arnold said, staring straight ahead, his neck and shoulders stiff and his knees still trembling.

"Then turn the key."

The Toyota's engine kicked over the first time, for which Mitch was grateful. Maybe tomorrow he'd add a wax job to the oil change, as a special reward for the little car.

"Now what?" Arnold asked, gripping the wheel until his fingers turned white at the edges.

"Turn on the lights." The windshield wipers flapped back and forth in front of them. "No, the other switch." The wipers settled back and the headlights came on. "There."

"Sorry."

"Don't worry about it. Most people turn on the wrong things when they get into an unfamiliar car. You can't be expected to know how all the stuff works until you've driven a car for a while."

Arnold looked relieved. "I don't want to break anything."

"You won't. Now, slowly let up on the clutch while you press down gently on the gas." The Toyota bucked forward, wheezing for nourishment. "More gas," Mitch said, using the calm voice he'd perfected for these situations. "Steer left. No, left. The other side. Left!" A metal crunch and a jolt told him the Toyota's right fender had grazed the lamppost he'd been trying to direct Arnold around.

With a frightened cry, Arnold took both feet off the pedals and stalled the car. "I hit something," he said, staring straight ahead. "Mitch, I hit something. I said I wouldn't and I did. I'll pay for it. Whatever it costs, I'll get a job. I can mow lawns. I can baby-sit. I can—"

"Relax, Arnold, and turn off the headlights," Mitch said. "Then restart the car, and turn the headlights back on."

"But—"

"It's only a little scrape. I have some touch-up paint in the trunk. Ready to try again?"

"I don't think so."

"Arnold, I don't care about the scrape. The Toyota's had a lot worse done to it. One time this kid, the quarterback on the football team—" Mitch threw that in on purpose "—backed into a brick wall. I had to have the trunk pulled back into shape, and it still doesn't close quite right."

"A brick wall?" Arnold's eyes widened as he looked at Mitch. "Did you let him drive after that?"

"Sure. People don't learn without making mistakes. If they're lucky, the mistakes are small, like bashing in a trunk."

"That's not small," Arnold insisted.

"Yes, it's very small," Mitch said. "Which makes your little scrape almost nonexistent. So come on, Arnold. Show some courage. Push in the clutch and turn the key." Mitch watched with pride as determination slowly replaced fear in Arnold's dark eyes.

"Okay," he said, and shoved his sneakered foot down on the clutch. "Okay, I'll do it."

The car bucked some more, but this time Arnold paid attention to his steering. They jack-rabbited around the parking lot, but eventually Mitch convinced Arnold to shift into second, and the ride smoothed out. A slow grin spread across Arnold's face.

"Now take your foot off the gas, put your left foot on the clutch and step down gradually on the brake," Mitch instructed.

Arnold brought the car to a jerky, but safe, stop.

"Turn off the lights. Now the ignition."

Arnold followed instructions, and when the car was quiet, he looked at Mitch. "I did it."

"You certainly did." He held up one hand and Arnold gave him a high five. "Congratulations." Mitch absorbed the heady feeling of Arnold's triumph and his part in it. How sweet to be needed, and to fulfill the need. With every positive experience he shared with Arnold, the pain he'd buried for three years became a little less sharp. No, he couldn't leave this kid on Sunday, even if staying meant he'd run the risk of disclosure. If Ginny thought she wanted him gone for her own reasons, he'd find a way to convince her otherwise. He'd advised Arnold to show some courage tonight. Mitch could do no less.

# CHAPTER SIX

USUALLY GINNY LIKED the focus group tours, liked ferreting out people's opinions, foibles and prejudices. Her enthusiasm for the job ordinarily made the days whisk by.

Not this time. She tried to rationalize her dislike of this tour as a dislike of her client. Meerstahl and his associate, a bootlicking sort named Edwards, insisted that she join them for dinner each night and then proceeded to guide the conversation inevitably to sports, which they obviously loved and she had to pretend some interest in. Odd, Ginny thought, that she'd lived with an athlete for over a week, and he hadn't pushed a discussion of sports on her once. These men, both overweight and no doubt incapable of walking a mile without resting at intervals, talked sports incessantly.

To add to Ginny's frustration, Arnold and Mitch hadn't been home either of the times she'd called. The first night she'd left a breezy message on the answering machine telling them she was glad the two of them were out enjoying themselves. The second night she'd reminded Arnold to be sure to get enough sleep. After leaving that message, she'd wanted to erase it.

In St. Louis on the third night she paced the length of her hotel room and debated whether to call again. Mitch had phone numbers for her at every hotel, so if something had gone wrong, he'd have contacted her. She should probably skip a night and not phone home.

Resolving to do that, she flipped on the television and changed into her nightgown. She'd left Meerstahl and Edwards having after-dinner drinks in the bar. She'd begged off from their booze-induced suggestion that they all take a taxi to see the six-hundred-thirty foot Gateway Arch at night. After an entire day and part of an evening in the company of the two men, she wanted to cocoon herself in her air-conditioned room, watch some TV, and go to bed.

Business trips were about the only time she watched television. She considered it a necessary way of heightening her marketing awareness, but seldom found time at home. When she was alone in a hotel room, however, television provided undemanding company as well as a useful research tool.

As if to taunt her, the channel she'd turned on showed a baseball game, and she switched the station with a groan. Eventually she settled on a family sitcom, expecting to pay more attention to the commercials than the show. She propped two pillows against the imitation black walnut headboard of her queen-size bed and tried to focus on the screen, but her attention wandered to the bedside table where the phone sat.

She calculated the time difference. Mitch and Arnold would be finished with dinner and were probably deciding what to do for the rest of the evening. Perhaps they were loading the dishwasher and joking around with each other, throwing those fake punches they'd become so fond of. In only a week of being around their horseplay, she'd grown used to it, although she hadn't given in on the issue of wrestling in the living room.

She wondered what they'd had to eat and what they were talking about. She wondered how Mitch was dressed, picturing him in his usual tank top and shorts. Most of all she wondered if he missed her.

If she believed what he'd said at the airport, he'd be thinking about her a lot as he debated whether they should keep their arrangement or abandon it on Sunday. Between Meerstahl and the focus groups, Ginny hadn't had much free time to think, but whenever her job didn't occupy her thoughts, Mitch did. After three days of sporadic inner arguments, she still didn't know what to do. If she'd hoped for an answer to surface during this trip, it hadn't presented itself so far.

She stared at the phone. Both her messages had promised to try to catch Arnold and Mitch later. This *was* later. After having missed being there for two calls, they might have stayed home to get her next one. They might be sitting around, wasting time, waiting to see if she tried to call again. She didn't want them to worry.

Feeling justified, Ginny dialed for an outside line and placed her call. After five rings she felt really sorry for herself. Arnold and Mitch weren't waiting anxiously for her call. After seven rings she became irritated. They'd left without bothering to turn on the answering machine. Arnold knew she required that machine to be on, for business reasons and in case of emergencies. After nine rings, she was frantic. Arnold *did* understand the importance of the answering machine, which meant if he hadn't turned it on, something was wrong. He was in the hospital. Or Mitch was. They both were. Unconscious. Or worse.

That damn Toyota. She should have insisted they always use the Volvo. She'd call the police. She'd call—

On the fifteenth ring, Arnold answered.

"Arnold!" She collapsed back against the pillows. "My goodness, where were you?"

"In the backyard, Mom. Sorry it took so long. We thought you might call, and we tried to listen, but we got involved in picking out the rings around Saturn, and—"

"So you're using the telescope?" Ginny slowly recovered her equilibrium. No one was hurt; all was well.

"Yeah. Mitch loves it. He's always wanted one, I guess."

"Then it's nice he has a chance to use yours." She battled the longing to be there with them, in the cool darkness of the backyard, taking turns peering through the telescope. She imagined the three of them stopping to have ice cream. She imagined the deep cadence of Mitch's voice as he sat in a lawn chair and discussed wonders like black holes, white giants and nebulas.

"Guess what, Mom?"

"What?" she asked indulgently. Mitch was so good for Arnold, she thought. All of her worries were foolish. She couldn't ask for a better caretaker. He was so considerate, so responsible, so—

"Mitch let me drive his car."

"He *what?*" She sat straight up in the bed.

"I thought you'd be surprised. It was great, Mom. I jerked it around a little at first, and I scratched the paint on this lamppost, but then I got the hang of steering, and I drove really great in second gear."

Ginny tried to make her lips work but they seemed carved in granite. She tried again. "Put Mitch on," she said tightly. "Please," she added as an afterthought.

"Are you okay, Mom? You sound funny."

"I'm fine, Arnold. Just get Mitch."

"He's still outside. Hang on a minute."

A minute. She sat for what seemed like hours, all the while heaping torrents of abuse on the head of the irresponsible jerk who'd had the colossal bad judgment to put a thirteen-year-old behind the wheel of a machine capable of killing him.

"Ginny?" Mitch's voice sounded close, as if he shared the bed with her.

"Hello, Mitch." She clutched the receiver tighter, unnerved by the intimate connection. It occurred to her that she'd never talked to him on the telephone before.

"Arnold said you wanted to discuss something with me."

"I certainly do," she said, grabbing hold of her indignation once more. "Arnold says, and I can hardly believe my ears, that you let him drive your car."

"Well, yes, I did."

Adrenaline rushed through her. "Are you out of your mind? He's thirteen, for God's sake. He doesn't know the first thing about cars. He could have been seriously hurt!"

"I take it you don't approve."

"Very perceptive of you, Mitch. Can you offer any justification for such an irresponsible action?"

He sighed. "I don't consider it irresponsible. I've taught driver's ed. I know what I'm doing. And it was my car."

"And my son! He hit a lamppost! And besides that, you were breaking the law."

"First of all, he didn't *hit* anything—he grazed it. Second of all, we were in a deserted parking lot so we weren't breaking any laws. Third of all, Arnold took a big step toward growing up that night, and I'm proud of him."

"Growing up? Is driving a car two and half years before it's legal to do so your idea of growing up?"

"Ginny, I'm sure if you'd been there, you would have understood."

"I'm sure I would not," she said, trembling with anger. "I want no more of such activities while I'm gone. Is that clear?"

"Ginny, the boy needs—"

"And don't you dare tell me what Arnold needs. You have no children. I'm so sick of people who have no children thinking they know exactly how to raise them."

"Could you be overreacting a little?" Mitch asked, an edge to his voice.

"No, but you're overstepping a little! Make that a lot. Listen, Mitch, if you have any more bright ideas about how to help Arnold grow up while I'm gone, forget them, okay?"

"Whatever you say." His tone was cool. "You're the boss."

"Exactly. And don't forget it. Good night, Mitch." She hung up the phone without waiting for his reply. Then she buried her face in her hands until she stopped shaking. Driving a car. Good Lord. And she'd thought Bambi's transgression with the beer had been bad. At least Bambi and Arnold had been sitting safely in Ginny's kitchen while they'd drunk it.

This was why she'd hired middle-aged women to take care of her son. None of them had seemed compelled to help Arnold grow up faster. Too bad if Arnold didn't approve of her choices. When she got home, she'd scour the city until she found a stable, dowdy woman to finish out the summer. Mitch Adamson had to go.

AT THE SEATTLE-TACOMA International Airport on Sunday, Ginny said her goodbyes to Meerstahl and Edwards as they walked down the roped-off area toward the concourse. Then, dreading the impending confrontation, she searched out Arnold and Mitch in the crowd of people waiting for arriving passengers. Arnold waved both hands and grinned, but Mitch looked wary. She tamped down a surge of excitement at seeing Mitch again, and instead, smiled at her son.

Arnold hugged her, something he hadn't done when she'd returned from a trip while Mrs. Waddell had been in charge. He'd been mad at her then. Well, he'd probably be mad at her again.

"We had a great time, Mom!" he said. "You shoulda been here. We went to a Mariners game, but they lost in extra innings, but that was okay. We played tennis and golf. And that night you called, we really saw the rings of Saturn plain. If it's not cloudy tonight, we should set up the telescope, so you can—"

"Your mom might be tired from her trip," Mitch said, guiding them toward the baggage area. "We discussed that, remember?"

"Oh, yeah." Arnold deflated a little.

"I'm not that tired," Ginny said, although she was exhausted. "We can get out the telescope if you like."

*And then, after you're in bed, I'll give Mitch the bad news,* she amended silently.

"I hope it's not cloudy," Arnold said. "Mom, you will freak out when you see Saturn. Oh, and I didn't tell you. I cooked dinner one night, and one pan got a little burned, but I scrubbed it and you can't tell. I think we should get a croquet set, Mom. For the backyard. Mitch and I thought that would be great." Arnold rattled on, full of tales about his week. Ginny couldn't remember the last time she'd returned from a trip and he'd been this excited. He was so exuberant he hadn't noticed her silence, or Mitch's.

Mitch and Arnold each took a suitcase so that all she carried to the car was her attaché case. Ginny remembered Mrs. Waddell's bad back, which had prevented her from carrying any luggage when Ginny arrived home from the last trip. She'd decided then to buy suitcases with wheels for the next trip, but hadn't had time. Mitch was handy to have around for carrying suitcases, she admitted grudgingly. But that didn't justify keeping him on. Not considering all the problems he presented.

In the parking lot, the Volvo sparkled from a fresh wash job. Mitch drove home, another perk she'd probably be giving up. The women she'd hired in the past hadn't been eager to take the wheel when Ginny was available to do it. But she also had to keep in mind that Mitch had also taken it upon himself to indoctrinate Arnold in the art of driving.

She glanced at Mitch from her position in the front passenger seat. His blue cotton sport shirt and wearsoftened jeans looked comfortable. Touchable. Huggable... No, darn it! His physical appeal could play no part in her decision. If anything, it would count against him. Just because his lean, muscled body was a refreshing change after a week of looking at Meerstahl and Edwards was no reason to change her mind. No reason.

"Wait'll we get home, Mom. We have a surprise for you," Arnold said from the back seat. "Don't we, Mitch?"

"I don't know about this 'we' stuff. You did most of it, Arnold. Don't go giving me the credit."

"Yeah, I will, too," Arnold replied, punching Mitch lightly on the shoulder. "I will if I want."

*A surprise,* Ginny thought, turning to gaze at Arnold. What next? "Arnold, you didn't take someone's offer of a free kitten or puppy, did you?"

"Nope. But now that you mention it, I've been thinking about a dog. Something like a Great Dane, maybe."

Ginny groaned. "You know that's out of the question. We've been over this before. We don't have the room and we don't have the time, not in the winter, anyway, when you're in school all day and I'm at work. You can't get a dog just because you'll play with him three months out of the year."

"Other kids have dogs," Arnold grumbled.

"Your mom's got a point," Mitch said. "It's not great for a dog if nobody's home all day. And your yard is a little small for a Great Dane."

Ginny appreciated the support, and she gave Mitch an approving glance. One intelligent statement about dogs didn't cancel out the incident with the car, but she noticed that Arnold dropped the subject of a dog. With her, he might have continued to argue, but Mitch could assuage him with a few well-chosen words. She was, she discovered, still jealous of that power, even when it served her best interests, as it did in this case.

Arnold would be tougher to handle once Mitch was gone, no doubt about that. But she was his mother, after all, and she could deal with her own son. She'd always been able to before, and a few hormones weren't going to stymie her. Not by a long shot.

"So I take it this surprise isn't a pet?" she asked, still wondering what awaited her at home.

"Nope," Arnold said, obviously pleased with himself for having a secret.

"You didn't paint the walls or anything, did you?"

Arnold snorted. "You think I'd be that stupid? You freaked out when we moved the furniture a little bit. I can imagine your reaction if we changed the color of the *walls.*"

"Well, I'm glad to know you wouldn't paint the walls without consulting me," Ginny said, thinking she wasn't crazy about the picture of herself that was emerging. Arnold's description of her behavior made her sound like a fussy, materialistic person who was more concerned about how things looked in her home than how people felt there. "Do you...do you like the color of the walls?" she asked, realizing she'd never asked before.

"What's to like or not like about white walls?" Arnold replied.

"Would you, um, like a different color in your room?"

"You'd let me?" Arnold asked.

Ginny wanted to crawl under the car seat. Mitch must think she was a totally controlling mother if she insisted on her preference for the color of the walls in her child's bedroom. "I—sure, I would. I didn't think you cared what color they were," she said, sneaking a peek at Mitch. He was smiling, the turkey.

"Care? Of course I care. Hey, maybe I could have one wall black, one red, one white, and one—no, two walls would have to be the same. Four colors is too much."

"Three colors is too much," Ginny said, and instantly regretted her comment. "I mean, maybe we need to go to the paint store and look around before you decide. Wouldn't that make sense?"

"If you want," Arnold said, in a tone that indicated his disinterest in hanging around a paint store.

Fool that she was, she glanced at Mitch in silent appeal. Maybe the all-powerful Mitch would say something against walls in red, black and white; maybe he would support her as he had with the dog idea. Mitch returned her gaze with a smile and said nothing. Clearly he didn't care if Arnold wanted polka dots on his walls. Of course, it wasn't his house. He could afford to be nonchalant. Ginny set her mouth in a grim line and stared out the windshield. Next to her, she thought she heard a soft chuckle.

When they reached the townhouse, Ginny saw nothing amiss. In fact, everything seemed perfect—the green grass in front cut exactly the right length, the flower beds weeded, the walkway swept. Of course, the ugly, brown Toyota, the vehicle of Mitch's transgression, sat at the curb. She didn't notice any new scrapes, though. "The yard looks wonderful," she said, turning to Arnold. "Is that the surprise?"

"Not really," he answered. "We worked on it a little, but that's not the surprise."

"Oh."

"You go on in, Mom," Arnold said as Mitch pulled the Volvo into the garage and turned off the engine. "Mitch and I will get the suitcases," he added, with the male tone of proprietorship he'd adopted since being around Mitch.

With a start Ginny realized the last sentence he'd spoken had also included a deeper note than she remembered, a bass where a treble used to be. Arnold's voice was changing.

She used her key to open the kitchen door leading from the garage. The aroma of roast beef wafted toward her as she stepped onto the spotless kitchen floor. They had dinner cooking and had cleaned the kitchen top to bottom; that much was obvious.

She put her attaché case and keys on the desk and opened the oven. Pot roast, one of her favorites. After so many days of eating restaurant food her mouth watered for the home-cooked meal. She appreciated the effort Mitch and Arnold had made, but of course Mrs. Waddell had done similar things for her. One thing Arnold could never complain about when they'd had middle-aged women taking care of him was the cooking.

Ginny continued walking through the house, planning to head upstairs to change clothes, but the scene in the dining room stopped her. An abundant bouquet of carnations, daisies, iris and one red rose graced the center of the table, which had been set with her best china and silver. Her crystal goblets sat at each place, and pink linen napkins were fan-folded on each plate. To complete the picture, Arnold had unearthed her silver candlesticks and bought graceful white (white! she thought) candles to go in them.

"You like it?" Arnold said from behind her.

"I love it," Ginny replied, turning to hug him. "What a beautiful thought."

"Mitch had the idea," Arnold said, his dark eyes glowing. "He said you deserved it, for all you do."

Tears welled in her eyes. It was a bribe, of course. All a bribe on Mitch's part. Still, she couldn't remember the last time anyone had shown, by word or gesture, that they realized how hard she worked, both as a career woman and as a mother. In spite of herself, she was touched. She gazed past Arnold and saw Mitch leaning in the doorway. "This is lovely."

"Welcome home," he said.

"Mom, there's more," Arnold said, almost twitching with excitement. "Go upstairs. To your bedroom."

Ginny obeyed, with Arnold following. She didn't have the courage to look back and see if Mitch was coming up, too. He was making this very difficult for her, being so sweet and understanding just when she'd had one of the most exhausting, miserable business trips of her life.

In the bedroom more fresh flowers graced her dresser. She breathed in the scent. "Nice," she said to Arnold. From the corner of her eye she looked for Mitch and noted that he had not come up, after all.

"Look in there," Arnold said, pointing to her bathroom.

Ginny looked, and gasped. Her tub sparkled; no sign of the hurried departure she'd made a week ago. On a small table beside the tub rested a bottle of champagne in an ice bucket. A plastic, fluted goblet, tied with a pink bow, was also on the table. Rimming the tub were three choices of bath salts, and newly laundered towels hung on the racks. "Did you fix this up?'' she asked Arnold, knowing he couldn't have, not with the champagne. Arnold would never have thought of bath salts, either.

"I helped, but Mitch did most of the stuff up here. He's pretty neat, huh, Mom?"

Ginny sagged against the doorway of her bathroom. "Arnold, I—"

"Mom, don't be mad at him about the driving thing."

"He told you I was mad?"

"No. He said you guys discussed it and decided it wasn't a good idea. But I could tell when I told you about it, and you made him come to the phone so fast. You were mad all right."

"Yes, I was. I thought he took a needless chance with your safety."

Arnold met her gaze, and she realized he had to look down to meet her eyes. Maybe he'd grown another inch in the few days she'd been gone....

"Let me tell you something, Mom," he said, and the bass notes crept in again, as they had earlier. "That night with the car was one of the best things that's ever happened to me."

"Oh, I'm sure you got a thrill out of it, Arnold, but—"

"That's not what I mean," he said, uncharacteristically interrupting her. "I mean that when I scraped the car, I got so scared, and I didn't want to try again. I'd hurt his car, and everything. I felt like scum. But Mitch got me to try again. He told me the car wasn't important, and I knew he meant it."

Ginny felt a twinge of remorse. Mitch's attitude toward his car was a far cry from her attitude about her living-room furniture.

Arnold took a deep breath. "So I tried again, Mom, and I did it. I did it! I didn't feel like scum anymore. And now I know, if some emergency came up or something, I could drive a car if I had to. I read about some kid my age who drove a car to get somebody to the hospital. I remember thinking I couldn't even do that. But now I can, Mom," he said, his expression earnest. "Now I can."

Ginny took his face in her hands. "Mitch really scared me with that driving stunt. I would die if something ever happened to you, Arnold."

He flushed and looked away. "I know."

She released him, not wanting to embarrass him further. "I'll think about what you said."

"While you're having champagne and taking your bubble bath, right?" he said with a hopeful lift of his eyebrows.

"Right." She took the chilled bottle from the ice bucket and handed it to Arnold. "If you'll go downstairs and get Mitch to open this, I'll begin that program right away."

"Sure thing." Arnold hurried out of the room.

Ginny removed her suit jacket and nudged off her shoes. A long soak in the tub and a glass of champagne were luxuries she hadn't allowed herself in ages. She started the water running and was debating which of the bath salts to use when someone cleared his throat behind her. She turned, expecting Arnold, and found Mitch standing with the open bottle of champagne.

"I wanted to say personally, when Arnold wasn't around, that I'm sorry about the car thing," he said. "I've thought a lot about it, and you're right, I should have checked with you first."

"What is this, a campaign? First Arnold and now you."

"Arnold?"

"He just asked me not to be mad at you for that."

Mitch looked puzzled. "I didn't tell him you were mad."

"He figured it out. Kids do that, especially sensitive kids like Arnold. Anyway, I appreciate all of this," she said, waving her hand around the bathroom. "For whatever reasons you did it."

"I can tell you exactly why I did it. I don't want you to fire me."

"And you thought I might?"

"After our last conversation, you bet I did. And after I cooled off, I realized you had grounds."

"Well, truthfully I did come home with that in mind," Ginny admitted. "But your honest apology makes a difference."

"I hope so."

"Besides, I promised Arnold I'd think about you some more while I soak in the tub."

"Oh?" His uneasiness waned, and a roguish look appeared in his eyes.

"Stop it," she said. "That's not what I meant."

"I didn't say a word."

"No, but that look..."

He winked at her. "Can't be blamed for looking," he said, his confidence obviously restored. "Here's your champagne." He handed her the bottle and left the bedroom, closing the door behind him. Even with the door closed, she could hear him whistle as he descended the stairs.

Ginny didn't know what sort of clarity of vision she hoped to gain by soaking in a warm tub and sipping champagne. What she did get was extremely mellow. By the time Mitch and Arnold served her a delicious meal by candlelight, and she'd unburdened herself of all the stories she'd collected about Meerstahl and Edwards—somewhat edited for Arnold's benefit—there was no way she could consider firing the golden-haired superman who'd provided her with such a terrific homecoming.

After dinner they set up the telescope and, as Ginny had fantasized while on her trip, they took a break for ice cream and sat in a semicircle in the cool darkness of the backyard talking about the mysteries of the universe. Eventually Arnold, who was sitting in the middle chair, yawned and announced he was going to bed. Ginny stayed where she was, her head resting on the cushioned back of the lawn chair, her eyes nearly closed. She felt too content to move.

Once Arnold was gone, Mitch switched to Arnold's chair and leaned toward her. "There's something we need to discuss," he said.

"Not tonight," she murmured, feeling relaxed and lazy. "We'll talk this all out tomorrow." She turned her head to gaze at him. "But if it makes you feel any better, I'm not nearly so convinced as I was that we should end this arrangement. It's been a wonderful evening, Mitch. Thanks."

He sighed and glanced across at the house, where Arnold's bedroom light threw a square of pale yellow on the grass of the side yard. "And I'm about to spoil it for you."

"How on earth are you going to do that?" A tiny ring of alarm sounded in her brain.

He continued to gaze at the house. Arnold's light flicked out. "I wasn't snooping, but now that I've found it, I think you should know."

"What are you talking about?" Panic began, curdling the sweet taste of ice cream in her mouth.

"The other night I asked Arnold where the telescope instructions were, and he told me to look in one of his desk drawers. I accidentally opened the wrong one. I'll bet he'd forgotten he'd hidden it in there."

"Hidden what, for God's sake?"

*"Bimbettes at the Beach."*

Ginny stared at him blankly.

"It's a porno movie, Ginny."

## CHAPTER SEVEN

GINNY GASPED. "I don't believe it. There's no way he could get such a thing."

"Sure there is. Mail order."

She remembered how Arnold always insisted on bringing in the mail. But that didn't necessarily mean anything. "Maybe you jumped to conclusions. Maybe it's some sort of science fiction or monster movie that only looks pornographic. Some of them do, with big-breasted women on the cover. People use sex to sell everything."

Mitch gazed at her in the quiet darkness. "I watched it."

Ginny groaned and covered her face in dismay and embarrassment. "I'm afraid to ask what's in it," she mumbled from behind her hands.

"You don't have to. You can judge for yourself. I smuggled it out again tonight so you could watch it, too. Tomorrow morning you can find some time to put it back. It goes in the middle left drawer of his desk, behind a pile of *Dungeons and Dragons* books."

"Me watch it?" Ginny glanced at him in surprise. "I don't want to see *Bimbettes at the Beach*."

"There's nothing too awful. Nobody gets tied up or anything."

Ginny made a face. "I should be grateful for that?"

"Yeah," he said with a chuckle. "I've seen worse. At least Arnold's not perverted. He just has a healthy interest in sex, like most boys his age."

"I still can't believe this. Not Arnold."

"Want me to get it?" He rose from his chair.

"No!" she said too quickly, too loudly. "I mean, since you have it now, why can't we simply destroy it and say nothing? I doubt Arnold will ask us where his *Bimbettes* video is." In the silence following her suggestion, Ginny read the answer. "Okay, you're right. I have to talk to him."

"And if you watch the video first, you might have a better idea of what to say to him," Mitch suggested.

Ginny sighed and flopped back in her chair. "Terrific. Not so long ago I was rereading *Heidi* and *Swiss Family Robinson* so Arnold and I could talk about them. Nobody told me the next item on the agenda was a discussion of X-rated movies."

"Have you ever seen one?"

Ginny glanced at him in the dim light. "Um, yeah. Once. A long time ago."

"Then this won't come as too much of a shock."

"What comes as a shock is that Arnold plotted to send away for this thing, has been hiding it in his drawer and probably used times when he was alone in the house to watch the bimbettes in action."

"That's really not all that shocking," Mitch said. "At his age I had a secret stash of *Playboy* magazines. This isn't much different, I guess."

"The heck it isn't. The girls in your magazines didn't move. They didn't..." Ginny hesitated, increasingly aware of the charged nature of this topic. Her overriding concern about Arnold had eliminated the erotic element of discussing this with Mitch, but now that the initial shock had subsided she was aware of Mitch as a man, an extremely virile man, sitting less than two feet from her.

"No, they didn't move. You're right about that." Mitch laughed. "From that standpoint, Arnold's self-education is better than mine was."

Ginny had put on a sweater against the evening chill, but she no longer felt chilly. She tried to shut out the inevitable images of men and women making love, of Mitch making love . . . to her.

"By the way," Mitch continued, "what have you told Arnold about sex?"

"Arnold?" she repeated, thinking that it would be a very good time for her to go inside. Except that inside was the video that Mitch wanted her to watch. Thank goodness she had a video recorder in her bedroom and wouldn't have to run the thing through the set in the living room.

"Yeah—Arnold. Your son." Mitch sounded amused.

"I bought him a book once." Ginny wondered how she'd face Arnold after she'd watched the video. Or how she'd face Mitch, for that matter.

"When?"

"I don't remember exactly." Ginny tried to concentrate on the conversation. "When he was about nine, I guess. He looked at it and gave it back to me." Maybe she'd watch the video on fast forward, to get it over with sooner. Then she pictured what that would look like, and began to laugh.

"What's so funny?" Mitch asked, smiling in response to her laughter.

"Never mind." Ginny tried to control herself, but the image stuck in her mind—a bionic couple performing at top speed. She pressed her hand to her mouth.

"You're not getting hysterical about this, are you?"

"No, I—" She gulped back a new wave of laughter. "At least, I don't think so. You see, I want to get this business of watching the movie over fast, so I'd decided to run it through on fast forward, but then I realized that I'd have—" She started laughing again.

Mitch grinned. "A marathon."

"Yeah," she said, still laughing. "Oh, my. Kids sure make life interesting."

"They do."

She smiled at him and realized a bond was developing between them, whether she wanted it to or not. They couldn't share these crisis points in Arnold's life without growing closer in the process.

Gradually she became aware that his smile had faded and the look in his eyes had changed from amusement to something else, something far more potent. The hushed darkness seemed to close around them. Even the noise of the crickets grew fainter, as if blocked by the intensity of his gaze.

"I missed you," he said.

Ginny swallowed. "I don't think we should—"

"I know. You're probably right. But just for the record, I missed you like the devil. When you walked off that plane, I wanted to trade places with Arnold, so I could hold you."

"Mitch, don't." Her whole body tingled. "You'll only make this more difficult for both of us."

"Right again. I must be a masochist, living here with you when I can't touch you."

"It has to be that way, Mitch," she said, her heart thudding in her ears. "The pornographic video makes that even more obvious. Arnold's at a delicate stage of his life, and the last thing he needs to further confuse the issue is for us to—''

''That doesn't help in the wee small hours of the night, when I'd give almost anything to be able to walk down the hall that separates us and take you in my arms.''

''Then perhaps you shouldn't stay,'' she said, her voice catching on the words.

''I'll stay. I'll stay because Arnold's got me hooked in, and because miserable as I am being near you and unable to do anything about my feelings, I'd probably be more miserable if I couldn't see you anymore.'' He rose abruptly from his chair. ''Good night, Ginny. I'll leave the video in your room.''

Long after he'd closed the back door, Ginny's fingers ached from clutching the arms of her chair. She massaged her stiff hands but continued to sit alone in the backyard listening to the crickets. The kitchen light flicked on for a few moments, telling her that Mitch had lingered downstairs, perhaps waiting to see if she would follow him in. Then the light winked out.

Surely she couldn't go on living in the same house with this man. He was clearly walking a thin line, and at any moment...she became lost in the possibilities as a delicious, familiar throbbing taunted her with the promise of what could be. But it could not be. If something happened between them, she would put a stop to it. Immediately. For Arnold's sake.

Yet Arnold wasn't the person on her mind as she walked inside and began locking up the house. As she climbed the stairs and walked past Mitch's room, she thought of him lying there near the window, with the breeze cooling his bare chest. She wondered if he slept nude, and if he locked his door. She could lock hers, for all the good it would do. Although she feared what Mitch might try, she feared her own impulses more.

The video lay on the bed, propped against her pillow. She approached it warily and finally picked it up. On the protective cover, two half-clothed women stared at the camera with a gaze Ginny hoped never to see in the eyes of any girl Arnold knew. She tried to imagine Arnold plotting to get this video. The idea wouldn't hold. He didn't even watch girls walk by on the street and had never had a date, let alone a girl-friend.

Maybe the video didn't belong to Arnold at all. Maybe somebody he knew, one of his friends from school or someone on the wrestling team, had given it to him. He might not even have watched it. Ginny rejected the last idea. He'd watched it. She recalled his lurking-by-the-bathroom routine with Bambi, and his wish that his mother hire another college girl. Ginny had forgotten that episode.

So, whether or not the video belonged to Arnold, she could assume he'd seen it, probably more than once. He'd had plenty of time when Mitch had driven her to the airport, for example, and there had been other occasions when he'd been alone for short periods of time. Ginny had worried about many things whenever she'd left Arnold by himself, but this hadn't been one of them. Welcome to puberty-land, she thought, shaking her head.

She laid the video on top of her bedroom television set, changed into her nightgown and began cleansing her face. She dragged the process out as long as possible. Then she checked her nails and decided they needed a little emery-board work and another coat of polish. While she was at it, she gave herself a mini-pedicure. She fooled with her short, blond hair, pulling it this way and that while she judged whether to get a haircut soon. Finally, she ran out of excuses, put the video into the recorder and settled on her bed to watch it.

Her face flamed as the actors disrobed in short order and began licking and nibbling each other. Arnold had viewed this, had witnessed this behavior, and she was supposed to discuss it with him. Then she remembered that Mitch had seen the video, too, and a different emotion assaulted her. Mitch, asleep down the hall—or more likely not asleep—had witnessed these scenes recently. One of the women was a blonde with short hair.

The coupling on the screen evolved into different combinations of men and women, but the effect remained the same—lust won the day, or night, in each case. Ginny didn't remember being aroused by the only other pornographic video she'd seen. Perhaps that had been because she'd watched it with a crowd of female friends who'd laughed and made fun of the action. How different to be here, in the privacy of her bedroom, with a desirable man only yards away.

At last the film ended. Ginny considered taking a cold shower, but that would mean admitting her condition. She turned off the VCR and the lights before climbing into bed. It was only a movie, anyway, a movie mostly geared toward men, if she evaluated the action objectively. She tried doing that, but it didn't help. Added to her dilemma was the suspicion that if she appeared in Mitch's room, he wouldn't turn her away.

Tense and wanting, she lay in her bed and prayed for the strength to stay there.

GINNY ARRANGED THINGS the following morning so that she ran late and only had time to dash through the kitchen, grab her insulated traveling mug full of coffee and charge out the door into the garage. She understood the escape was cowardly, but she needed more time before she could look Arnold, but most of all Mitch, in the eye.

At the office she poured herself another cup of coffee, told Claudia she wasn't officially in the office yet and waited for Maggie to come in. Her message spindle bristled with more paper than a trash collector's spear, but she ignored it. When she heard Maggie's voice in the outer office, she picked up her coffee mug and met Maggie at the entrance to her office with a terse "I need to see you."

"Okay," Maggie responded. "Let me get my coffee and I'll be right with you. And welcome back."

She returned moments later, flipped on the light and gestured toward one of the chintz chairs in front of the desk. When Ginny sat down, Maggie sat beside her. "Was Meerstahl that bad?" she asked, setting her steaming mug on the desk in front of her.

"He's pretty obnoxious, but that's not what I want to talk to you about. Mitch found a porn movie hidden away in one of Arnold's desk drawers."

"I don't believe it. Are we talking about the same Arnold? The clarinet player? The goody-two-shoes?"

"Apparently neither of us knows him as well as we thought we did," Ginny said, picking up her coffee mug and leaning back in the chair. "Anyway, now I suppose I have to confront him about it."

"Then he doesn't know that you know?"

"I don't think so. This morning I put it back in his drawer while he was out of the room."

"You watched the movie?" Maggie asked, her eyes bright.

"Yeah. Did I ever." Ginny took a calming sip of her coffee. Last night was still a vivid memory, including Mitch's comment about wanting to hold her in his arms. "It's titled *Bimbettes at the Beach*," she said, glancing at Maggie to catch her reaction.

Maggie rolled her eyes and reached for her coffee cup. "Wonderful. So it's sexist, too. That bothers me more than the idea of Arnold watching a pornographic video." She blew across the surface of her cup. "But I suppose all those movies are exploitive, huh?"

"Don't ask me. I'm no expert. Mitch said I should be happy it's not some sado-masochistic flick with whips and chains."

Maggie nearly dropped her coffee in her lap. "You watched the movie with Mitch?"

"No." Ginny laughed at Maggie's astonishment. "Does that sound like something I'd do?"

"Not really, but for a minute there, I thought we were getting into something really juicy."

"Absolutely not," Ginny said with more conviction that she felt. "I have enough problems dealing with this latest episode in Arnold's life. Oh, and his voice is changing. You can really tell now."

"Is it really?" Maggie tasted her coffee, grimaced and returned her mug to the desk. "Claudia's coffee is getting worse," she muttered. Then she turned back to Ginny. "So, little Arnold is growing up." Her tone and gestures grew expansive. "Why, it seems only yesterday that we took him to see Walt Disney cartoons, and now, in the blink of an eye he's graduated to porn."

"Maggie, listen, this isn't funny. I need some ideas about how to handle my discussion with Arnold."

"Well—" Maggie pursed her lips "—I don't suppose you could watch the movie together and discuss it afterward."

"Maggie!"

"Okay, okay. Let me think." She picked up her mug again and circled the rim with one finger. "I'm at a disadvantage here, never having smuggled dirty magazines into my room. There weren't any dirty magazines for girls when I was growing up. Ever think about that? The boys got all the important info while we learned how to color-coordinate our eye shadow and lipstick."

"No, I never thought about that. My big awakening came when I smuggled in a copy of *Lady Chatterley's Lover*, but I was already sixteen then, three years older than Arnold is now."

"I didn't read that book until I was in my twenties, but kids grow up faster, now."

"That's what Mitch said."

Maggie sighed. "I really don't know what to tell you, Ginny."

"But you're the one with the Chippendale calendar."

"That hardly makes me an expert on porn, sweetie."

"I know." Ginny sighed, too. "This is the blind leading the blind."

"Mitch seems to have some knowledge on the subject. What does he suggest?"

Ginny was taken aback. "I didn't ask him. This is *my* job, to handle as I see fit."

"Except that you just admitted you don't know where to start."

Ginny gazed at her friend and colleague. "Help me figure this out, Maggie. I'm not asking Mitch for his advice, and that's that."

"Ah. I see. A little tension in the Westerfelt hacienda?"

"I'll handle it. But first I have to plan what I'll say to Arnold about his foray into X-rated videos."

"Okay." Maggie stared at the ceiling. "How's this? You tell him that you know he has the video, *Bimbettes on the Beach,* which you try to pronounce without gagging. Then you ask if he has any questions."

Ginny took another sip of coffee and considered the approach. "I like it. Nonjudgmental, sensitive, willing to listen. I'll open the door to communication." She smiled. "Thanks, Maggie. I didn't realize how simple this could be."

"You're welcome. Now that the important part of the day is completed, shall we move on to Meerstahl and cat litter? I assume we have a final presentation to prepare."

Ginny grinned and rose from her chair. "Oh, that. Cheer up, Maggie. The summer will be over before you know it, and then I'll be able to concentrate on business for a change."

"Speaking for the 'and Associates' part of this operation, I certainly hope so."

Flashing a smile of gratitude, Ginny returned to her office buoyed by the conversation and Maggie's suggestion. She tackled her stack of messages with renewed energy. Life wasn't so difficult, after all.

GINNY'S GOOD SPIRITS lasted until she walked into the kitchen of her townhouse and realized that her moment of discussion with Arnold was almost at hand. She'd wait until after supper, she decided. Mitch and Arnold weren't home, and she vaguely remembered Mitch calling out to her this morning, as she dashed out the door, that he and Arnold would bring pizza home at around six o'clock. Ginny glanced at her watch. They'd be home any minute.

Hurrying upstairs, she changed into sweats and sneakers. While doing that, she heard Mitch and Arnold come home, then Arnold's step on the stairs.

"Mom!" he called. "Pizza's here. Getting cold!"

"Be right down. Go ahead and start," she called back. Then she dawdled, brushing her hair. Finally, a little angry with herself for being intimidated by a stupid porno movie, she went downstairs.

If Arnold suspected that she or Mitch knew his movie secret, he was a more accomplished actor than she'd ever imagined. He grinned at her, his mouth full of pizza, and asked why she'd taken so long.

"Slow, I guess," she said, taking her seat at the kitchen table. Her gaze skittered across Mitch. He, too, looked as if nothing were amiss. She couldn't believe that he'd had a restful night, either. He'd already watched the video, and had known that as he lay in bed, she was right down the hall watching the same orgy he'd witnessed.

But he smiled, as if they were merely casual friends, and asked her about her day. She contributed her share of dinner conversation and then asked about wrestling practice. Wrestling talk lasted until the last slice of pepperoni pizza disappeared from the cardboard container. Then Mitch excused himself and said he had to go upstairs and write a long-overdue letter to his parents. Ginny knew why he was leaving. He was giving her a chance to talk with Arnold.

"Guess I'll watch TV," Arnold said, throwing the pizza box in the trash and rinsing his milk glass in the sink.

*Or you could stick a certain tape in the VCR,* Ginny thought, *if you were alone.* She didn't want to have this talk. She didn't want Arnold to own a pornographic video. But he did. She took a deep breath. "Arnold, before you do, would you sit back down for a minute? I have something to talk to you about."

"Sure." He sprawled in a chair opposite her at the round, oak table. "Shoot."

She gazed at her son. He still had the same boyish face she treasured. The curly hair would always make him look younger than he was, but when the braces came off a year from now, he'd look more mature. "You still have some pizza in your braces."

Arnold explored the area with his tongue. "Is that what you wanted to talk about? I'm brushing and using the Water Pik, Mom, just like I'm supposed to."

"That's good. When's your next orthodontist appointment?"

"About two weeks from now, I think. It's on the calendar. What's all this about my teeth?" Arnold shifted restlessly in his chair. His attention span seemed shorter these days.

*It's called breaking the ice,* Ginny thought. "Nothing really. I just wondered if we'd remembered to schedule your appointment for after wrestling practice."

"Yeah, we did." Arnold pushed his chair back and crossed his ankle over his knee, displaying one of the running shoes he was so proud of, another purchase she'd warned was motivated by slick marketing techniques. He hadn't cared. At the moment he looked bored. And older. A few hairs poked out of his chin. The beginnings of a beard.

"Arnold, I have something to discuss with you." Ginny tried to remember exactly how Maggie had phrased the introduction to this talk.

"You already said that, Mom."

"Okay." She dovetailed her fingers and put her clasped hands on the table. "I, um, know that you have a video in your desk drawer," she mumbled, not looking at him. She couldn't make herself say the title, or the word "pornographic." She was afraid she was blushing.

"Aw, geez."

"And I wondered if you had any questions," she rushed on, still not looking at him.

Silence.

Finally, she found the courage to look up. His face was red, and he was fooling with the lace on his running shoe. "Well?" she prompted.

"Do we have to talk about this?" He wound the lace around his finger, unwound it and wound it back.

"I think we do."

He glanced at her, his dark gaze agonized. "But you're a *girl*, Mom."

"I'm also your mother, and the only parent you have. I was...surprised when Mitch told me about the video." Ginny wasn't sure she should admit even surprise. She vaguely remembered reading that parents should stay unruffled when confronted with a child's behavior, no matter what it was.

"Mitch told you? How'd he know?"

"He didn't mean to pry," Ginny said, hurrying to Mitch's defense. "He was looking for the telescope instructions and opened the wrong drawer by mistake."

"Oh. Oh, yeah. I forgot, when I told him to look there. . . . Damn. But still," he said, his voice picking up volume, "he shouldn't have ratted on me! That's low, really low."

"That's not 'ratting' in my book." She kept her hands clenched on top of the table. "Mitch is doing his job by making me aware of something I didn't know was going on. I'd expect him to tell me that kind of thing."

"So, you two can just gang up on me, is that right?"

"Arnold, of course not. We—"

"Real nice, Mom," Arnold sneered, thrusting back his chair and leaping to his feet. "Now I find out you've hired a spy. I thought this was a free country. I guess I was wrong about that, huh?"

"Wait a minute, Arnold." She hardly recognized this boy as her quiet, well-behaved son. "Mitch is concerned, as I am, about your welfare."

"Oh, yeah? Well, the best thing you can do, both of you, is leave me the hell alone!" Arnold stomped out of the room, hurled himself up the stairs and slammed his bedroom door.

## CHAPTER EIGHT

GINNY SAT at the table in a daze, wondering how a session that was supposed to have left Arnold contrite had ended with her feeling guilty, instead. He had a porno movie hidden in his room, for heaven's sake. She suspected that for someone his age to possess such a thing was illegal, so in effect he'd broken the law, yet he'd put her and Mitch in the wrong for presumably conspiring against him.

"I heard his door slam," Mitch said, coming into the kitchen and occupying the chair Arnold had recently vacated. "I gather the talk didn't go well."

"He's making us out to be the gestapo or something." Ginny still couldn't believe the injustice of it. "He accused me of hiring you to spy on him."

Mitch laughed.

"I'm glad you think it's funny. Arnold's never talked to me that way before." She recognized another emotion surfacing along with guilt. Her feelings were hurt.

"I'm sorry. It's just that he's behaving like such a typical kid of his age."

"Is he?" Ginny challenged, ready to do battle with someone, anyone. "I never talked to my mother that way."

"There could be lots of reasons for that. Girls aren't socialized to attack when they're confronted. Some do, anyway, but I'm sure you didn't. Remember what you told me the day you hired me? You said you weren't used to conflict."

"I do remember. I also said Arnold wasn't used to it, either." Ginny paused. "At least he hasn't been until now," she added, gazing at Mitch.

"Uh-*huh*." Mitch got up and walked over to the cupboard. He took out a glass and ran water into it from the kitchen faucet. "Want some?"

She shook her head. Let him try to get out of this one, she thought.

"You're implying that I have something to do with the change in Arnold's behavior, and the wrestling class does, too."

"I think that's a reasonable conclusion."

"Maybe it is," he said, taking a swallow of the water.

Ginny smiled. A small victory. A victory over a bronzed god who stood in her kitchen in a loose, white tank top and gray shorts, his caramel-colored skin stretched tight over muscles that commanded her attention every time he moved. He could afford to be generous—his sensual appeal rendered her almost powerless.

"Just remember that Arnold would have sent away for the video whether he'd met me or not," Mitch continued, gesturing with the glass.

"You don't know that," she said, trying to maintain her edge.

"I think I do. Considering how long mail orders usually take, he must have sent away for the tape before the wrestling program started. In fact, I think he had it before I moved in. Although he's been Johnny-on-the-spot bringing in the mail, I usually notice what's in his hand, and I would have seen a package. Everything's been magazines and letters since I've been here."

Ginny couldn't disagree with Mitch's logic. She shifted back to her original argument. "Okay," she agreed. "Let's assume he already had the video. Maybe I would have found it, maybe not. But if I had, he wouldn't have reacted with such aggression. I believe the training he's had recently accounts for that behavior."

Mitch drained the glass and put it in the dishwasher. "You don't know that, but I'm willing to say you're right."

"So you admit that you've helped him become more difficult to handle?"

"Sure." Mitch leaned against the counter and folded his arms, which made his biceps more prominent. "And you're implying that's bad."

"I'm not implying. I'm saying it straight out. You've taken a gentle, easygoing kid and turned him into a combative, rebellious teenager. I want the old Arnold back."

His gaze flickered but his voice remained calm. "Maybe that would be easier for you, but not for Arnold. You might have a peaceful existence with him until he left home, but he'd be a sacrificial lamb once he encountered the world outside this house. He's already had a little taste of that reality with Billy Herman."

"Do you want to turn him into Rambo?"

"We've had this discussion before, Ginny. Obviously we don't agree. But Arnold's a long way from becoming Rambo. He's reacting like a normal thirteen-year-old."

"*Your* version of normal."

"Lots of people's version. I'm a teacher, Ginny. I can match you on childhood psychology, book for book. You know, even if you've conveniently forgotten, that psychologists worry about kids who never talk back to their parents."

She had read that. Damn. Mitch looked like such a jock that she kept forgetting he was a teacher. She sighed. "So, he's normal. Let's assume that you've saved him from becoming abnormal. Unfortunately, he doesn't seem to appreciate what you've done for him, Mitch. He thinks you ratted on him. And right now he doesn't like me much, either. Where do we go from here, Mr. Psychology Expert?"

"In the interests of solving the problem, I'll ignore that sarcastic tone."

Ginny glared at him.

"Or would you rather I bowed out of this one?" He challenged her with a look. "As you stated so clearly on the phone the other night, you're the boss."

She hesitated. She'd love to tell him that he'd done quite enough, and she'd deal with her own son, but she hadn't performed very well a few minutes ago with Arnold. She needed an ally, not an enemy. "I certainly don't feel like the boss tonight," she admitted.

Mitch pulled out the chair and sat down again. "Nevertheless you are. He's your kid."

"Technically, that's true, but with every day that passes I lose more ground. I hate to say this, but I'm stymied on this video business. I don't know whether to march up there and demand the tape and an apology or let the matter ride for a few days."

Mitch rubbed one finger along the edge of the table. "I could talk to him. Or try."

"What would you say?" She remained wary.

"I'd ask him what he knows about sex, for óne thing."

She drew back. "I, uh—that is, I don't—"

"You don't want me to discuss that with him?"

Ginny forced her brain to work. Sex was certainly a charged topic for her and Mitch to handle, but apparently she had to handle it. "Well," she began, avoiding his gaze, "I don't seem to be the right person to discuss the subject with him, and I guess someone should, in case he has any misconceptions."

"Exactly," Mitch glanced at her. "I didn't notice any birth control used in the video, did you?"

Ginny felt warm. "Not that I noticed, no."

"Besides giving him that book you mentioned, what have you told Arnold?"

"Uh, not much, I guess. He—he didn't ask. There was a class in school, and Arnold always seemed so uninterested in girls that I just..." But Ginny knew that wasn't strictly true. Arnold had demonstrated a definite interest in girls when he'd begun lurking around Bambi. Ginny had recognized Arnold's preoccupation, and instead of dealing with it, she'd fired Bambi. "I guess I fell down on the job," she said at last.

"Don't berate yourself," Mitch said gently. "He probably understands the basics."

"No thanks to me." Ginny found the courage to meet his gaze. "I wonder if it's my fault that he sent away for the video, because I didn't explain sex properly to him."

"I doubt that. I knew a lot about sex when I rented my first adult video, but that didn't stop me from being curious about X-rated movies."

"Are you . . . uh, have you had a lot of sexual experience?"

Mitch laughed. "A lot of experience? I don't know. How would you define that?"

"Lots of partners," Ginny said, more harshly than she'd intended.

"Then I'm not," he said, leaning toward her and drawing her in with his gaze. "I believe in the depth of a relationship, not a breadth of conquests."

"Oh. That's good." She swallowed. "I mean, for Arnold's sake. Along with facts, I want him to be given some moral principles." Her heart pumped wildly.

"Maybe I should give you an idea of what I'd say to Arnold, once I clarified what goes where, and how to prevent getting a girl pregnant."

"F-fine." Ginny's palms began to sweat.

Mitch held her with a steady look. "I'd tell him that sex is nice, but sex with someone you love and cherish is five hundred times better. I'd tell him that people with any self-respect usually won't settle for sex without love."

"That sounds . . . pretty good."

"I happen to believe it," he said softly, watching her. "Don't you?"

"I—yes, of course," she mumbled.

"The video he has is pure sex, wouldn't you agree?"

Ginny nodded, her power of speech gone.

"And it has a certain amount of provocative appeal."

Ginny nodded again.

"But I want Arnold to know that sex with love makes that video seem dumb by comparison. Maybe it's time to introduce Arnold to some of the great love

stories, either in books or movies, since he doesn't—''
Mitch paused.

"Doesn't what?" Ginny croaked.

"Well, he doesn't have a real-life situation to observe," Mitch finished, continuing to gaze at her.

"Oh. Right." Ginny looked down and discovered
she was gripping the edge of the table.

"So, shall I talk with him?"

"That would be...fine." Ginny wondered if
someone could die from wanting to be touched. Mitch
had described sex as being nice, and sex with love as
being wonderful, but she hadn't had either version in
a very long time. She ached to have him wrap his arms
around her. She ached for more than that, but she
would have settled for an embrace.

"Ginny."

She glanced up and saw passion in his eyes. He
knew. "Please go talk with Arnold," she said.

"We could work this out so that all three of us are
happy. Give Arnold credit. I think he'd understand."

"Do you *know* he would, without a shadow of a
doubt?"

"Of course not. Only a fool would make such an
absolute prediction, but—"

"Then I'm afraid the case is closed."

"But—"

"I can't risk it, Mitch."

Frustration replaced passion. "Right," he said, and
left the kitchen.

MITCH HAD WATCHED her struggle with herself, and
he had to admire her will, even as he wished she'd give
up and let him love her. He longed to confide his past
to her, to ease the burden of carrying the secret about

the child molesting charge. He could only take that risk in the context of loving intimacy.

But Ginny had the final say about their relationship. Arnold was her kid, and Mitch didn't have all the answers. Maybe Arnold would be terribly upset if his coach and his mother were lovers. Maybe he'd be jealous, too, that they wanted to focus on each other and not on him. Personally, Mitch saw some value in teaching Arnold that he wasn't the center of the universe.

As Mitch climbed the stairs, he wondered if his relationship with the boy would withstand what Arnold had interpreted as a betrayal. Mitch rapped on Arnold's door, loud enough to be heard over the rock music blasting away inside. "It's me," he called through the door.

He half expected Arnold to refuse to open the door, but the knob turned, and the door swung open. Arnold turned away and sprawled on his unmade bed, beneath a recently hung poster of the entire Mariners team.

"Could we turn that down?" Mitch glanced at the rack stereo system in the corner of the room.

Arnold picked up the remote and pushed a button, lowering the volume of the music so that intelligible conversation was possible.

Mitch waited until Arnold looked at him again. "I understand you're not happy with me," he said.

"That's right." His expression remained flat as a dinner plate.

"One of us had to tell her," Mitch said. "Maybe I should have let it be you, but I made a command decision and decided I would."

"Why did somebody have to tell her?"

Mitch gestured to the desk chair. "Can I sit down?"

Arnold shrugged again.

"Somebody had to tell her because this is her house, and what goes on here concerns her," Mitch said, straddling the chair backward. "You had the potential for causing her great embarrassment, if she'd come home unexpectedly and found you watching that video. She might even have brought a client home with her. Can you imagine that scene?"

"She doesn't do that. It wouldn't have happened."

"You can't guarantee it wouldn't have. It's sort of like having a pet snake in the house. If there is one, people who live there should know about it. It's only fair, sort of an unspoken rule of living together."

Arnold stared at him. Gradually his sullen expression eased. "A pet snake?"

Mitch shrugged. "Seemed like a good comparison."

"I wonder if Mom would let me have one instead of a dog." Arnold grinned.

"I wouldn't bet on it."

"Me, neither."

"But you might have the wall paint situation knocked," Mitch said, glancing around. "Red, black and white, huh?"

"I think it would look outstanding, don't you?"

Mitch nodded. "Pretty intense." Then he returned his gaze to Arnold. "Listen, your Mom's worried about the video. She thinks maybe she hasn't given you enough information about sex, so that's why you ordered it. She's blaming herself, in a way."

"That's dumb. I don't *want* information from her. She's my *mother*."

Mitch relaxed. It looked as if he'd be able to do this favor for Ginny, and discuss the birds and the bees with Arnold. "Well, I know you've had some classes at school, but just for my benefit, will you tell me what you know about how the process works?"

"Why?" Arnold winked. "You need some advice?"

*Not the kind you could give me,* Mitch thought. "I'm just checking how well these courses are going over. You know, professional interest, as a teacher."

"I know it all," Arnold said.

Mitch bit his lip to keep from laughing. "Then maybe you do have something to teach me. Tell me what you know."

"If you say so." Arnold rolled his eyes at the ceiling and recited a litany of body parts and processes in the singsong of a bored pupil.

Mitch wasn't fooled. This was the only way Arnold could say the words out loud. When he'd finished speaking, including in his recitation several methods of birth control, Mitch felt satisfied that Arnold had the information right; attitude, however, might be another matter. "So, what did you think of the video?" he asked.

Arnold gave him a furtive glance. "You saw it?"

Mitch nodded.

Arnold tried to achieve a knowing smirk, but only managed a nervous smile. "Pretty cool, huh?"

The video had aroused Mitch, but these days, living with Ginny, that wasn't a difficult assignment. "It was okay," he said. "Except I didn't like the way people treated one another in the movie."

Arnold's laughter barked out and his face turned red. "The girls treated that one guy pretty sweet, if you ask me."

"I mean, people were treated like *objects,* not people."

Arnold looked at him, and gradually understanding replaced the excited gleam in his eyes. "Yeah, I guess."

"And I promise you, no matter how much fun those people seemed to be having, they'd have a lot better time with someone they loved. Those are actors, pretending. When you love someone, you don't have to pretend anything, and it's better than what you saw, Arnold. Much better."

"Yeah? So?"

"So, Arnold, don't have sex just to have sex. That's using another person as an object. But when you love someone, and they love you back, and you have sex with that person, then..." Mitch paused. He was in love with Ginny. He'd been blind not to realize it. And his love was growing stronger, despite her rejection.

"Whatever, it's a long ways away for me," Arnold said with a sigh.

Mitch brought himself back to the business at hand. "That's probably true. Loving someone enough to have a sexual relationship with them means you're willing to take full responsibility for your actions, Arnold. You have to be careful you won't hurt someone else's feelings, or compromise their beliefs, and if the birth control fails, you have to be willing to be a father."

"Hey, not me!" Arnold held up both hands. "No way. Don't look at this boy."

"Just the facts of life, Arnold." Mitch smiled.

"I get the picture."

"Good."

"Can I keep the video?"

Mitch hesitated. "You know that set of wrist and ankle weights you wanted?"

"Yeah."

"Did the video cost that much?"

"More," Arnold said.

"So if I gave you the money for the video, you could buy the weights, right?"

Arnold smirked. "You wanna buy the video?"

"No. If you sell it to me, I'm shredding it."

"Aw, gee."

"That's my offer. Take it or leave it."

Arnold thought for a moment. "I'll take it," he said. "I've seen the video six times, and I could use the weights."

Mitch pulled out his wallet while Arnold retrieved the video from his desk drawer. Soon they'd made the exchange, and Mitch rose to leave.

"You sure you're gonna shred the video?" Arnold asked.

Mitch thought of what watching it could do to his already inflamed passions. "I'm sure," he said grimly, and left to destroy the tape.


MITCH HELD to his belief that Ginny had to make the first move, but she remained distant as days and nights piled on top of each other, and his own tolerance became paper-thin. The Fourth of July weekend would bring four days and nights uninterrupted by Ginny's work or his wrestling practice. Mitch couldn't imagine how he could spend those four days in her constant presence, loving her and unable to touch her. He searched for a solution but none presented itself to him.

Then, one day while browsing in a sporting goods store with Arnold, Mitch gazed at the tents and remembered that another teacher in the science department, Stan Gaston, often took his family camping in the summer. He'd issued an open invitation for Mitch and anyone he cared to invite to join them. At the time, Mitch had been clinging to his privacy, unwilling to get too close to anyone for fear he'd be drawn into revealing the secret of his past.

"Ever been camping, Arnold?" Mitch asked, peering into the four-person dome tent on display.

Arnold laughed. "Can you picture my mother in a tent? Once I asked her if we could try one weekend, and she told me a story about grizzly bears that tear up tents and attack people in their sleep."

*Good,* Mitch thought. *She won't want to go.* "So your mom isn't an outdoors person. How about you?" he asked, wandering over to the sleeping bags. "Think you'd like it?"

"I'd *love* it. Could we?"

"I have this teacher friend who invited me to go camping with him and his family any time I wanted. He has three kids, two of them about your age, as I remember. I thought I might call and see if they're going camping over the Fourth of July weekend. You'd be welcome, too, I'm sure. Stan always says the more the merrier."

Arnold hesitated. "What about Mom?"

"From what you've said, I can't imagine she'd want to come along. We could ask her, though. *And pray she turns us down,* he added to himself.

"Nah, she wouldn't go," Arnold said. "But if we went, would we just leave her alone all weekend?"

"Well, yes. But don't worry, Arnold, your mother's a resourceful woman. I'm sure she'd find things to do."

"I don't know." Arnold appeared torn between the lure of a camping trip and the guilt of leaving Ginny by herself.

Mitch tried a different tack. "Arnold, are you going to college when you graduate?"

"Yeah, of course. Why?"

"Will you go to the university and live at home?"

"Heck no! I'm gonna get a scholarship to somewhere back East, like maybe even Harvard or Yale. If I keep my grades up, and maybe do some wrestling in high school—" He slid a glance toward Mitch, who nodded encouragement. "I should get a scholarship, easy, don't you think?"

"Don't see why not." Mitch thought about Jason, Bob and Ruby Taylor's not-so-bright son. If Jason could get a scholarship, Arnold could get a scholarship, especially if he kept growing and had Mitch helping him hone his wrestling skills. His performance had already improved dramatically. Billy Herman and his gang hadn't shown up again to distract him, and Arnold had nearly won his last two matches, against fairly tough opponents.

"So what's all this about college?" Arnold asked.

"Oh, I just thought I'd make the point that in four years you'll be leaving your mom alone for months at a time. Maybe it's a good idea to break her in gradually with a four-day trip."

Arnold digested this concept. "I never thought about it that way. She does kind of depend on me, you know?"

"I know."

"Like, she's saying all the time that if anything ever happened to me, she doesn't know *what* she'd do."

"You've very important to her, Arnold. You two have been a real team ever since your dad died."

"Yeah." Arnold gazed into space. "But sometimes..." He paused and shook his head.

"What?"

"Well, sometimes, it's like a big weight, you know?"

"You mean you worry about her?"

"I guess. Like now, when you said let's go camping, and I really wanted to, but I knew she wouldn't want to, and I didn't see how I could leave her alone for four days, so I almost said no, let's not. But maybe you're right." Arnold looked at Mitch and a new maturity glimmered in the boy's eyes. "Maybe it would be a good thing, so she can start getting used to the idea that I won't be around forever."

"Maybe so." Mitch had only suggested this idea as a convenient escape for himself, but somehow the camping trip had evolved into a growth experience for Arnold and Ginny, as well. "Listen, if my friend Stan isn't going camping over the Fourth, you and I will go anyway, okay?"

"You've got the stuff we need?"

"Not yet, but I've always wanted a tent." Mitch fingered the lightweight nylon of the dome model. "Thanks to you and your mom, I'm making extra money this summer, so I can certainly afford a few camping supplies."

"Great!" Arnold smiled broadly. "Then it's settled."

"Not quite. We still have to get your mom's permission for you to go."

A twinge of uncertainty shadowed Arnold's expression. "She'll let me," he said, but he didn't sound absolutely sure.

"Let's hope so." Mitch knew that he'd go camping, with or without Arnold, but now that he understood Arnold's feelings of entrapment, he was determined that Arnold would go with him.

## CHAPTER NINE

"ARNOLD DOESN'T KNOW the first thing about the outdoor life," Ginny protested. "Anything could happen to him."

She and Mitch walked up the neighborhood street through clear twilight, a soft evening tailor-made for compromise, in Mitch's opinion. The crest of the hill brought a view of Mount Rainier, brushed pink by the vestiges of the sunset. The rounded, hulking mountain always reminded Mitch of a giant serving of baked Alaska. Below them down the hill, the waters of Lake Washington darkened, throwing into relief the stark white sails of boats skittering toward their moorings.

Ginny seemed unmoved by the setting. She'd agreed to a walk so they could discuss the camping trip, about which she had serious reservations. "Think about poison ivy," she continued, walking with a much quicker stride than the gentle night required. "Think about skunks. Think about bears. Bears have been known to—"

"Arnold told me your bear story," Mitch said.

"Arnold thinks I'm a fussy old woman, and I suppose you do, too, but the fact remains that he has no experience to guide him in this."

"I don't think you're a fussy old woman. Quite the contrary." Mitch took the plunge. "You're the main reason I'm planning to get out of town."

That stopped her. She turned to him, her eyes wide. "You're leaving to get away from me?"

"Yep." He shoved his hands into his pockets. Better that than touching her. "I'll admit it. I can't take the heat, Westerfelt, so I'm getting out of the kitchen, at least for a few days."

"I thought...I thought you were okay. You've been so cheerful, that I assumed that maybe you'd—I don't know, gotten over—"

"Nope. The longer I live with you the more I care about you. And I'm not made of stone, Ginny. Every day I watch you go off to work in those clingy silk suits you like to wear, smelling so sweet from the shower and whatever lotions and potions you put on that provocative body of yours, and I can't get you out of my head for the rest of the day. That's not even discussing what my nights are like, when we're in the house together."

There, he thought, watching for her reaction. At least she was aware of the way things were. He studied her eyes for an answering spark. It appeared, and his pulse raced. "There's another option," he said softly. "I'll bet Stan would take Arnold on the camping trip without me. Arnold would have a fantastic time, and we—"

"No." She was breathing fast, as if they'd run not walked the last block. "Go on the camping trip. And take Arnold. I...I know he's dying to go."

He was silent for a minute. Then he lowered his voice another notch. "Can't you even admit that you feel something for me, too?"

"No. Because I don't." She looked away.

He wanted to tilt her face back to his so that he could more easily judge what was going through her mind, but that would mean touching her, and he didn't trust himself to do that. "You're a hard woman, Ginny Westerfelt. And a lousy liar," he added.

"Do you want to end our arrangement? You certainly have that option." She faced him and the words came evenly. She'd regained most of her composure, apparently.

"Under these conditions, I sure as hell do, but there's Arnold to consider. I care about that kid, too."

"Yes, but—"

"We'll take it one day at a time," he said, his tone as brisk as hers. "Ready to go back?"

She took a deep breath. "Yes," she said, putting her hands into the pockets of her sweatpants to match his action. "Yes, I am."

They walked home in silence. Mitch worked to shut down all his natural reactions. The fragrance of her that he'd mentioned still lingered at the end of the day. A breeze ruffled her short, blond hair. He knew, without experiencing it, how her hair would feel if he ran his fingers through it and cupped the back of her head while he— Oh, Lord, he was in trouble. The only answer was to keep away from her as much as possible, and never, under any circumstances, allow himself to be alone with her. He lengthened his stride.

GINNY CONSIDERED HERSELF a self-reliant woman, able to amuse herself when she found herself on her own. Yet, she'd never faced four days in an Arnold-less house. He'd stayed overnight a few times with

Billy Herman, but otherwise he'd always been around. She had left *him,* of course, on business trips, but that, she was quickly discovering, didn't mean she was self-reliant at home. She found herself wandering through rooms devoid of life and flipping on the television, which she seldom watched, not to do research on marketing techniques, but just to hear voices again.

When Maggie had been told about the arrangements for the holiday weekend, she'd been miffed at Arnold and Mitch for running out on Ginny. Ginny had conveniently left out Mitch's motivation for taking the camping trip, not wanting to add fuel to Maggie's already active imagination. Ginny had pretended that she was looking forward to four days of worrying about no one but herself. She'd stay up late reading novels, she'd said, and take long baths, have her hair and nails done—in short, pamper herself.

By the evening of the first day, she was going crazy. At last, realizing she'd never last another three days taking long baths and reading novels, she called Maggie.

"I'm miserable," she confessed when Maggie answered the phone. "I'm lonesome and worried about Arnold." *And I miss Mitch,* she wanted to add, but didn't.

"Want to sleep in the guest room?" Maggie offered immediately. "We'd love to have you. Phil was just saying that he hadn't seen you in ages, and—"

"Maggie, that's sweet, but my pride wouldn't let me. However, I'd like to come over and sit on your roof to watch the fireworks on Saturday, even if Arnold won't be there this year. I think we all used him as an excuse, anyway."

"Great. Phil and I had already decided to watch fireworks this year, Arnold or no Arnold. I'd planned to call you and announce we were doing it and ask you to come over, even if you couldn't bring the requisite kid."

"Let me help with the food," Ginny said.

"Goodness, no. I can fix a buffet, like always."

"Maggie, please. Let me bring something. I need projects for the next forty-eight hours. I'll make German potato salad, and maybe some fancy dessert that takes hours of preparation."

Maggie laughed. "Sounds like the ravings of a desperate woman. Listen, you won't mind if someone else comes over Saturday night, will you?"

"Of course not, Maggie," Ginny said, although she felt disappointed that she wouldn't have her old friends to herself. "It's your roof."

"There's this guy Phil works with, and he's new in town, so Phil asked him."

Ginny had a premonition. "Does he have a family?"

"No, he's single," Maggie said with a revealing lilt in her voice.

Ginny groaned. "Maggie, this is a setup, isn't it? You were planning to ask me after this man said he'd come. You're trying to fix me up again."

"Well, you don't seem to be getting anywhere with that wrestling coach of yours. If he'd choose to take Arnold off camping for the weekend, instead of spending the time with you, he can't be worth much."

"Oh, Maggie." Ginny considered canceling and spending the Fourth alone, after all. She had zero interest in meeting some new man. She'd never liked being set up, anyway, and now...now the presence of

Mitch in her life crowded out even the slightest desire
to meet someone else. Despite her denials to everyone, she feared she was falling in love with Mitch
Adamson.

"So. German potato salad and some sinful dessert,
right?" Maggie prompted. "About six o'clock."

"Oh, Maggie," Ginny said again, this time adding
a sigh. "I've never wanted you to fix me up with dates.
You know that."

"Don't make such a big thing of it," Maggie said.
"We'll just be four people watching the fireworks together. Unless you have some other reason for not
wanting to meet this guy. Unless there's something
you're not telling me, about your involvement with
Mitch?" Maggie allowed the question to drift casually over the line.

"I'll be there Saturday night," Ginny said. "At
six."

WES COCHORAN, an engineer with Boeing, had removed his sport coat for the climb to the roof but had
left his paisley tie knotted carefully around his neck.
Ginny acknowledged that he was attractive, with dark
hair slicked back from features that many women
would label handsome. He seemed interested in her
work, and asked good questions. Maggie had already
informed her, during a moment when Wes and Phil
weren't around, that he made a very respectable salary with Boeing and was valued by the company. He'd
be in Seattle for many years, no doubt, Maggie had
said with a satisfied smile.

Ginny tried to be fair in her evaluation, but every
time Wes cleared his throat, which he did often, or
waved his hand in a nervous gesture, or fiddled with

the high school class ring he still wore, Ginny thought of Mitch's self-assured manner. Compared to Mitch's easygoing attitude, Wes seemed unduly fussy. When he wasn't adjusting his own clothing, he straightened framed pictures on Maggie's wall, picked dead leaves from her potted plants and rearranged her throw pillows on the sofa. He made Ginny think she should be checking her sleeves for dangling threads or finding a mirror to repair her makeup. Had it not been for her loyalty to Maggie and Phil, Ginny would have left before the fireworks began.

"So, you have a little boy, I understand," Wes said, settling his deck chair next to hers as the first shower of colored sparks appeared over Lake Washington.

"He's thirteen, almost fourteen," Ginny said. "And he's taller than I am already, so I don't think of him as little anymore."

"I can hardly believe you have a son that old." Wes ran his thumb and forefinger down the crease in his slacks. "You must have had him when you were very young."

Ginny knew she was supposed to be flattered. Instead, she felt irritated at such an obvious ploy. "Do you have children?" she asked, pretty positive he didn't, because Maggie hadn't mentioned an ex-wife or kids.

"None I know of," he said with what was supposed to be a roguish wink designed to inform her that he'd been around, and anything was possible.

How different, she thought, from Mitch's declaration that he believed in depth of relationships, not breadth. She couldn't even find a suitable way to respond to Wes's remark.

"Teenagers," Wes said, shaking his head. "Aren't they a pain?"

Ginny wouldn't have admitted her frustrations on a bet. "Actually, I like this stage," she said. "Arnold's more interesting now."

Wes snorted. "Interesting. That's a word for it. Weird haircuts, loud music, driving those junk heaps they call cars as if they were on the Indianapolis Speedway. They're interesting, all right."

"You must not care for teenagers," Ginny observed.

"I think all children should be frozen at age twelve and unthawed when they're twenty."

Ginny wanted to knock his pompous ass off the roof. She wondered if she could make it look like an accident. Finally, unable to sit beside him another moment, she got up. "It's colder than I thought it would be up here," she announced. "I'm going down for a sweater."

Phil offered to go, instead, but Ginny warned him off with a look. When she returned, she made a great production of deciding she'd rather have her chair wedged between Phil's and Maggie's because the view was so much better from that angle. Maggie, who had obviously heard Wes's remarks about teenagers, didn't object.

THE DISASTROUS social event of Saturday night heightened Ginny's anticipation of the return of her men. She'd begun to think in those terms—*her men*— at about three o'clock in the afternoon, as she scrubbed and polished every inch of the townhouse. In her fantasy she was the keeper of the hearth and they were the adventurers coming home at last from the dangers of the world beyond. Ginny conveniently forgot that the usual order of things placed her in the role of adventurer, while Arnold and Mitch stayed home to tend the hearth.

She fried chicken and baked yeast rolls. She thought about decorating the dining room the way they had for her; she abandoned the idea when she realized that they were men, after all, who had been living in the great outdoors and were used to the simple life of hearty food served in plain surroundings. The longer she worked, the more Ginny pictured herself as a character in *Little House on the Prairie*. A real pioneer woman, keeping hearth and home together.

The image was completed when Mitch and Arnold walked into the kitchen at five o'clock, smelling of wood smoke and wearing plaid flannel shirts.

"Hi, Mom!" Arnold seemed to have grown another two inches. "We brought home fish."

"How nice." Ginny barely glanced at the ice chest Arnold carried. Her vision filled with the sight of Mitch. His tousled, blond hair and four-day growth of beard broadcast a rugged maleness that stirred elemental yearnings within her. And the look in his eyes. She knew that only the presence of Arnold prevented Mitch from taking her, unresisting, into his arms.

But Arnold was there, holding the ice chest out to her. "Five rainbow trout, Mom. Wanna see?"

"Um, sure." She wrenched her gaze away from Mitch to focus on the ice chest Arnold had deposited on her polished kitchen floor.

"Ta-da!" Arnold flung back the cover and the stink of dead fish filled the room. "Take a look at those babies."

Ginny held her breath and stepped back. "Wow."

"Pretty impressive, huh?" Arnold said, beaming. He picked up the top fish by the tail and waggled it in front of Ginny. "*I* caught this one. Biggest fish of anybody, right, Mitch?"

"That's right."

"We'll keep these in the freezer, and we can eat 'em," Arnold announced. "Mine last, though. I hate to destroy the evidence too soon."

Ginny stared at the fish and its dead eyes stared back. "That's... that's terrific, Arnold," she said, trying to imagine this thing, and four more of its kind, lying in her freezer, impaling her with that stare each time she opened the freezer door.

"Angela caught one almost as big. She's gonna eat hers last, too. Maybe we'll eat them at the same time."

"Who's Angela?" Ginny asked, relieved when Arnold returned the fish to the ice chest and closed the lid.

"Oh, this girl." Arnold remained bent over the ice chest, so that Ginny couldn't see his face, but his ears turned pink.

Ginny glanced at Mitch for more explanation.

"Angela is Stan's daughter. She's Arnold's age," Mitch said. "I guess they'd seen each other at school before, but they'd never really talked to each other."

"Oh? That's nice," Ginny said, raising her eyebrows in Mitch's direction.

He shook his head and mouthed the word *later*.

"Yeah, she's okay," Arnold said, picking up the ice chest. "Where shall I put this?"

"In the garage for now," Mitch suggested. "Looks like your mom has dinner ready. We can clean the fish afterward."

# NO COST! NO OBLIGATION TO BUY! NO PURCHASE NECESSARY!

## PLAY "LUCKY 7" AND GET AS MANY AS SIX FREE GIFTS...

## HOW TO PLAY:

1. With a coin, carefully scratch off the silver box at the right. This makes you eligible to receive two or more free books, and possibly other gifts, depending on what is revealed beneath the scratch-off area.

2. You'll receive brand-new Harlequin Superromance® novels. When you return this card, we'll send you the books and gifts you qualify for *absolutely free!*

3. If we don't hear from you, every month, we'll send you 4 additional novels to read and enjoy. You can return them and owe nothing but if you decide to keep them, you'll pay only $2.96* per book, a saving of 43¢ each off the cover price. There is **no** extra charge for postage and handling. There are **no** hidden extras.

4. When you join the Harlequin Reader Service®, you'll get our subscribers'-only newsletter, as well as additional free gifts from time to time just for being a subscriber.

5. You must be completely satisfied. You may cancel at any time simply by sending us a note or a shipping statement marked "cancel" or by returning any shipment to us at our cost.

*This lovely heart-shaped box is richly detailed with cut-glass decorations, perfect for holding a precious memento or keepsake—and it's yours absolutely free when you accept our no-risk offer.*

# PLAY "LUCKY 7"

**Just scratch off the silver box with a coin.**
**Then check below to see which gifts you get.**

**YES!** I have scratched off the silver box. Please send me all the gifts for which I qualify. I understand I am under no obligation to purchase any books, as explained on the opposite page.

134 CIH AEL3
(U-H-SR-05/92)

NAME

ADDRESS                                                    APT

CITY                    STATE                    ZIP

 WORTH FOUR FREE BOOKS, FREE HEART-SHAPED GLASS BOX AND MYSTERY BONUS

 WORTH FOUR FREE BOOKS AND MYSTERY BONUS

 WORTH THREE FREE BOOKS

 WORTH TWO FREE BOOKS

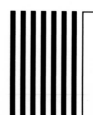

BUSINESS REPLY MAIL

FIRST CLASS MAIL    PERMIT NO. 717    BUFFALO, NY

POSTAGE WILL BE PAID BY ADDRESSEE

**HARLEQUIN READER SERVICE**
3010 WALDEN AVE
PO BOX 1867
BUFFALO NY 14240-9952

NO POSTAGE
NECESSARY
IF MAILED
IN THE
UNITED STATES

"But we have to leave the heads and tails on, right? Especially on my fish. So I can prove how big it was."

"Sure, we can do that," Mitch said.

Arnold carried the ice chest out to the garage, but he left the door open, so Ginny didn't feel free to question Mitch about Angela. She contented herself with one question. "Did you know Stan had a daughter Arnold's age?" she asked, keeping her tone neutral.

"No, I didn't." He copied her tone. "I knew he had three kids, two boys and a girl, but I didn't know the ages."

"I see."

"Oh, and Arnold told me about his fight with Billy Herman," Mitch said in a lower key. "You're right—he wants revenge. And I should tell you that he didn't like our coming to his rescue at the gym. He wants a chance to handle Billy by himself."

Ginny groaned. "That would be a disaster."

"Maybe not."

"Mitch, you can't seriously think that—"

Mitch put his finger to his lips and cocked his head in the direction of the garage.

Ginny nodded. This discussion should be continued later, out of Arnold's earshot. Still, she had no intention of ever allowing Arnold a rematch with Billy Herman, whether or not Mitch thought the odds had changed.

"And how was your weekend?" Mitch asked, maintaining a polite level of conversation.

She didn't know what made her do it. "Fine," she said. "On Saturday I went over to Maggie's to see the fireworks and met a nice guy who works for Boeing." When she saw the hurt and anger in Mitch's expression, she felt like a louse. "Actually, he was a pain in the rear," she amended.

"Who was a pain in the rear?" Arnold asked, coming back into the kitchen.

"People who eavesdrop," Mitch said, but he continued to gaze at Ginny, as if trying to puzzle something through. At last, he shook his head and turned to Arnold. "Come on, buddy. Let's go wash up so we can eat some of that delicious fried chicken I smell."

During dinner, Ginny learned that no bears had appeared at the campsite, much to Arnold's disappointment, but there had been deer and raccoon and skunks. Throughout the narration, mostly conducted by Arnold, the name of Angela came up regularly. Arnold's voice deepened whenever he said her name, and by the end of the meal, Ginny didn't need Mitch to tell her that Arnold had a girlfriend. After the dishes were done, Mitch went out to clean the fish and Arnold excused himself to "make a phone call." Ginny knew exactly who he'd be calling.

She put on a sweater and went out to the backyard, where Mitch had spread newspapers on the redwood picnic table and was preparing to clean the fish in the fading light of the setting sun. Ginny didn't want to watch the process, and the fish smelled as awful as she remembered, but she had to ask about Angela while she had a chance to talk to Mitch alone.

He glanced up when she appeared. He didn't smile. "Have you come out to help?"

"I'd rather not, if you don't mind." She positioned herself to the right of the table.

"Didn't think you'd want to." He gazed at her. "Nothing down-and-dirty for this lady."

Ginny ignored the crack. "I wanted to ask you about the romance between Arnold and Angela."

"It's just the usual." Mitch turned back to his work and slit the first fish open. "Puppy love."

Ginny averted her eyes from the cleaning of the fish. "And you're sure you didn't know that Angela was Arnold's age when you set up this camping trip?"

Mitch tossed down the knife with an oath.

Instantly concerned, Ginny started toward him. "Did you cut yourself?"

He whirled. "No, I didn't cut myself. You think I'm going to play matchmaker for Arnold, when I can't even run my own love life?"

She paused, heart thumping.

"That's right, look innocent. What was all that about the 'nice guy' from Boeing, anyway? You won't give me the time of day, yet you parade some other jerk in front of my nose, when you know how I—oh, forget it." He returned to the table and picked up the fish knife.

"Mitch, I—"

"Never mind. But if you're worried about Arnold and Angela, don't be. They're two young kids who just discovered their first soul mates. Angela's kind of like Arnold, a good student who hasn't been singled out much by the opposite sex, partly because of her scholastic abilities. The two of them talked endlessly."

"Talking's okay," Ginny said, determined to say her piece, regardless of Mitch's attitude. "I'm just concerned that, since you were there three nights, Arnold and Angela may have engaged in something more serious than talking." She noticed, even from watching the cleaning out of the corner of her eye, that

Mitch attacked the fish as if he was enjoying the grisly process.

"You mean, did they kiss?" Mitch glanced up, his jaw tight. "I think they might have kissed. I didn't spy on them, but I made sure Arnold slept in my tent all night, if that's what you want to know. Our campsite was very pure, just like this damned house."

"You don't have to swear."

"Yes, I do. It's one of the only pleasures left to me. Now, if your curiosity is satisfied, will you be so kind as to let me disembowel these fish in peace?"

Ginny couldn't think of any more relevant questions. Slowly she backed away. "Certainly," she said. "Excuse me for intruding." She hurried into the house and escaped into her room. Arnold's door was closed when she passed by, but she could hear murmurings. He was still talking to Angela.

Mitch was furious with her, Ginny acknowledged as she threw herself on the bed. She could pretend his anger stemmed from her unwillingness to let down the barriers between them, but that wasn't the reason. He'd been frustrated about that, but not really angry. He'd tried hard to understand her point of view and respect it. She couldn't fault him for his behavior, not in the least.

She could, however, fault herself. After anticipating his return with such pleasure, after cleaning house and cooking a meal entirely with him in mind, she'd ruined the whole homecoming by mentioning her Saturday-night escort, and worse yet, making it appear, at first, as if Wes were an eligible man. Why had she done such an insensitive and cruel thing? She knew how Mitch felt about her.

There could be only one answer; subconsciously she wanted to provoke Mitch into losing patience. If he'd have grabbed her, despite her protests, and insisted on making love to her, she knew she'd have given in, but it wouldn't have been her responsibility. He would have made the first move and forced the encounter. Apparently, somewhere twisted in her mind was the idea that if Mitch swept her away in a tide of emotion, the decision to become lovers wouldn't be her fault.

She was a coward. Pure and simple. More than that, she owed Mitch an apology. Once Arnold was in bed, she'd seek out an appropriate moment and tell Mitch she was sorry.

She stayed in her room until after the sounds of Arnold's preparations for bed ended. She hadn't heard the back door open and close, so she assumed Mitch was still in the yard. Moments later, she found him sitting in a lawn chair, his head resting against the cushion, his eyes closed. She walked quietly toward him and leaned down to see if he was asleep.

He grasped her arm and pulled her into his lap.

"Mitch, wait," she cried.

"Not anymore," he muttered, capturing her chin with strong fingers. "Not anymore."

She squirmed in his unrelenting grip as he lowered his mouth to hers. He was reacting exactly as she'd subconsciously wanted him to, and it was wrong, all wrong, for him to do this and take the blame when she had goaded him into it. She struggled harder, but he held her tight.

"I *am* going to kiss you, dammit," he said.

From the first touch of his lips, her resistance vanished, as she'd known it would. Her mouth softened under the pressure of his, and her skin tingled from the friction of his beard. With a soft moan she wound her arm around his neck and absorbed the heat radiating through his shirt. His breath came fast; he was on fire for her and she loved knowing it.

She made room for the demanding thrust of his tongue, and the force of this new intimacy swept away barriers she'd been erecting for years. She'd thought herself mistress of her passions, but Mitch was proving her wrong. She wanted him. She wanted his hands on her bare skin, his mouth tasting her feminine secrets, his passion deep within her.

As if sensing her unspoken wish, he released her chin and caressed her throat. Gradually, he moved to the first button of her blouse, and the second. Ginny's heartbeat thundered in her ears, drowning out the voice of reason as Mitch slid his hand beneath the lace cup of her bra. Oh, yes. His knowing caress fulfilled all her forbidden fantasies of how he would touch her, how he would tease and stroke her flesh until she writhed against him and asked for more. But this had to stop. Dimly she remembered the boy asleep in the house, the promises she'd made to herself.

She ended the kiss, but he only took that as a signal to nuzzle her throat and then the cleft between her breasts.

"Mitch," she gasped. "We can't—"

"I think we are," he murmured, pulling her bra strap from her shoulder and nudging her breast free.

"Mitch," she tried again, but her plea became a moan as he drew her nipple into his mouth. Her fingers dug into his scalp as pleasure fed her starved senses. Another moment and she'd forget everything but the sweet suction that spiraled downward and opened a moist, aching void within her. He'd already unfastened the belt of her slacks. Another moment and nothing would stop the pulsing surge of their coupling.

# CHAPTER TEN

"No." Her denial came out as a hoarse croak. She pushed his head from her breast, nearly crying out at the loss. "No," she repeated.

Mitch's hands stilled. He gazed into her face.

"We're not doing this," she said, her voice shaky.

"Yes, we are." He started to kiss her again.

"No, we're not." She pushed him back.

"Ginny, don't."

"I mean it, Mitch." She struggled out of his lap. "We can't do this."

"Tell me this isn't happening. First you tease me with another guy—"

"That was stupid."

"—and now you lead me on, just to...I can't believe you're that cruel."

"I don't mean to be cruel," she said, almost in tears as she fought her own frustration. "I want to make love to you."

"Ginny!"

"But we can't. Not like this, with Arnold so close that he could walk out at any minute and find us."

"He's asleep, Ginny." Mitch's tone was desperate. "He sleeps like the dead."

"This would be the night he wouldn't. Please understand, Mitch. Please. I told you I couldn't do this, become lovers right under Arnold's nose, no matter how much I might want you."

"You're serious, aren't you? You aren't going to make love to me tonight, even though a minute ago you were acting exactly like a woman who wants a man to love her."

"That was a terrible mistake." Ginny adjusted her bra and buttoned her blouse. "I should never have lost control like that."

"No joke! And what did you expect to happen, when you come traipsing out here and lean down as if you're about to kiss me? Did you think we'd play spin the bottle and then stop when things got too hot and heavy?" He stared at her. "Maybe you did, at that."

"I didn't lean down to kiss you. I was trying to see if you were asleep."

"Why? Why didn't you just leave me alone in my misery? Did you come out to rub salt in my wounds?"

"No!" Ginny shouted, and then realized the neighbors might be able to hear. "No," she said more softly. "I came out to apologize for my behavior."

Mitch's laugh sounded sarcastic. "I don't know if there's an apology that covers this sort of behavior, but there's certainly a term for it."

"You're right. That's what I've been," Ginny said, shivering. She buttoned her sweater. "I've been the kind of tease that men complain about, and that was why I wanted to apologize. Only—"

"Only it came a bit late. I was already panting after you so much that when you leaned over me, your breath so sweet on my face, I reacted like some sex-crazed animal and grabbed you."

Ginny closed her eyes. How she wanted to fling herself back into his arms and complete the union her body craved, even now, with a clamoring she couldn't subdue. "That's the point," she made herself say. "I realized tonight that I want you, but I also don't think it's the right thing, because of Arnold. My solution, subconsciously, was to make you desire me so much that you'd sort of...propel me into becoming your lover. Then I wouldn't have to take responsibility for something I thought was a mistake, but wanted anyway."

Mitch gazed at her. "You are one mixed-up lady."

"Mitch, I—"

"You wanted me to force you, is that it?"

"Well, not exactly."

"Okay. I understand the routine," he said quietly. "Come here," he continued, holding out his hand. "I can accommodate you. I'll take the responsibility, if that's what you want."

"No." She backed away. "I don't want it to happen that way now. I'll take full blame for whatever we do, or don't do. And I know one thing. We will not make love in this house, or in this yard, and risk Arnold's finding out. That's final."

Mitch stood, looming ominously in the dark. "Well, that pretty much means we won't make love, doesn't it? You and I don't have many excuses to go off together without Arnold, do we? That's not the setup."

"You're right, it's not."

"Let me get this straight. Are you saying that if we could be alone together, away from this house, so that Arnold wouldn't notice, you'd—"

"But that's impossible," Ginny interrupted.

"How perfectly ironic." Mitch shook his head. "What we need is a damn baby-sitter. Except that's my job."

"What we need is to act like mature adults and put this aside. It's not appropriate for our lives right now. We need to consider Arnold and his needs, not our own selfish desires."

"Wonderful speech. Personally, though, I don't consider my desire for you selfish. And it's not only sexual gratification. I care about you, and I think you care about me, but the way we're living, denying ourselves the freedom to express how we feel about each other isn't natural, Ginny."

"I think that's called being civilized," Ginny said, straightening her shoulders.

"Ah." He shoved his hands into the back pockets of his jeans and faced her, legs braced apart. "Then what we just experienced is uncivilized?"

She steeled herself against the primitive lure of his aggressive stance. She wasn't out of danger yet. "I think it's better if we agree not to refer to what happened tonight."

"All right." He took his hands from his pockets and stepped closer, his gaze intense and his voice low. "I won't refer to it, but I'll be thinking about how you felt and tasted and moaned when I touched you. I'll think about it tonight and tomorrow and the next night, and so will you."

"No."

"Yes. Let's leave it this way. If the corset of civilization ever pinches that soft skin a little too tightly, you know where I'll be." He gazed at her a moment longer, then strode past her into the house.

Ginny stood in the yard and steeled her whole body to keep herself from running after him. He was right. She'd play tonight's moments of passion over and over in her memory. And each time, desire would well fresh and demanding, begging her to go to him. She would have to be strong.

SEVERAL TENSE DAYS LATER, Arnold asked if Angela could come to his wrestling match, and Ginny agreed. She was curious about the girl, and the wrestling match would give her a chance to talk with Angela when Arnold was otherwise occupied.

On Thursday night, Ginny, Mitch and Arnold picked Angela up at her house. The girl must have been watching for the Volvo, because the minute they pulled up at the curb, she bounded out of the house and barely gave Arnold time to open the car door for her. Ginny liked that. At least Angela wasn't coy.

She looked as if she could have been Arnold's sister, with dark, curly hair down to her shoulders and brown eyes only a shade lighter than Arnold's. They even shared the same orthodontist. At about five foot seven, Angela was almost Arnold's height, but that would probably change. Arnold, built so much like his father, would top six feet before he graduated from high school.

On the way to the wrestling match, the two sat in the back seat of the Volvo, seat belts buckled, holding hands. Ginny detected the hand-holding by glancing surreptitiously in the rearview mirror. Talk on the way to the gym consisted mostly of rehashing the camping trip, which included lots of inside jokes that Ginny didn't understand. For the first time in her life, she wondered whether she had been wrong about camping. Camping with someone like Mitch might not be all bad.

When they reached the gym, Ginny and Angela sat together on the bleachers while Arnold stayed below with his team. At least his body stayed with his team, Ginny decided. His attention remained with Angela; he kept glancing back at her uncertainly, as if to assure himself she hadn't disappeared.

With Mitch and Arnold sitting several rows beneath them, Ginny made use of her first fact-finding opportunity. Offering an encouraging smile, she threw out the first conversational bait. "Arnold tells me you like to read," she said.

"Yeah. I read a lot," Angela said, bobbing her head.

"What sorts of things?"

"Oh, all kinds of stuff," Angela said. "I love the Walter Farley series about the Black Stallion, and just about any kind of animal book."

*Good,* thought Ginny. *Wholesome.*

"And I like mysteries," Angela continued. "Agatha Christie, and Sherlock Holmes. Oh, and Stephen King. I love his horror stories."

Ginny continued to smile. Of course they had lots to discuss, her son and this girl. Arnold had found a bookish little playmate who shared his love of Stephen King. Ginny relaxed a little.

"And I just finished *Lady Chatterley's Lover,* you know, by D.H. Lawrence."

Ginny stiffened and her smile faded. "You did? Well, uh—" Ginny paused to clear her throat "—what did you think?"

"Mmm." Angela looked dreamy. "What a love story."

"Yes, I guess it is," Ginny said, frantically trying to remember how sexually explicit the book was. As far as she remembered, D.H. didn't pull any punches.

"Haven't you read it?" Angela asked.

"Years ago," Ginny said, thinking that Angela and Arnold made quite a pair. Between Angela's adventure with D.H. Lawrence and Arnold's exploration into the world of bimbettes, the two teenagers probably knew more about sex than Ginny had when she got married. She felt betrayed, as if someone should have warned her to prepare herself for this stage three years ago. Clearly, she wasn't ready.

"You know, I think it's really neat that Mitch is staying with you guys for the summer," Angela said.

Taken aback by the mention of Mitch, so soon after the discussion of *Lady Chatterley,* Ginny blinked. "You do?"

"Yeah. I really like him, don't you?"

Ginny gazed at her brown-eyed, innocent stare and wondered if Angela was all that innocent. Perhaps she imagined a secret relationship between Ginny and Mitch similar to the one between Lady Chatterley and the caretaker. "Yes, I like Mitch," Ginny said. "And Arnold adores him."

"Yeah, I know. He said he wished he could go to Westwood and have Mitch for a teacher, but then I reminded him that he wouldn't be in the same high school with *me,* so he dropped that idea."

Ginny looked at Angela in amazement. Already the girl assumed a magic hold over Arnold. With the relationship only a week old, she could boast that Arnold naturally would choose to be with her instead of his beloved Mitch. It seemed, Ginny mused, that overcoming envy would be her lesson for the summer. First, she'd had to deal with Arnold's defection to Mitch. Now, he'd apparently switched loyalties again, and Angela was the favored person for whom he'd climb the highest mountain and swim the deepest sea. Intellectually Ginny had known that someday Arnold would place another woman in the favored spot. She just hadn't expected it to happen before he was fourteen.

"Did you know that Arnold writes poetry?" Angela asked, her fresh young face without pretense.

"Yes." Ginny longed to remind this cherub that she was Arnold's mother, the person who had nurtured him for thirteen years, and who had encouraged all his gifts, including the writing of poetry. "He's written a few for me," Ginny said, wishing she'd have felt secure enough not to have said it.

"Really? That's nice. I'm keeping all the ones he wrote for me in a folder. They're wonderful."

The last thing Ginny wanted to hear was that she'd fostered Arnold's poetic ability so that he could dash off sentimental love notes to this adoring ingenue, but she'd had to face many unsettling truths lately. "I'm sure they are wonderful," she forced herself to say.

"Look, Arnold's going out. It's Arnold's turn," Angela said, leaning forward. She cupped both hands to her mouth and screamed, "Go get him, Arnold!"

Ginny flinched and expected everyone to turn and stare at the loud young girl. No one did. The only person who turned was Arnold, who, serious as a knight at the jousts, gave Angela a salute. She, in turn, blew him a kiss.

The match began, and a very different Arnold wrestled on the blue mat below them. Ginny could hardly believe the transformation. The other boy never had a chance. As Arnold demonstrated complete control of the outcome, Angela went crazy beside her, cheering and whistling through her teeth. When Arnold pinned the other boy, Angela leaped to her feet, screeching out Arnold's name.

The referee's whistle ended the match, and Arnold, the conquering hero, got to his feet with deliberate slowness. Then he gazed up into the bleachers. Ginny didn't foolishly imagine he looked for her. The brilliant smile, the flash of braces, the lifted face—all were bestowed on the skinny, brown-eyed nymph next to her who read D.H. Lawrence in her spare time.

Then Ginny became aware of another face turned their way, gray eyes that were seeking her. She gazed at Mitch, who held up two fingers in the victory sign. Smiling, she responded with the same gesture. If she couldn't share this triumph with Arnold, she could share it with the man who'd made it possible. Feeling emotionally abandoned by her son, Ginny took refuge in Mitch's warm gaze. In spite of all they'd been through, she wouldn't want to give up a single minute of knowing him.

During the ride home, Ginny broached the subject of the victory. "I'll bet you feel good about winning," she said.

"Sure do," Arnold said from the back seat.

She waited for him to elaborate, perhaps to describe the match, but instead Ginny heard rustlings and an occasional whisper from the back seat.

"You seemed really in control," she added.

"Pretty much." More rustling and whispers.

Ginny took the hint and gave up. The interior of the car was darker than it had been on the ride to the gym, so Ginny couldn't identify the activities behind her.

She suspected Arnold and Angela were maneuvering themselves for some furtive kissing and were battling the constraints of the seat belts.

A memory floated up, of a double date Ginny had shared with her best friend Joan. Joan's steady hadn't had a car, but his friend had had one. They'd fixed Ginny up with the friend. Ginny remembered riding in the front seat trying to think of something to say to this boy she'd just met, while Joan and her steady made out in the back seat.

She glanced at Mitch, who returned her glance with a smile. "Arnold's really improved," she said in a low voice, although she doubted Arnold and Angela would be listening. "You've done a good job."

"I don't think I can take the credit. Apparently he only needed some motivation."

"Amazing, isn't it?"

Mitch glanced in the rearview mirror. "The power of love," he murmured just loud enough for Ginny to hear. His gaze flicked over toward her. "They say it moves mountains."

"So they say." Ginny swallowed. They hadn't spoken much since Sunday night, and only then to impart information about Arnold or some housekeeping chore. She reverted to that safe haven now. "The orthodontist called me at the office today. He needs to reschedule Arnold's appointment for next Monday afternoon instead of tomorrow afternoon. I figured that would be okay, so long as it was after wrestling practice."

Mitch frowned. "What time?"

"Two."

"I can't make it."

"Oh." Ginny sat in puzzled silence. Other than checking on his apartment once a week and collecting his mail, which he could do any time, she hadn't thought Mitch had any obligations besides wrestling. True, she hadn't asked him to account for every minute, and she'd assumed he left Arnold alone once in a while when he went to the grocery store or the gas station, but those errands could be done at any time, too. Now, it seemed, Mitch had an appointment of some sort.

"I apologize for not checking with you before I agreed to the appointment," she said, her tone stiff and formal. "I suppose, in the future, I should do that when we have a schedule change."

"I suppose you should."

"I assume Arnold will be taken care of?"

"I've already made arrangements with the Gastons."

"Do you—does this have something to do with your teaching job?" She wanted desperately to know without seeming to pry.

"No. It's personal."

*Personal.* A cold chill slid through her. *He had a date.* She couldn't blame him, of course. Sunday night's episode must have been the final straw. He'd talked about having needs, and he'd given her ample evidence of what those needs were. If he'd had other women friends, perhaps he'd abandoned them temporarily in hopes that she . . .

Well, she hadn't, and virile, healthy male animal that he was, Mitch wasn't accepting celibacy anymore. She couldn't blame him for that, she thought again. She couldn't, but she did. She had no right to feel hurt and betrayed, but she did. Logically she couldn't expect a man like Mitch to hang around begging for her favors, not when she'd made her position clear. If she didn't like his going out with someone else, too bad. She'd had a chance to say yes, and she'd said no.

She should even be glad that he'd taken this step. The pressure would be off, and the two of them could interact as employer and employee without all the underlying tension they'd experienced recently. This new arrangement could benefit Arnold, who could use Mitch and his new girlfriend as a role model for his relationship with Angela. Maybe the four of them could sometimes go places together.

Arnold would like Mitch's girlfriend; Mitch had good taste. Ginny would probably even like her, except that she never wanted to see her sweet, lovely, sickening face as long as she lived. A lump rose in Ginny's throat. Self-sacrifice might be noble, but it sure made her feel awful. That night, for the first time in years, Ginny cried herself to sleep.

ARNOLD'S INTEREST in Angela transformed the summer routine. The teenagers spent most afternoons together, either at Angela's house or Arnold's. The day after the wrestling match, Ginny instructed Mitch to chaperone the young couple closely when they chose the townhouse for their afternoon's entertainment. She mentioned that Angela was a worldly thirteen-year-old who had read *Lady Chatterley's Lover*. Mitch laughed and asked if he should follow them through the stacks when they went to the library, too. "Yes," Ginny replied before stomping out of the room.

The following Monday afternoon, during Mitch's two o'clock "appointment," Ginny couldn't concentrate on her work for thinking about him with another woman. That evening, she studied him for evidence of a torrid afternoon—a love-bite on the neck, perhaps, or chapped lips from excessive kissing. She found nothing and Mitch behaved the same as ever, only once raising his eyebrows in a silent question when he caught her staring at him. She looked away and said nothing.

After that, Ginny imagined Mitch with this unknown other woman every time Arnold spent the afternoon at Angela's house. Soon, Ginny thought, Mitch would start announcing that he had plans for the evening, or Arnold would make a passing reference to Mitch's new girlfriend. Ginny braced herself for the moment when suspicion became reality.

Finally, she decided that Mitch was concealing his new paramour from both her and Arnold. Why he would do that eluded her, but that would explain his presence in the house night after night. Unless, of course, the woman was married and Mitch was seeing her on the sly. Ginny dismissed that notion immediately. She might not know everything about Mitch, but carrying on with someone else's wife would be out of character for him.

Arnold continued to spend lots of time with Angela and her family, so Ginny wasn't surprised when the Gastons invited him on a Saturday trip up the coast to Vancouver and Victoria. She notified Mitch that he could have the day off, and the evening, too, if he liked. He shrugged and made no comment.

On Saturday, Angela's family picked up Arnold at nine o'clock. Ginny expected Mitch to leave, too, but when he didn't, she drove to the closest shopping mall, both to pick up a few things she needed—nylons, makeup and a refill of her cologne—and to get out of the house until Mitch had the good grace to disappear. He seemed intent on puttering at chores she ranked unimportant. She could deal with a squeaky hinge, a few weeds in the flower bed and an undusted bookcase. What she couldn't deal with was being alone with him. Yet not having the courage to tell him that, she left.

Three hours later she returned to find him on the sofa in front of the television watching a baseball game. Her heart ached to think what they might have had together if circumstances had been different. Her gaze traveled lovingly over the muscled curve of his shoulder. His white tank top emphasized his deep tan, and his gym shorts, though loose in the legs, were pulled snug across his groin. Some other woman enjoyed the delight of looking at him, too, Ginny reminded herself.

She stood in the doorway between the dining and living room. "Don't you have someone you'd like to visit today?" she asked.

He glanced toward her, all innocence, as if he hadn't heard her come in, as if he hadn't realized she was standing there until she'd spoken. "Not particularly. Why?"

She couldn't believe he'd keep up the pretense, even to the point of staying away from his girlfriend on a Saturday just to throw Ginny off the track. "I would have thought you'd like some time off," she persisted. "Arnold's not here to worry about, and I'm certainly capable of taking care of the house in your absence. You're free to do whatever you like, with whomever you like."

He challenged her statement with a wry smile. "Not quite."

"You most certainly are," she said, tiring of the game. "Look, I'm aware you're dating someone, and I can't see the point in pretending any longer."

"Dating someone?"

"Stop it, Mitch! You couldn't make that orthodontist's appointment with Arnold, remember? You said the reason was personal. How dense do you think I am?"

The puzzled look disappeared. "Oh, that."

"Yes, that. And you've had plenty of time to see her since then, with Arnold traipsing over to Angela's two or three afternoons a week. But as far as I'm concerned, you can bring this romance out of hiding, Mitch."

He stood and walked over to the television set. "Sorry to disappoint you, Ginny," he said, flicking it off and walking toward her, "but I had a doctor's appointment that Monday, not a date."

"A doctor's appointment?" Relief, enormous beyond all reason, rolled over her. "Why didn't you tell me that?"

He shrugged. "Lots of reasons. I was ticked off at you, for one thing."

"So you made it seem like a date, sort of on purpose?"

"Maybe I did. If you can trot out your Boeing guy, I can use my doctor's appointment to get under your skin." He gazed at her and smiled. "Did I?"

The significance of what he was saying began to take hold of her. He had no other woman in his life. Moreover, he'd deliberately tried to pretend that he had one, to give her the same sort of jealous feelings he'd suffered when she'd tried that ploy. Ginny recalled the hours she'd spent imagining him with someone else. He was under her skin, all right. Deeper than she cared to admit, especially now, when they were alone in the house, and Arnold wasn't due back until supper time.

"You're being pretty quiet," Mitch said, stepping closer.

She backed up. "I'm thinking of all the things I have to do today. There's laundry, and I think we're out of milk and eggs, so I need to go to the store."

"You just got back from the store." He advanced another step. "How come you didn't pick up groceries on the way home?"

*Because I was thinking about you, and your mythical girlfriend,* she thought. "I must have so much on my mind that I'm getting forgetful," she said, stating the truth if not in exact terms.

"I wonder if it's the same thing I have on my mind?" Mitch asked, narrowing the distance between them again.

"I doubt it." She retreated and encountered the hard edge of the dining-room table.

"I don't." Definite purpose etched his features. "I think your mind's filled with the same thing that goes around in mine, day after day, hour after hour. I want to make love to you, Ginny. And you want to make love to me. Furthermore, Arnold's out of town."

She struggled to draw a breath. One more step and he'd be touching her. "For the day."

"That's long enough." He started forward, and the telephone rang.

"I'll get it," she cried, ducking away from him and racing into the kitchen.

He followed her. She'd known he would. He stood
by the desk while she talked. The caller was Arnold.
The Gaston's fifteen-year-old station wagon had broken down in Vancouver. The mechanic couldn't get the
necessary parts until the next day. The Gastons, and
Arnold, were spending the night in a motel.

# CHAPTER ELEVEN

GINNY HUNG UP the phone and turned to face Mitch. She couldn't avoid his question about the call. He had heard her say Arnold's name.

"What's the story?" he asked. "Is everyone all right?"

"Everyone's fine." Ginny took a deep breath. "They had car trouble in Vancouver. The car's old, as you know, and they can't get the parts until tomorrow. They'll drive home then."

He greeted her explanation with silence.

As she met his gaze, memories tumbled in her mind: Mitch suffering through the symphony concert, Mitch scrubbing her bathtub and buying champagne, Mitch helping her deal with the porn movie, Mitch giving her the victory sign after Arnold had won his first wrestling match. His laughter, his tolerance and his warmth had strengthened the fabric of her life with unbreakable threads, threads spun, she realized now, with love. Love like that deserved expression. She'd denied herself, and him, long enough.

He moved toward her.

"Not here," she murmured.

He paused.

"That may sound silly to you," she said.

"No, it doesn't." His expression gentled. "Get what you need. We'll go to my apartment."

FROM THE MOMENT she stepped inside the door of Mitch's furnished one-bedroom apartment, Ginny felt liberated from her carefully constructed self-image. Here she could fling off the conservative role of reputation-conscious mother and businesswoman. Here she could be as anonymous as the surroundings.

The decor, bland enough not to offend anyone, suited no one in particular. Two plaid chairs flanked a tweed sofa. The trio faced a bookshelf containing a television set, stereo components and speakers, and a haphazard collection of books.

The apartment was small, very small. Ginny liked that. False modesty withered and intimacy flourished in a place where she could stand in the kitchen and look right through the living area to the bedroom. Inside these nondescript walls nobody cared if the furniture matched, or the bedspread hung straight, or the towels were coordinated. Most of all, nobody cared if Ginny Westerfelt made love to Mitch Adamson.

"It's nothing fancy," Mitch said, tossing his keys on a laminated wood coffee table. He crossed to the windows, which looked across to the second story of another apartment building, and opened them to allow the afternoon breeze inside. Faint noises drifted from the street, a car motor, a child's shout, a snatch of a song on someone's radio. Mitch closed the brown drapes, muffling the intrusive sounds from the outside world.

"It's perfect," Ginny said, relishing the beige half-light that reminded her of the cozy interior of a tent. Excitement built within her as Mitch approached. At last, she thought, shivering slightly in anticipation.

"Not quite perfect." He took the small satchel from her unresisting hand. "But you are." He dropped the satchel to the carpet, where its soft thunk created the only noise in the apartment besides their breathing.

"You must realize," Ginny said, gazing up at him, "that it's been a long time. I may not be very—"

"Hush." He laid one finger against her lips and circled her waist with his arm. "I wouldn't worry about that, if I were you."

He was already aroused. She felt the firm ridge against her stomach and her heartbeat accelerated. She wanted to please him, but she was worried. She was out of practice. He might be disappointed.

"Ginny, sweetheart," he murmured, gazing into her eyes. "We'll be fine."

*We.* With a single word he'd encircled them with the magic of a shared quest. Ginny guided his head downward. "Kiss me," she whispered.

His lips moved lightly against hers. She tasted the mint of toothpaste and the smoothness of his freshly shaved upper lip. She liked this better, so much better, than the anger that had driven his passion that night in the backyard. He outlined her mouth with the tip of his tongue before dipping inside. As he explored the recesses of her mouth, emotion from that first night when he'd kissed her came flooding back. She remembered his hand on her breast, and her nipples ached for that touch again. Winding her arms around his neck, she pressed closer.

He lifted his mouth. "I've waited so long," he said. "I can't do this slow, Ginny." In one deft motion he swept her up in his arms and carried her through the bedroom doorway. He tumbled them both onto the bed, rolling over once so she was on top of him. Then he kicked off his shoes before burying his fingers in her hair and guiding her head down for another kiss.

As her needs grew stronger, Ginny slid one hand beneath his tank top and caressed the hair-covered expanse of his chest. She laid her palm over his heart and felt the rapid thumping as his tongue plunged more urgently into her mouth.

He rolled her to her back. "How I want you," he said, kissing her temple, her cheeks, her throat as he worked with trembling fingers on the buttons of her blouse. In his impatience, one popped off. "Damn," he swore softly. "I didn't mean to—"

"Never mind. I don't care about buttons," she said, anticipation squeezing the air from her lungs.

He pushed aside the blouse and unfastened the front catch of her bra. For a moment he gazed at her breasts, heaving and sheened with moisture. Then he glanced into her face. "If we'd made love that night, we would have been in the dark and that would have been such a waste."

"I know." She understood that he cherished the light, for so did she. All those days of waiting and yearning demanded the fullest of rewards, the richest of sensual experiences. They deserved to touch, to smell, to taste and see what they'd longed for. She wanted to know him, all of him.

He gazed down at her. "Your eyes look like Christmas morning," he said. "And you'd thought you'd be shy." His voice grew rough, although his touch was smooth as whipped cream. "I don't think I'm going fast enough for you."

"You're doing fine," she whispered.

"I can do better," he said, unbuttoning her slacks and sliding the zipper down. His hand moved inside the silken casing of her underwear, and she gasped as his gentle fingers probed deep, finding the wellspring of her need. "Ginny," he breathed, drawing her name out as he stroked her. "I've dreamed of touching you this way, dreamed how your eyes would grow bright, your skin turn pink... And now... at last...."

His head lowered to her breast, and she moaned as the twin assault on her senses made her arch her back and her shoulders rubbed against the nubby material of the bedspread. Wanting more, she reached for him and pushed at the elastic of his gym shorts.

He lifted his head and looked deep into her eyes.

"I want to touch you, too," she said, her voice choked with longing.

The emotion etched in his expression took on a new intensity. "Good," he said, pressing his palm against the core of her desire and rotating his hand until she gasped his name. "Because I want that, too, Ginny. I want your hands on me, and your sweet mouth." Slowly he withdrew his hand, leaving her aching and damp, incomplete.

Bestowing kisses as he worked, he removed the rest of her clothes before taking off his own. He kicked the discarded garments to the foot of the bed and gathered her in his arms once more. "Now," he sighed.

Ginny closed her eyes as their bodies met, bare skin against bare skin, the smoothness of her breasts against the dark blond hair covering his chest. He pulled her in close, leaving no doubt that he was ready for her, so ready. She opened her eyes and found him gazing at her.

"I've fantasized this so many times," he murmured. "I can't believe you're here beside me."

"I've imagined it, too," she admitted.

"Tell me. Tell me how you imagined it would be."

"Like this. Close together. Touching you…all those muscles you work so hard to build." She ran one hand over his hip.

He nibbled her lower lip. "So you do care about that."

"I care about you," Ginny said, caressing his back, his firm bottom. "I wouldn't be here if I didn't, no matter how many muscles you have."

He stopped kissing her and looked into her eyes. "And I care about you," he said. "I want this to be okay. I don't want you to be tied up with guilt because we've made love."

"No guilt," she said, meeting his gaze without hesitation. She kissed him again. Then she began to satisfy the urges that had been driving her crazy for weeks, as she roamed his heated body with hands and lips. She loved hearing him groan and feeling him twist beneath her, telling her without words that she pleased him.

Ah, but he smelled and tasted good. Instead of making her more timid, her years of abstinence had made her bolder. Or perhaps Mitch was the reason. Mitch, who could be tender one moment and excitingly aggressive the next. And hers to love at last.

"Ginny, I can't wait any longer. I need you…now," he gasped, stilling her hands and guiding her away from him.

She waited, heart pounding, while he fumbled in the bedside table drawer. She heard the rip of cellophane and a moment later he turned back to her.

"I'm shaking," he said, touching her cheek with the back of his hand so she could feel him tremble. "That's what you've done to me, Ginny. You . . . you give so much of yourself."

She held out her arms. "I want to give more," she said, her words choked by the emotion rising in her as she looked into his face. She loved him. That was why she'd been able to lose her inhibitions so easily, to forget about herself.

"You're wonderful," he murmured, moving over her. Arms braced, he held her gaze as he thrust forward.

He filled her perfectly with pressure so sweet, she cried out softly.

He eased back. "Did I hurt you? I didn't want to—"

"No," she said, almost laughing in her delirious pleasure as she grasped his hips and urged him back. She arched upward. "Please don't stop."

"I don't think I could." He moved within her. "Not now. Not when I feel you close around me, when I know you want me there."

"I want you there," she whispered, gazing up at him as he stroked back and forth, increasing the pace.

"Ginny, we were meant to be together like this." He pushed against her deep within, reviving the dizzy whirling she'd felt earlier.

"Yes." She tried to concentrate on his eyes, so loving, so filled with desire. The tension built inside her and her breathing turned into short gasps. His beloved face kept sliding out of her vision. She heard his voice, but she lost the sense of what he was saying as the rhythm of their bodies carried her beyond words to pure sensation. There. Now. *Yes.* The explosion wracked her with convulsions and she grabbed his shoulders for support. Gradually she realized the moans she heard were her own.

As the haze cleared, she lay exhausted beneath him. Slowly she focused on his eyes, his smiling lips. "Amazing," she breathed.

"Yes, you are." He turned his head and kissed her fingertips where they still gripped his shoulders.

"But . . . you? . . ."

"I wanted to enjoy the view. You're so beautiful. All rosy. Here," he said bending to kiss her cheek. "And here," he added, leaning down to nuzzle her breast.

As he circled her nipple with his tongue, Ginny felt the stirrings of need again. She rotated her hips and ran her fingers lightly up his back.

"Oh, Ginny," he moaned, thrusting deep within her once more. "You're everything a man could ask."

Ginny lay in the late-afternoon light listening to Mitch breathe as he slept on his side, one arm tucked around her waist. They'd finally taken time to pull back the spread, and they'd made love again on the cool sheets before Mitch had drifted into sleep.

She'd longed to join him, but she'd never been able to fall asleep easily in strange beds. Arnold was the same way. She'd read once that firstborn and only children had that problem. Mitch, the youngest in a large family, could probably sleep anywhere, adapt himself to any setting. That was why he'd fit into her household so easily.

No, that wasn't the only reason, she amended, turning her head to gaze at him. He'd fit in because he was a good man, kind and considerate. Slowly and steadily he'd built her trust. Even letting Arnold drive his car now seemed the right thing to do—a growth-oriented experience, as Mitch had first explained it.

Thanks to Mitch, Arnold and Ginny might survive Arnold's rush into puberty this summer.

Ginny didn't want to get ahead of herself, though, and plan events beyond the end of this summer. Just because she'd made love to Mitch didn't mean she knew enough about him to make any lifetime commitments. Besides, he hadn't indicated he wanted that, either. Still, he had said that he didn't enter into relationships for the short-term. She had no reason not to believe him.

They both needed time to nurture this new arrangement. Ginny wanted to keep things as they were for now, or as they'd recently become. She still wasn't comfortable with the idea of making love in the townhouse. Mitch's apartment offered the perfect retreat, and they could use it whenever Arnold was out with Angela for any length of time. If Mitch and Ginny were circumspect whenever Arnold was around, he wouldn't have to know about the changed circumstances until they were ready to tell him. But that was getting too far in the future, Ginny reminded herself.

For now, she should learn more about Mitch Adamson, and he about her. She longed to hear stories of his childhood in Minnesota and a description of his family. From the bed where she lay, she could see several framed pictures on the double dresser across the room. They looked like family photographs—one large picture and several smaller ones. More snapshots were stuck in the frame of the mirror over the dresser.

Moving carefully, Ginny eased out from under Mitch's arm. He didn't wake up. She tiptoed into the bathroom and quietly closed the door. A small window over the tub gave her enough light to finger-comb her hair and splash water on her face. Until she retrieved her satchel from the living room, that would have to do.

A black, silk kimono hung on the back of the bathroom door. She slipped it on. The sleeves hung past her fingertips and the hem brushed her knees. She figured it hit Mitch about midthigh. She looked forward to seeing him in it and didn't have to wonder why he'd never worn it around the townhouse. That would have been unfair temptation. She sniffed the collar; it smelled faintly of his after-shave.

Tying the belt of the robe around her waist, Ginny returned to the bedroom, where Mitch continued to sleep on his side, his arm curved as if still holding her against his body. He looked vulnerable, lying there without even a sheet to protect him.

He looked so defenseless that Ginny was struck again by the thought that Mitch, too, was in danger of getting hurt if their relationship didn't work. She'd been concerned for Arnold, and then for herself; Mitch had always seemed so solid and self-sufficient. He didn't look invincible now, however, with his blond hair tousled and his penetrating gray eyes closed, and his glorious body uncovered. She considered pulling the sheet over him, but didn't want to wake him yet. She had some exploring to do.

Crossing to the dresser, she leaned over to inspect the pictures displayed there. There was a family reunion sort of photograph taken outdoors in the summer. She found the small oval of Mitch's grinning face in the back row. His muscular arm was hooked around a blond girl who looked very much like him—a sister, perhaps.

More than half the people in the picture were blond, including the woman Ginny picked out as Mitch's mother. His father was completely bald. A gray-haired woman who sat in the center of the front row could have been a grandmother or great-aunt, and there were children ranging from babies to teenagers.

Ginny counted the people in the picture—thirty-two. She marveled at such a crowd of relatives, compared to the few she could claim. Her mother and father each came from families of only two children, which gave her two aunts and two uncles, whom she rarely saw. One couple had remained childless and the other had a boy, her only cousin, who lived in Europe now and was married, but Ginny didn't know whether or not he had any children. Face it, she thought, she'd be hard put to gather such a crowd. To her surprise, she felt a pang of regret.

The smaller framed picture included a formal portrait of the man and woman Ginny had decided were Mitch's parents, one of the gray-haired woman when she was much younger, an Irish setter on a braided rug in front of a gigantic fireplace, and a photograph of Mitch with a dark-haired boy that might have been taken when they both were in high school. They had on letter jackets and had their arms slung around each other's shoulders. The snapshots around the mirror were all of kids—nieces and nephews, Ginny decided.

The entire array gave her a warm image of Mitch surrounded by a large, loving family, yet he'd hardly spoken of them since she'd known him. He'd made a few phone calls, written some letters, but he hadn't said things like "You should see how my dad would handle this," or "That's my mom's favorite color"— nothing to indicate his relatives were often in his thoughts. Ginny decided to ask him questions about his family after he woke up.

She continued her exploration in the living room. The stereo system and tape collection indicated exactly what Mitch had said about himself. He liked popular music with words. Mitch's bookshelf didn't offer many surprises, either. She found science textbooks and books on wrestling, along with science fiction and astronomy books and charts. There were two sets of high school yearbooks, one dating from Mitch's school years and the other from his former school in Cedarville, Idaho. The Idaho yearbooks were closest, and Ginny pulled one from the shelf.

She found two pictures of Mitch, one in the classroom surrounded by stainless steel sinks and test tubes, and the other standing beside his wrestling team. She saw a slightly younger Mitch in the pictures than the man she knew, someone who looked—she searched for the right word—less intense. *Carefree,* she thought, studying the two pictures. She wouldn't apply that adjective to him now, although he was funny and warm and easy to be around.

Maggie's theory of a ruined love affair would explain the apparent change in Mitch, Ginny mused, and his departure from Cedarville. She closed the yearbook and pulled out the next one, dated a year later. Immediately following the title page she found a large, studio portrait of Mitch with the words Teacher of the Year underneath. Scrawled messages of affection from students decorated the borders of the page and spilled onto adjoining pages.

As Ginny read the messages, she absorbed the love they represented. Mitch's students had idolized him. Even a disastrous love affair didn't seem cause enough to leave a nurturing environment like Cedarville High. The Mitch she knew wasn't the kind of man to allow a personal crisis to affect his work. Thinking about that some more, she turned the pages of the yearbook.

MITCH AWOKE SLOWLY, disoriented by the late-afternoon light and his surroundings. These days he was used to waking up in Ginny's townhouse, not his apartment. Then he remembered. She wasn't there, but her clothes still cluttered the end of the bed, so she hadn't left. He smiled. What a wondrous woman. For all her reservations about making love, when she'd finally committed herself to the concept, she'd *really* committed herself. He'd been thoroughly loved. And that was the right word, too. Love, or something very near it, had motivated Ginny this afternoon. He recognized the emotion, because it mirrored his own. At last perhaps they could throw aside the silly rules and regulations she'd set up and get down to the business of building a solid relationship. Mitch was ready for that.

He rolled over and sat on the edge of the bed. Time to search for Ginny. In this apartment that wouldn't take long. He considered looking for her as he was, naked, but decided they might not have reached that stage yet. Without bothering to put on his underwear, he pulled on his gym shorts. The way he was feeling, he wouldn't have them on long, anyway. Considering that option, he opened the bedside table drawer and unwrapped a cellophane package before putting the contents into his pocket.

He walked into the living room and found her, sitting cross-legged on the floor, wearing his black, silk kimono and looking sexier than a centerfold. She hadn't heard him. She sat absorbed in a book open in her lap. Then he recognized the book, and the warm anticipation he'd felt at seeing her again evaporated like water on a hot griddle.

This could be the moment to tell her, he thought as a knot tightened in his gut. Surely he'd proven himself with his treatment of Arnold, and Ginny had shown complete trust this afternoon, when they'd made love. But he was afraid. Even his family, who loved him completely and had never doubted his integrity—even they treated him differently now. They were conservative people, and no Adamson had ever been on trial before, least of all for something like child molesting.

After the trial, he'd gone home to Minnesota for a week and discovered he made everyone uncomfortable. His family's awkwardness had hurt, and he hadn't returned in three years. Letters replaced phone calls; in letters he couldn't hear the hesitations and embarrassed coughing. Mitch hoped that eventually his family would forget their shame and his part in having caused it, but for now, he was tainted.

He could hardly expect a more liberal reaction from Ginny, who'd known him such a short time. He would tell her some day, of course, but rushing his confession could be as foolish a thing as he'd ever done, and he'd done some pretty foolish things in his life.

He leaned in the doorway in a deliberately nonchalant stance. "Ancient history," he said. "Pretty boring stuff."

Ginny glanced up, and his heart turned over at the softness in her blue eyes. He longed to grab the book from her and carry her back to the bedroom. Now that he knew the joyous abandonment with which she made love, he wanted her more than ever.

"I hope you don't think I'm prying," she said. "But you hardly ever talk about yourself. My goodness, Teacher of the Year! You were a hero in Cedarville."

He shrugged and forced himself to smile. *Hero. Right.* "Oh, you know these awards," he said. "Schools are always giving them out. No big deal."

Ginny closed the book she'd been studying and reached for another lying beside her on the carpet. He recognized it as last year's and guessed she might be looking for the award winner in it. She wouldn't find one.

"They didn't give it that year," he said.

"How about the year before that?" she asked, closing the book and gazing up at him.

He remembered that she conducted interviews for a living. Just his luck. "I—um, no. The year I got it was the first time they gave the award."

"They created it for you?"

"I'm sure not for me. Lots of teachers—"

"Was anyone else up for the award the year you got it?"

He shouldn't have had the darn books in the shelves, but he hadn't thought she'd be here, browsing through his apartment, either. "No," he said, wondering how to get out of this discussion.

"So." She gazed at him. "The award was created specifically to honor you, which means the faculty and staff at Cedarville High, after you'd been there only a year, thought you were somebody pretty special."

"They were easily impressed," he said, crossing the room and dropping to the carpet beside her. "How about you?" he said, easing the book away from her.

"Are you easily impressed? I sure hope so." He reached for the belt of the silk robe.

"Stop trying to change the subject." She pushed his hand away but she was smiling, and he could tell from the look in her eyes that he excited her. "Here you were practically crowned king at this school, and yet you moved away. I don't get it."

"If you'll stop talking," he said, this time successfully untying the sash, "you might get all kinds of things."

"You're avoiding the issue." She closed her eyes when he reached inside the robe and cradled her breast in his palm.

The pliant weight of her breast and the feel of her soft skin under his fingers made his mouth moist at the thought of tasting her again. "I have more important issues on my mind." He tried not to think of this as the cowardly way out. When he'd loved her for days, and not merely hours, he'd tell her the whole truth and take his chances. But for now, with her dusky pink nipple puckering under the gentle stroking of his thumb, and her lips parting in expectation of his kisses, he'd be crazy to lose his advantage. He'd taught his wrestlers that. Timing is everything.

"Tell me why you left Cedarville," she murmured, her head lolling back and her outstretched hands braced on the floor.

"I will," he said, cupping her breast and leaning down. "But not now." He drew her nipple into his mouth and the throbbing began in his groin. She moaned, and that single, breathless sound was enough to bring him to surging readiness.

Lowering her to the carpet, he pushed aside the kimono and ran his hand with firm purpose up her inner thigh. Nothing mattered but this, he thought as he kissed her breasts, her throat, her sweet mouth.

He stripped away his shorts and sheathed himself. He had no time to take her back to the bedroom. He needed her now. The carpet scratched his knees, but he didn't care. The silk robe, fanned out beneath her, would protect her from the rough carpet.

He gazed down at her, pink and creamy against the black robe, her breasts quivering with each rapid breath, her eyes bright. He supported her hips with his hands and delved deep. Her eyes opened wide. He drew back and stroked forward again, loving the way her pupils widened and her cheeks flushed.

"Oh, Mitch," she crooned.

"I know." He pushed into her again. He wanted to stay like this, inside her, forever. "I know."

She did the lifting now, eagerly thrusting upward to meet him, and he braced his arms on either side of her head and buried himself in her warmth over and over. Fortunately her release came quickly, because he couldn't have controlled the burst of passion that shook him soon afterward. He slumped forward, and one hand struck a hard object, the spine of a book. He pushed the book away with a groan and settled his head in the comforting curve of Ginny's soft shoulder. Not yet, he thought. A little more time. Please.

## CHAPTER TWELVE

WHEN GINNY COULDN'T COAX Mitch into reminiscing about Cedarville, the theory of a love gone wrong reasserted itself in her mind. He demonstrated his passionate nature throughout the memorable night, and Ginny could imagine that if he'd given himself so completely to someone else back in Cedarville, and been ultimately rejected, he might have suffered enough to want to leave town, despite the adulation of his students.

Ginny decided to bide her time and see if Mitch offered an explanation of his former love life and of its pain. Perhaps he needed more assurance that *she* had no intention of rejecting him. In the hours they held each other, she found assurance easy to provide.

Early the following morning, they discussed returning to the townhouse in case Arnold called again. Yet they delayed the moment. They showered together in Mitch's small bathroom and cavorted like otters at play. Then Mitch bought Ginny breakfast at a waffle house, and they finally arrived home in the middle of the morning. The answering machine was empty of calls, and Ginny sighed with relief that she wouldn't have to fabricate reasons for not having been home.

"What now?" Mitch asked as they stood together in the middle of the kitchen.

Ginny put her satchel down on the kitchen table. "You mean right this minute, or is that a more far-reaching question?"

"I want to know where we are in this, how we proceed from here."

"As the female porcupine said to the male, with extreme caution."

He gave her a wry smile. "You still don't want to tell him."

"Not yet. But obviously we can't go back to things as they were. I'd go crazy if I thought I couldn't make love to you."

"That makes two of us." Mitch rubbed the back of his neck and looked relieved. "I'm glad that much is settled, at least. For a minute I thought you might say we couldn't—"

"Not here," Ginny interrupted. "I still can't imagine making love in this house, even after Arnold's asleep."

His silent gaze questioned her reluctance.

"Mitch, Arnold's room shares a wall with mine. I can hear his stereo when he turns it up loud. I'm afraid that he might . . . well, hear us or something."

"We'll use my room, then."

Ginny shook her head. "You're right across the hall from him. That's not any better. He'd find out. I know he would."

"I still don't understand why that's so terrible. Sooner or later he'll have to—"

"Not necessarily. We don't know where this is going yet."

"Don't we?" Mitch stepped toward her. "I've always liked being around you, and now—" He circled her waist and drew her close, ignoring her stiff resistance. "Now I crave being with you and beneath you and on top of you, kissing every—"

"Mitch, don't." She tried to hold herself aloof, but his warmth seeped into her, relaxing her tense muscles.

"Don't? That isn't what you said early this morning." He cupped her breast and rubbed gently across the cotton of her blouse. "Your body isn't saying *don't.*"

"Not in this house." She covered his hand and stopped the caress.

"Your eyes are getting all misty, the way they do when you want me," he murmured.

She closed her giveaway eyes and sighed. "I believe that. I'm amazed at what happens to me when you touch me, but I don't want Arnold even to sense we have a physical relationship. First you and I need to get used to each other, to this change in our situation."

"What change? Sounds like everything will be back to normal, both of us frustrated as hell."

"Well, whenever Arnold goes to Angela's on the weekend, we can drive to your apartment, as long as we're back before he is."

Mitch frowned. "That's ridiculous. We'd only have a Saturday or Sunday afternoon once in a while."

"I guess so."

"You can't be serious." Mitch lowered his head and kissed the corners of her mouth.

"Mitch—"

"You can't believe that every night we'll sleep down the hall from each other," he murmured, interspersing his words with nibbling kisses, "peacefully settled in our own sterile beds, secure in the knowledge that once every two weeks, if we're lucky, we'll be allowed to make love."

"I didn't say...it was a terrific solution. Mitch, you have to stop this. I'm really—"

"Really getting hot and bothered? Me, too."

"Maybe...maybe I could take off from work some afternoons when Arnold's at Angela's house, and make up the time by bringing more stuff home at night."

"That has promise." Mitch slid his hand down and caressed between her thighs. "Keep thinking."

"I can't think. Not when you do that."

"Push me away, then."

Ginny groaned. She was becoming a glutton for pleasure.

"We could tell Arnold."

"No." Summoning her willpower, Ginny extricated herself from Mitch's embrace. "No, not yet," she said, backing away.

He moved closer.

"Now, stop." She held out both hands. "Play fair, Mitch. You've said before that Arnold is my kid, and decisions concerning him are mine."

"Yes, I did say that. But this decision concerns more than Arnold."

"Please don't push me on this issue. I'll do what I can to give us time to be alone. That's all I can promise for now. And yes, we'll stay in our own rooms, in our own beds, each night. If you can't handle that—" she shrugged "—then I guess you could always drive back to your apartment every night."

"You're a tough woman. Besides, that wouldn't solve my problem. The cold shower works here just as well as it does there."

"Have we got a deal, then?"

"A reluctant deal. Want to shake on it?"

"No," Ginny said, backing away. "I'm going up to my bedroom."

"And I'm not to follow."

"Mitch, this is just as difficult for me as it is for you."

His smile came slowly. "I certainly hope so," he murmured.


GINNY CONCLUDED that the only way she'd be able to take time off in the afternoon, which she'd never done before, would be to confide in Maggie. Not wanting to risk having Claudia overhear such a conversation, she suggested that she and Maggie go out for lunch on Monday.

"We should do this more often," Maggie said, glancing around at the rustic decor of a restaurant in Pike's Place Market near the waterfront. "In fact, Phil and I should come down here once in a while. A world-famous farmer's market right here, and we hardly ever see the place."

"I've always loved it, too," Ginny said, although she wasn't paying much attention to the atmosphere. She'd chosen this particular setting because it was a noisy place. Ginny didn't want anyone except Maggie to hear her confessions. The last thing she needed was a client or survey respondent to overhear her conversation.

"You look wonderful, by the way," Maggie said, leaning her crossed arms on the table and smiling at Ginny. "Did you buy some new makeup over the weekend or something?"

Ginny flushed.

"Goodness, you're blushing! You have a secret, don't you? Tell me right this minute."

"I'm sure you can guess." Ginny reached for her water glass and discovered she had the shakes. "Mitch and I—" she stopped and gulped some water "—well, it's not exactly a platonic relationship anymore."

Maggie's eyes sparkled. "Get outta here. Really?"

"Really."

"I am impressed." Maggie offered her hand across the table. "Congratulations."

Ginny shook her partner's hand and blushed a brighter shade of red. "It's not exactly the way you think."

"How do you know? I have a terrific imagination."

"I don't want Arnold to find out, at least at this stage, so we don't . . . do anything in the townhouse."

Maggie clucked her tongue. "You're such a prude, Ginny Westerfelt. Honestly. You could certainly—" She paused as the waiter approached. Then she glanced at Ginny. "Does this call for champagne?"

"No. Heavens, no." She gave the menu a quick once-over. "I'll have the crab and avocado salad and iced tea," she told the waiter.

"No wine or anything?" Maggie asked, pouting.

"Go ahead if you want. I have two appointments this afternoon."

"Oh, all right." Maggie sighed. "Make my order the same as hers, the sensible one." After the waiter left, Maggie leaned forward again. "I hope you're not such a wet blanket with this new relationship. You'll bore that gorgeous hunk to death."

"I probably am a wet blanket. That's probably exactly what I am, but I have to consider Arnold."

Maggie studied her for a moment. "Just remember, sweetie, that Arnold's not always going to consider you in return."

"I know." Ginny smiled ruefully, thinking of all the times recently Arnold hadn't considered her. Angela came first now, Mitch second, and she a poor third. "But he's a kid, and kids are often self-centered. I'm supposed to be an adult who isn't."

"So there's no hanky-panky going on in the townhouse."

"That's right."

"There's certainly something going on somewhere," Maggie said. "It's written all over your face."

Ginny refolded her napkin. "Mitch kept his apartment for the summer."

"So you two sneaked over there? What a kick!"

"We didn't *sneak.*" Ginny bristled because secretly she felt that word described their behavior exactly. "Arnold went to Vancouver with his girlfriend's family, and the car broke down. They all had to spend the night in Vancouver, and so... because we were unexpectedly alone, one thing led to another, and we..."

"Got in the car and drove over to his apartment? Arnold was a hundred and fifty miles away. I don't get it."

Ginny noticed the waiter coming with iced tea, and she waited until he left before answering. "I know it's a fine distinction," she said. "But if I—" she lowered her voice "—if I made love to Mitch in the townhouse, even with Arnold gone, I'd feel strange about it when he came back. Does that make any sense?"

Maggie dumped artificial sweetener into her tea. "For you, I guess it does. You're convinced the walls have ears. Frankly, if it were me, I wouldn't go through these contortions. I'd tell Arnold that Mommy and Mitch have a lovely relationship and they'll be sleeping in the same room from now on. Simple as that."

Ginny groaned. "You make it sound simple, but I can't picture myself saying that to him, let alone doing it."

"That's what you get for setting yourself up as some paragon of virtue all these years."

"I happen to think that was the right thing to do."

"To a point, maybe you're right. Goodness knows, Ginny, I don't believe that mothers, or fathers, either, for that matter, should demonstrate to their kids that they'll jump into bed with any old partner at the drop of a hat. But you, after five years of abstinence, can hardly be accused of promiscuity. Don't you think Arnold would understand?"

"I don't know, but there's another thing. Mitch and I have made no commitment to each other. I don't want Arnold fantasizing that Mitch will be his new father and then have the whole thing blow up in his face. Mitch and I need more time to discover where this is going. If we should decide it's a permanent deal, then of course I'll tell Arnold."

Maggie grimaced. "Let's hope you tell him in time for him to rent a tux for the wedding."

"Maggie, you're impossible."

"It's one of my finer qualities," Maggie said, fluffing her hair.

"I guess if I didn't trust you as much as I do, I wouldn't have the nerve to be telling you all this, or to ask about something else, something that has to be kept absolutely quiet."

"Oh?" Maggie's expression became alert. "I am the soul of discretion."

"I hope so, because I want to start taking a few afternoons off to... be with Mitch."

Maggie clasped her hands. "Love in the afternoon. How poetic."

"I'll be doing some juggling, of course."

"Juggling?" Maggie's eyebrows rose. "I take back the wet blanket remark. You're more sexually innovative than I thought, honey."

"Maggie, for heaven's sake! I meant juggling of the office work."

"Oh." Maggie regarded her with a merry expression. "Sorry."

"You should be concerned about the work schedule," Ginny said. "Both our paychecks depend on everything running smoothly."

"I haven't the slightest worry about efficiency in that office. I doubt you'd allow an earthquake to disrupt your duties, and this is merely a love affair. You probably have everything planned out, and you'll take work home if you don't get it done during the day. Am I right?"

"Yes, but—"

"So all you need from me, because you certainly have my blessing, is a zipped lip. If anyone asks, I'll say you've taken on a special consulting assignment."

"Even Claudia."

"Even Claudia," Maggie agreed. "Even Phil. This is between you and me, kiddo, until you tell me otherwise."

"Thanks, Maggie." Ginny reached across the table and squeezed her arm.

"You're welcome. Am I permitted one tiny bit of advice?"

Ginny laughed. "You give me huge chunks of advice all the time, Maggie. What's another tiny bit going to matter?"

"But this time I'm really serious. This is important."

"Okay."

"I have the feeling that right now, if you had to choose between Mitch and Arnold, you'd choose Arnold."

"You're right. I would."

"Arnold will only be around a few more years, Ginny. Mitch has lifetime potential. Don't be hasty."

Ginny gazed at her friend. "That's what all this caution is about, Maggie. I'm trying to arrange everything so that I don't have to make that choice, ever."

MITCH HAD an extra key made to his apartment. On weekday afternoons, when Arnold announced his plans to ride his bike over to Angela's, Mitch would call Ginny at the office and find out if she was free. Sometimes she couldn't get away, and she'd force herself to concentrate on a client's problems while privately longing to be enclosed in Mitch's strong arms.

Sometimes, however, she could shove her unfinished paperwork into her briefcase, inform Maggie that she was leaving and drive at a speed slightly above the limit to Mitch's apartment. If she got there ahead of him, she'd take off all her clothes and hang them carefully in his closet. If he arrived before her, she always had to remind him to be careful of her outfit,

because she had to put it back on and look present-
able when she returned home or to the office, whichever they'd arranged.

But she loved his frenzy to undress her, despite the
danger to her wardrobe. Their lovemaking bubbled
over with impatience borne of long hours spent together when they couldn't touch. Ginny marveled that
Arnold hadn't noticed the charged atmosphere in the
townhouse whenever Ginny and Mitch were in the
same room. Apparently his own severe case of puppy
love had blinded him to everything else.

Ginny couldn't remember the last time she'd possessed an energy level equal to this. The frustration of
not being able to hold Mitch whenever she wanted to
drove her to long hours of work at the small com-
puter in her bedroom. One day at the office Maggie
remarked that the new regime had resulted in more
productivity, not less.

She and Ginny found themselves ahead of schedule
in planning for the next focus group tour. The client,
wooed by Maggie for more than a year, was an ad
agency needing ideas for a company that produced
adhesive tape. Ginny threw herself into the project as
a distraction, all the while dreading the week that she'd
be away from Mitch.

At least she knew that Arnold would be well taken
care of while she was gone. Between Mitch and Angela's attentions, Arnold's self-confidence had soared.
He won nearly every wrestling match now, and when
he didn't, he accepted the loss with the good grace of
someone who knows his worth.

After meets, he and Angela had formed the habit of
asking for the car keys as soon as the last match had
ended. Mitch had encouraged Ginny to indulge their

wish to be alone in the car for a few minutes before the adults showed up, and Ginny had conceded Arnold and Angela's need for some privacy. She stayed with Mitch while he congratulated his team and conferred with parents. Ginny had made a few friends among the parents, too, and had sheepishly admitted to herself that she now looked forward to the meets.

On a Monday night near the end of July, she stood talking with Julia, the woman with the permed hair who had spoken to her during Arnold's first match so many weeks ago. As they exchanged compliments about Arnold and about Julia's son David, Angela raced into the gym.

"Coach!" she panted. "Billy Herman's out there! He says he's going to beat Arnold up!"

Mitch dropped his clipboard on the bleachers and ran toward the double metal doors with Ginny hurrying after him as fast as her high heels would allow. Her stomach churned with fear. She shouldn't have allowed Angela and Arnold to go outside the gym alone, no matter how urgent their need for privacy. Once again, she'd been too lax. But this time Billy wouldn't lay a hand on Arnold if she had anything to say about it.

The summer-night sky still glowed with a streak of daylight splashed across the horizon, but the security lights in the parking lot had flicked on in the twilight. Ginny saw Arnold immediately, his shower-wet hair glistening under the light of the security lamp. His back straight and shoulders squared, he stood in the middle of a circle of boys, facing Billy, who was crouched and ready to swing.

As Ginny drew closer, she noted Arnold's pale face, his heaving chest. He was scared.

Billy, on the other hand, seemed unintimidated. "Think you're pretty big stuff, huh?" he sneered. "Won a few wrestling matches, got yourself a girl-friend? Well, you're still a wimp in my book, Wester-felt. Let's see what you can do against fists, nerd-face."

Adrenaline rushed through Ginny as she broke into a run and clenched her purse strap. Her purse was heavy, and she had no reservation about using it as a weapon. Just before she reached the circle, someone caught her arm, and she wheeled, ready to swing her purse at whoever had stopped her.

"Wait," Mitch said in a low voice as he gripped her arm tighter.

"For what?" Ginny said harshly. "For that Nean-derthal to bash Arnold's braces down his throat? Let me go, Mitch."

"If you wade in there now and don't give Arnold a chance to regain his self-respect, he'll hate you, Ginny."

"Let him. At least he'll be in one piece."

"I promise I won't let the fight get out of hand," Mitch continued urgently. "But I don't think it will."

"Because Arnold's won a few wrestling matches? Billy's a star football player, Mitch. He loves to hit people."

"She's right, Coach," Angela said. She stood on his other side. "Billy's mean. He really whomped on Ar-nold in the cafeteria last year."

Mitch glanced toward the circle where Arnold had altered his stance. He crouched now, like Billy, and flexed his arms. "I don't think Billy will whomp Ar-nold now," he said.

"Mitch," Ginny protested. "I hate this."

"He saw me standing here," Mitch said. "He could have called out for help. He didn't. Arnold wants to do this himself, like he said on the camping trip. Don't you think, after all his work this summer, that he's earned that right?"

Ginny trembled. "You'll stop it if he starts beating Arnold up?"

"I'll stop it."

Ginny stared at the lamplit circle and wished she could close her eyes. But she had to watch every second, to be ready to race forward, Mitch or no Mitch, if necessary.

"Come on, wimp," Billy taunted. "Take a swing. Show your girlfriend how brave you are."

"Leave Angela out of this," Arnold said, his new baritone squeaking at the end of the declaration.

"That's right. Angela Gaston. Pretty cute chick for a loser like you, Westerfelt. Think I'll ask her out."

Arnold swung wildly and missed.

Billy laughed and glanced in the direction of his friends standing in the circle. "Needs some lessons, don't you think, guys? Better pay attention and see how it's done, wimp." Billy's first blow glanced against Arnold's nose. Arnold shook his head and drops of blood spattered on his sweatshirt. Angela gasped.

Ginny's heart pounded at the sight of Arnold's blood and she clutched Mitch's arm. "Stop it now," she said. "He's bleeding."

"Not yet." He covered Ginny's hand with his. "He's not hurt," he soothed. "He's still okay."

"Keep watching," Billy said, dancing on his toes. Then his grin faded as he threw a right and put his whole body behind it.

Ginny stared in horror as Billy's fist seemed to come toward Arnold's jaw in slow motion. She tensed for the moment when Arnold's jaw would crack and he'd topple to the asphalt unconscious. The crack never came.

She watched in disbelief as Arnold sidestepped the punch and grabbed Billy's arm.

"Yes!" Mitch shouted.

Arnold twisted his tormentor's arm, and when Billy turned, Arnold put him neatly into a headlock. The crowd of boys fell silent. Billy's struggles spun the pair around, but didn't dislodge Arnold's grip.

"You gotta let me go sometime!" Billy screamed, trying to hit Arnold on the back. "Then I'll break your face!"

Arnold clenched his jaw and tightened his grip around Billy's neck. Billy swore and threatened to kill Arnold when he got loose.

"Could Arnold choke him to death?" Ginny asked nervously.

"He could, but he won't," Mitch said, never taking his eyes off Arnold.

"Get him, Arnold!" Angela cried. "For all he did to you!"

Arnold glanced in their direction. Blood had crusted under one nostril. He seemed to lose himself in thought for a moment, and then with one last squeeze, he released Billy.

Ginny held her breath as Billy started toward Arnold again. Arnold crouched and flexed his arms. He looked Billy straight in the eye. Billy's glance wavered.

"Come on," Arnold said, and this time his voice didn't break. "What's keeping you?"

Slowly Billy edged back toward the perimeter of the circle. "Maybe I got better things to do," he said, nudging into his crowd of jock friends. They moved away from him. "I'll get you later."

Arnold straightened. "Suit yourself," he said with a shrug.

Mitch squeezed Ginny's arm. "Now you can go."

She rushed forward with Angela right behind her and both of them in tears. They hugged Arnold together, and Ginny felt him quivering. "I was so scared, Arnold," Ginny said, looking at him with swimming eyes.

"Me, too," Arnold admitted.

"What if he'd wanted to keep fighting?" Angela asked.

Arnold looked over at Mitch, who stood a few feet away with his arms folded and a wide grin on his face. "I would have handled him, right, Coach?"

"Damn right you would have," Mitch said.

## CHAPTER THIRTEEN

ARNOLD'S VICTORY over Billy Herman erased all his remaining insecurities. Ginny could hardly believe the transformation in Arnold's walk, his gestures and his tone of voice. Billy made good on his threat to call Angela for a date, and Arnold was so sure of himself that he took Billy's attempt to move in on his girl as a joke. Billy called Angela more than once, and Arnold reported with pride that Angela had turned him down flat. Arnold announced that if Billy became a pest, he'd have to have another "talk" with him.

Angela looked upon Arnold as her knight in shining armor. The two were together as often as their parents would permit. On weekends, Arnold alternately spent time with Angela's family or asked Ginny and Mitch to plan activities in which Angela could participate. Those outings proved difficult for Ginny and Mitch, who were forced to observe the two teenagers holding hands and stealing kisses. Meanwhile, Ginny hardly dared exchange a glance with Mitch for fear of igniting the sparks ever present between them.

On a Saturday early in August, Ginny had braced herself for another one of those days. To make matters worse, business had been hectic and she and Mitch hadn't had a single afternoon together all week. Still, Arnold had requested that he, Mitch, Angela and Ginny take a ferry ride across Puget Sound, and Ginny had agreed, remembering that the previous weekend Angela's family had taken Arnold to the Seattle Aquarium. Ginny wanted to be fair and do her part, even if she'd be a bundle of repressed sexual energy for days afterward.

Right after breakfast, however, Angela called and said she didn't feel like going and asked Arnold to come over to her house, instead. Arnold looked disappointed, but Ginny assured him they'd go another time. Meanwhile, she tried to control her own jubilation at the unexpected reprieve, and the possibilities that opened up for her and Mitch.

"I suppose we could still take the ferry ride," Mitch said after Arnold headed into the garage to get his bike.

"If you'd like." Ginny smiled at him.

"You know what I'd like." Mitch tilted his head toward the garage. "Chances are he'll be gone all day." He yawned and stretched. "I feel a little weary. I think I'll spend the day in bed."

"And which bed will you spend the day in?"

"Whichever one you choose."

"You know which one I'll choose," she said.

"Yeah, but I know of two others a whole lot closer."

"Everything's going so well." Ginny watched out the kitchen window until Arnold pedaled to the end of the street and turned out of sight. "I don't want to risk spoiling what we have."

"How about improving what we have?"

She glanced at him and her heartbeat quickened with apprehension. If he said he loved her, if he asked her to marry him, the status quo would change. Arnold would have to be told.

"Does that scare you?" Mitch asked, challenging her just a bit.

"Maybe."

Mitch stayed where he was, with several feet of space separating them, and gazed at her. "Okay. Then I guess we shouldn't stand around here talking all morning, when we could be doing those things that don't scare you."

"Mitch, I—"

"It's all right, Ginny. Believe me, it's all right. Only a fool would push for more when he has heaven in his arms, at least part of the time."

Ginny stood there, uncertain. She loved him. Of course she did, yet she hadn't spoken the words aloud. Neither had he. He might be waiting for her to take the initiative. She had the most at risk, with Arnold in the picture.

"Come on," he said gently. "Don't think. Come with me to the apartment, like always, and we'll make beautiful love there, like always. That's enough for now. More than enough." He stretched out his hand and she walked forward and placed hers within it. "Let's just go," he said, drawing her toward the kitchen door.

"I haven't finished cleaning up." She glanced back at the dishes stacked on the counter.

"Forget the dishes. Come with me."

She looked into his eyes and the primitive longing awakened within her once more.

He smiled and guided her out the door.

Later, they stood in his bedroom at the apartment, and undressed each other with elaborate care. This time Ginny's Saturday outfit of jeans and short-sleeved sweater didn't require the attention that her work clothes demanded.

"Maybe this has been too fast," Mitch said, unfastening her bra and pulling it slowly from her breasts. "All of it. We never seem to have time to slow down, do we?"

Ginny shook her head.

"We'll be slow now. We'll take our time."

"I don't mind it when you hurry, though," Ginny said, wanting him to know how he'd pleased her with his urgency. "I know it's because you want me so much."

He leaned down and kissed the tip of her breast. "I do. I do now. Remember that." He slid his hands beneath the elastic of her panties. As he eased them down, he stooped to kiss his way down the hollow between her ribs, over her flat stomach, past the pale triangle of hair to her soft inner thigh. "But sometimes, when a man takes his time, he wants a woman just as much, but he doesn't want the loving to be over," he said, his breath warm against her skin. "He wants it to go on forever," he added, leaning his cheek against her thigh as he lifted each of her feet and released the panties.

Ginny trembled as he ran both hands up the backs of her legs and cupped her bottom. Kneeling before her, he urged her forward, guiding her toward an intimate kiss. She tangled her fingers in his hair as his tongue and lips found her. As he'd promised, his touch was slow, leisurely, deliberate.

Her knees weakened, but he held her firmly and supported her weight while he continued to tease her. When the tension became so much that she thought he'd catapult her over the edge, he paused until she regained equilibrium. Then he began the sweet assault again.

"You're torturing me," she gasped.

"And you love it," he murmured.

"I love you." The words came as a surprise to her. She hadn't meant to say them.

Mitch tensed. Slowly he got to his feet and stood before her, his hands at his sides. He swallowed. "I need to know..." He paused and took a breath. "Ginny, don't tell me that unless you mean it."

She looked deep into his eyes and she could barely breathe. "I mean it," she said. "I didn't think I could tell you yet, but I mean it."

"Why didn't you think you could tell me?"

"Because then everything...everything would be different."

He hesitated. "You're right, everything is different. Not because you love me. I knew you did. I knew you couldn't be this way with me unless there was love."

"You love me, too."

"Yes. More than you can imagine."

"Mitch, I'm scared."

"Me, too. I don't know what you'll do."

The idea that he was frightened startled her. "What do you mean?"

"You're so worried about Arnold and how our relationship will affect him. I'm in love with you, and I don't know if one of these days you'll tell me to take a hike. What I mean is, you may love me, but you may also sacrifice that feeling for Arnold's sake, if necessary."

Ginny remembered that Maggie had said the same thing.

"You see?" Mitch flexed both hands. "You're not denying that Arnold comes first."

Ginny gazed at him standing before her, uncertain and vulnerable. She loved his laugh, his touch, his kindness. Most of all she loved the strength of character that allowed him to risk so much for the chance of loving her. She couldn't picture life without Mitch, couldn't picture giving him up. "That's just it, Mitch. I don't know if Arnold comes first anymore. And I wonder if I'm a terrible mother because I want you so much that I'm not all that concerned about Arnold right now."

The tension eased from his body. "Is that true?"

She nodded.

"Thank the Lord." He gathered her into his arms and buried his face against her neck. "I love you so much."

"But Mitch, maybe I'm not being responsible, maybe I'm allowing emotion to—"

"Come to bed," Mitch said, guiding her there. "There is no more responsible woman in the world than you, Ginny Westerfelt."

She smiled and stretched out on the sheets. "I can't help it. That's my nature."

He lay down beside her and wrapped his arm around her waist. "I know, and I treasure you for it, but what we have together is not going to hurt Arnold. We won't let that happen."

"All right." Close to him, feeling his strength, she was soothed.

"Ginny, thank you."

"For what?"

"Finally telling me. I've bitten my tongue so many times to keep from saying that I loved you. I didn't want to put the pressure on."

"The pressure's gone," she said, nudging him until he lay on his back. "And now I'm not only going to tell you I love you, I'm going to show you."

"You've been doing that all along, without realizing it."

"Maybe, but loving each other will be different, now that we can say the words," Ginny promised as she caressed his furred chest. "You'll see."

Their loving was different. Magic flowed through their fingers with each touch, turning pleasure to joy, satisfaction to ecstasy. When at last their bodies joined, the fusion celebrated their confessed love, love that became a shout of exaltation at the moment of release.

They stayed at the apartment as long as they dared, cherishing the moments of loving each other without restraint. Finally, at midafternoon they forced themselves to drive back to the townhouse.

As they approached Ginny's street, Mitch cast her a sideways glance. "Any chance you'd be willing to discuss this with Arnold tonight?"

She'd been expecting the question. "Let's wait a little while longer," she said, knowing Mitch wouldn't like her answer.

"You are planning to tell him soon, though?"

"Well, yes. But we haven't talked about the future, you and I."

"That's easy. Let's have one together."

"Mitch, I know where this discussion is heading." She laid her hand on his arm. "I'm not quite ready to make those kinds of decisions yet. Can we hold off just a bit? I want to have time to talk this out between us before we bring Arnold into the picture. Everything should be settled when we tell him. We love each other, but that's not all there is to it."

"If you want a proposal, I—"

"No. I don't. Not this minute."

"Okay." He set his jaw.

"Don't be hurt, Mitch. Please. I love you. Can that be enough for a while?"

He didn't answer.

"Mitch . . ."

"You'd better get out the garage door opener. We're almost there."

She took the opener from the glove compartment of the Volvo and pressed the button. "Listen, maybe after Arnold's in bed tonight, we can discuss—" She forgot the rest of the sentence. The garage door opened to reveal Arnold's bike parked inside. He was home.

"Oh no," she whispered. "I left the dishes in the sink and everything. What on earth will we say we've been doing all day?"

"Tell him we went shopping," Mitch said.

"But we don't have any packages with us."

"Then, tell him we went to a movie."

"All day? Besides, he'd be mad we didn't wait and take him along, or that we didn't ask him and Angela to come with us."

Mitch sighed. "Then tell him we went for a drive to enjoy the nice day. I don't know. Tell him anything. Aren't you entitled to a life?"

"Mitch, you know we're not in the habit of traipsing out somewhere together. He'll be suspicious."

Mitch switched off the ignition and turned to her. "Then you could tell him the truth."

She met his gaze. "Maybe I'll have to."

"Maybe it would be a godsend."

"Well, we can't sit out here in the car any longer, or he *will* wonder what we're up to," Ginny said, unbuckling her seat belt.

Mitch caught her hand before she got out the door. "I love you, Ginny."

She turned back at him and tried to tamp down the guilt that was tying knots in her stomach. "I love you, too." The words, spoken so joyfully earlier in the day, didn't ease her nervousness. She'd never lied to Arnold. Lying to a child was one of the things she believed a parent shouldn't do. But this time, if he asked, and she felt certain he would, she wasn't ready to tell him the truth.

She walked into the kitchen with a bright smile. Breezy, that was the tone. Ask Arnold about his day first and maybe he wouldn't ask her about hers.

The kitchen was empty, but she heard Arnold's stereo turned up loud. If his window was open, the neighbors next door were being treated to a concert. She might have heard the music from the garage, if she'd been listening, but she'd been concentrating on her problem and hadn't noticed.

"He's either deliriously happy or miserable," Mitch said, closing the door behind him as he came into the kitchen behind her. "And the reason probably has big, brown eyes and long, curly, dark hair."

Ginny turned to him. "I don't know which to hope for. I've been worried that their relationship is getting too serious."

Mitch gazed at her silently. "Like ours?" he said at last.

She returned his gaze without answering.

"Oh, Ginny, you may break my heart yet."

"I'm going upstairs to see Arnold."

"Want me to come along?"

"That's okay. I'll . . . I'll handle this."

"Which means you're not telling him about us, right?" Mitch shoved his hands into the pockets of his gym shorts.

"I don't know."

"Think I'll cut the grass," Mitch said, turning abruptly and opening the door into the garage.

"I'll keep you posted."

"I'd appreciate that," he said over his shoulder before closing the door.

Ginny felt like a louse, but she couldn't imagine going upstairs and announcing to Arnold that she was in love with Mitch. Nothing would be accomplished by such a confession, and much could be lost. She and Mitch needed more time before going public with the information. Or she did, at least. Mitch seemed ready to tell the world. And that, she decided, was why she felt so terrible. He was proud of their love, and her behavior suggested she was ashamed. No wonder his feelings were hurt. With a sigh, Ginny headed for the stairs.

She started to knock on Arnold's door and then hesitated, wondering how she looked. She hadn't thought of it until now. Detouring to her bedroom, she washed her face, brushed her hair and quickly applied new makeup. Now she didn't look as if she'd recently made passionate love. Ginny glanced out her bedroom window into the yard, where Mitch pushed

the lawn mower at a furious pace. Fleetingly she recalled that Lady Chatterley's lover had been the caretaker and had probably cut grass, too.

Feeling a little better, Ginny returned to Arnold's
door and knocked vigorously. She waited, and
knocked harder. She had one moment of panic in
which she imagined Arnold and Angela in there together, on Arnold's bed—but no, that was a fear based
on her own recent activities, she decided. Besides,
Angela's bike hadn't been in the garage.

Finally, the volume of the stereo receded, and the
door opened. Arnold stood there, bleary-eyed and
slouching, with misery wrapped around him like soggy
newspaper. "Yeah?"

As she gazed at her son, Ginny realized this wasn't
the alternative she would have chosen, whether the
relationship with Angela was getting too serious or
not. "The stereo's a little loud," she ventured.

"I'll turn it down. I didn't think anybody was
home."

"I . . . I'm home now." Ginny realized she wouldn't
have to discuss where she'd been. Arnold was too engrossed in his pain to care. "Did something go wrong
at Angela's?" The question sounded stupid, the answer obvious but Ginny couldn't figure out how to ask
him if his romance was over.

Arnold stared at her. Then he scratched his head
and looked away.

"Arnold . . ." Ginny wanted to take him in her arms,
as she'd done when he was five and had skinned his
knee. She didn't dare. If he pushed her away, it would
hurt too much.

"She broke up with me," he said, not looking at
her.

"Oh, Arnold, I'm sorry." A lump rose in Ginny's throat. Poor kid. His first love, and she'd dumped him. Ginny wondered how she could have resented the whispers and hand-holding and stolen kisses, when they had made Arnold so happy. "Did she say what the problem was?"

"Oh, yeah." Arnold's voice broke from baritone to tenor. "She doesn't think we should be going with someone when we start high school. She says that's too limiting."

"Oh." Wonderful logic, Ginny thought, but it sounded a little like parental logic to her. Maybe Angela's parents also had worried about the close involvement between the two teenagers, and had handed down an edict. But Ginny didn't suggest that to Arnold. She didn't see how that would help.

"So, anyway, I guess I'll be around here more often," Arnold said. "Think I'll paint my walls."

"That's fine," Ginny said, but even as she said it the realization hit her that Angela had provided the distraction that had allowed her time alone with Mitch. No Angela, no time with Mitch. Besides that, Arnold would notice everything that went on in the household now. Before this catastrophe, he'd walked around in a romantic haze and hadn't tuned in on the sexual tension between his mother and Mitch. The party was over.

"Did you have something you wanted to tell me, Mom?"

Ginny looked at him. Did she? "Just that I'm home, and the stereo was a bit loud." Coward. Shameless coward. "I'm sorry about Angela, Arnold. Maybe you and Mitch and I can go out to dinner tonight, to that spaghetti place you love so much. Would you like that?''

"Not really."

"Well, pizza, then. You can choose the kind. We can eat it there if you want, and play video games, and—''

"Mom, that's okay."

"I just wish I could *do* something for you."

Arnold shrugged. "You can buy me a couple of cans of paint, one red, one black."

"I will." Ginny put her hand on his arm. "You're a terrific person, Arnold. She's missing the boat."

He smiled sadly. "Thanks, Mom." He fidgeted for a moment. "The tape's over," he said with a hopeful glance at her. Obviously he wanted her gone.

"I'll be downstairs if you need anything," she said, backing away from the door. "We can get the paint this afternoon."

"Okay." He closed the door.

As Ginny started down the stairs, the stereo came to life again, and the volume was up, but not quite to the level it had been. Ginny didn't go back to ask him to turn it down. The neighbors would have to tolerate a little noise for a while.

MITCH FINISHED the last swath and turned off the motor. Thank God for lawns, he thought, unhooking the grass catcher and dumping the contents into a trash bag. He wondered how cavemen had battled their frustrations. Not too much in the way of yard work around the old cave. Of course, cavemen probably hadn't experienced his type of frustration. They'd simply taken what they wanted from a woman. Then again, what they got back couldn't have been anything like the loving Ginny gave him. He wished she'd stop all this secrecy stuff.

Not that he had any room to talk. He, the man who had stood trial for sexually harassing a child, was carrying around the biggest secret of all and hadn't had the guts to tell her about it. He wondered if Ginny somehow sensed he was keeping secrets. She had good instincts. Maybe she knew there was something he hadn't revealed.

Mitch wheeled the mower around to the front yard. *Face it,* he thought, *you want Ginny to tell Arnold now, before you risk bringing up Cedarville and what happened there. You know that once Arnold's brought into it, Ginny won't be so quick to break things off, no matter what she finds out about you.*

He flicked the motor on and started across the smaller patch of front lawn. He realized that some people might consider him weak for wanting to line up his reinforcements in advance. But dammit, he'd lost a lot because of this thing in Cedarville, and he didn't want to lose any more. Once he told Ginny about his past, she'd need something to steady her until she recovered from the initial shock. Wedding plans, especially if those plans had been shared with Arnold, would be that steadying influence.

Having thought that through, Mitch felt better. He enjoyed the sun on his back and the harvest aroma of freshly cut grass. He couldn't propose to Ginny right away. She'd already said she didn't want that. So he'd wait a couple of weeks, give them time to absorb the impact of admitting their love for each other.

As he wheeled the mower around to finish the last section of the yard, Ginny opened the front door and walked out onto the small, covered stoop. He waved to indicate he'd seen her, and finished the last stretch before turning off the motor. Then he left the mower where it was and went over to sit beside her on the sun-warmed concrete steps. She looked so beautiful, with her hair shining like twenty-four-carat gold in a jeweler's window, and her cheeks pink as cotton candy, probably a bit whisker-burned from all the loving they'd done that day.

He forced himself to keep his hands away from her. "So, what's up with Arnold?"

Ginny propped her cheek on her fist and gazed at him. "Angela dumped him."

"Damn." A sympathetic ache squeezed his heart. "I'll bet he's a mess."

"I think so, but I don't know what either of us can do for him, except buy him paint. He's ready to paint his walls red and black."

Mitch nodded. "Decent therapy."

"Maybe, but it won't last long. It isn't a very big room."

"Then we'll think of other things. Which reminds me. On the days that it rains, is there anywhere Arnold and I can practice wrestling holds?"

Ginny hesitated. "I don't know."

"I could always take him over to my apartment, I guess." Mitch figured she wouldn't go for that, and he was right.

"Our living room is better," Ginny said immediately. "Just move the furniture carefully, and spread a blanket or something on the carpet, in case one of you gets a bloody nose or something."

"Okay." Mitch relaxed. At least this debacle with Angela had served one good purpose. He'd arranged it so Arnold had a little roughhouse room. "So now we have painting and wrestling to occupy him and make him forget."

Ginny sighed. "I still feel really helpless. I have half a mind to call her mother. Apparently, Angela said they shouldn't be going with someone when they start high school, but that sounds like a parent's statement, not a kid's."

"You're right, it does, but don't forget that Angela went along with it."

"I haven't forgotten. Besides, what would I say to Mrs. Gaston? 'I think you should let Angela go with Arnold because he's miserable without her'? I may be an overprotective mother, but I have some idea where to draw the line."

"Good."

She raised her eyebrows.

"I'm just confirming that you're right not to interfere," he said with a smile.

"Let's hope so, because I'm not in the mood for much besides agreement right now."

"And I'm agreeing with you. Arnold's miserable, and we have to stay out of it, except to keep him occupied with other things."

Ginny gazed across the clipped grass. "I even offered to take him out for a spaghetti dinner, or pizza, and we'd play video games. He didn't want to."

"Do you remember when you lost your first love?"

"Yeah. I wanted to kill myself." She tensed beside him and turned an alarmed face toward his. "Mitch, you don't think—"

"No, I don't think he would do that." Mitch longed to put his arm around her, but he was afraid of where a simple consoling touch might lead. "It's an expression, one I'm sure you didn't really mean when you were that age, either. Besides, he wants to paint his room. That's a healthy sign, wanting to improve his surroundings.''

Ginny made a face.

"By his standards," Mitch added.

"I guess painting is better than gorging on food," she agreed, clasping her hands around her knees and gazing across the street. "Come to think of it, I refused a nice family dinner when I lost my first love, too."

"Was it the guy with the muscles?"

Ginny didn't look at him, but he could see the beginnings of her smile. "Uh-huh."

"Who broke it off?"

"Oh, he did. Seems I wouldn't go as far as he wanted, if you know what I mean."

Mitch laughed. "I do. And you haven't changed all that much."

She turned to him, her mouth open. "How can you say that, after all we—"

"I should have added that you've switched priorities. I'll bet you told that boy you loved him, but you wouldn't sleep with him."

"That's precisely what I told him."

"Now you've switched it around. You slept with me, but look how long it took for you to tell me you loved me. It's all part of the same idea, withholding something precious."

"You make me sound manipulative."

"No. Cautious. I understand. There's a cautious side to me, too."

"Not much of one," she said, smiling again.

"Sure there is. Like right now, every part of me wants to kiss you, but I'm exercising caution."

"Good darn thing. I'd be forced to slap you, just to put on a convincing show for the neighbors."

"Then I'll have to wait until we're showing off in front of my neighbors instead of yours."

Ginny stopped smiling. "Mitch, that's the other thing. We won't be able to go to your apartment anymore."

The sun's warmth seemed to vanish. He'd been so caught up in admiring her that he'd missed the implications of Angela's decision. "Doesn't Arnold have other friends he could go see?"

"Not since he had the fight in the cafeteria with Billy Herman. He lost a lot of confidence with that episode, and he's pretty shy to begin with." Ginny paused. "Or was," she said with a smile.

"Right. I'll bet that deal in the gym parking lot earned Arnold some respect. Maybe now that Angela's finked out, Arnold will get in touch with some of his former buddies."

Ginny shook her head. "From what I just saw upstairs, the look on his face, I wouldn't count on it. Or more to the point, we shouldn't count on it. Arnold's ego was in great shape until today, but..." She shrugged. "Anyway, I also don't want us to seem to be pushing him out of the house right when he needs our love and support."

"I guess." Mitch gazed at her. "You know, this is not good."

"I know."

"I can't imagine having no chance to hold you, to love you."

"But Arnold will be around all the time now, unless they make up, and if I'm right about Angela's parents being behind this, they won't be making up."

Mitch gazed across the yard and rested his elbows on his knees. His hands dangled, useless to his cause because he couldn't touch her. If he could, he might be able to coax the answer to their problem out of her. He knew what it was, and so did she. If they told Arnold about their relationship, they wouldn't have to wait for times when he was gone to be together.

"I know what you want me to do," Ginny said at last. "And I can't. I can't just announce to Arnold that we're lovers and you'll be sharing my bed."

"Would you like me to tell him?"

"That wouldn't help, at least not much. I'd still have to face Arnold after you told him. I can't imagine what it would be like at night, with you and me walking into that bedroom together and Arnold in his bathroom, brushing his teeth or something, and thinking Lord knows what about his mother."

"He might just think you were normal."

She shook her head, and the sunlight flashed against the bright strands. "No. That's a cute answer, but not good enough. Arnold doesn't think of me in that way. I'm convinced most kids don't think of their parents that way. They don't want to. They want us to be mommy and daddy, and sexless."

"You may be right."

"I think I am."

"If you are, I know one way we can establish the right air of dull respectability that seems to be required." Mitch paused. He had to go for broke. His heart beat a nervous rhythm as he considered the stakes. "We can get married," he said, turning to her. He liked the reaction his words got. A spark of anticipation lit her eyes, and a flush spread over her al-

ready pink cheeks. Her lips parted, and her breasts
rose and fell more rapidly as her breathing accelerated. "I love you, Ginny," he said more softly.
"Please marry me."

CRITICAL MASS

Mitch and Ginny. My first and last adventure together. I have to ask her now, before forming Tekk circle. "I have the courage," he said, to give this one more try...

## CHAPTER FOURTEEN

"IT'S SO SOON," Ginny said.

"I know, but the circumstances dictate that I propose now." Mitch paused. "I wanted to wait and ask you later, but now I don't have the luxury of courting you for a few more weeks or spending a few more long afternoons with you in my apartment. Angela changed everything."

"One young girl. Such power." Ginny shook her head. She seemed dazed and disoriented.

Mitch put all he had into his plea. "Please. I need you, Ginny. Don't put us on some regimen of enforced celibacy when all you have to do is say yes and we can enjoy each other. I'll even install soundproof paneling in your room, so you won't have to worry about noise. Not that we have to worry, I guess, once we become respectable and Arnold dismisses us as parents who never have sex."

That got her, and she laughed. "Oh, Mitch, there are so many things we haven't talked about yet. Important things."

Mitch tensed. Here it was. She'd ask him for specifics about his past. "Like what?"

"More children, for example. A man like you probably wants a child, but I don't want to interrupt my career again for motherhood."

"I wouldn't ask you to," he said, experiencing great relief. "I honestly never imagined you and me having a child together. I'm a teacher. I work with kids all the time. That's my contribution, and for me, I think having a houseful of kids might cut down on my effectiveness at school. I always assumed I'd marry someone who'd want kids, and I'd have to compromise that belief, but now I don't have to."

"All this time and I didn't know that," Ginny said.

"We've been busy with other things," Mitch said, remembering exactly what those other things were and feeling his groin tighten. "Talking seemed like a waste of time."

"And when we're around Arnold, it's difficult to ask really personal questions like whether you want children of your own," Ginny added.

"Now you know I don't."

"What about your family? I don't know much about them."

"They'll love you." Mitch realized the truth of his words as he spoke. This marriage could bridge the gap that had opened up between him and his family since the unfortunate business in Cedarville. "I don't know much about your father, either. Does he even know I'm living here?"

"No." Ginny looked remorseful. "I was afraid of what he'd think, so I've kept my distance this summer. We're not really close, anyway. That's why I'm sort of fascinated with that huge clan of yours."

"We'll go there," Mitch said, getting excited about the prospect. "Maybe at Christmas. We'll—"

"Mitch."

He looked down and saw that he'd grabbed her hand. Instead of releasing it, he brought it to his lips and kissed her fingertips. "I love you so much," he murmured.

"I love you, too."

"Then it's settled."

"No."

He felt as if a stone had been dropped from a great height into his gut. "No?"

"I need some time. You have to give me time to think about this. Today we admitted we loved each other. Only a few hours ago, Mitch. Now you're planning our marriage. I can't go that fast, no matter what Angela has or hasn't done to make us consider marriage as an option. You have to let me think this through. I have to consider how it will affect Arnold, and me, and . . . everybody."

He forced himself not to grab her and shake her, and then kiss her until she agreed to marry him as soon as possible. "How long do you need?" He kept her hand in his and caressed her palm with his thumb.

She fell silent for a moment. "Well, I'm going on another focus group tour the week after next. I think . . . I should be able to give you an answer when I come back from that trip."

Mitch groaned.

"We've been through this much. Another two weeks won't matter if we're talking about a lifetime."

"Another two weeks *is* a lifetime, if I can't make love to you at all." He gazed at her and battled his impatience. "But I see your point. Getting married right away and then having you leave the week after wouldn't be the best situation."

"I don't think so, either. And you'll have time to think, too, without the distraction of having me around. I don't want this to be a rushed decision for either of us."

"This isn't a rushed decision. I've known what I wanted ever since I met you, even if I didn't quite admit it to myself. You're the one, Ginny."

She met his gaze, and he read all the things he wanted to read there. But she wouldn't say them. He told himself that her cautious nature was one of the things he loved about her, trusted about her. He wouldn't be happy with a wildly impulsive, helter-skelter woman. At the moment, however, her caution was working against his desires. And his desires clamored to be satisfied.

She shifted position on the concrete steps. "We should probably go in. Arnold might be looking for one of us. I promised we'd buy paint today."

Mitch held her hand for a few seconds longer. "Two weeks," he said, and it sounded like a funeral dirge.

"The time will go fast."

"No, it won't, but I'll do my best." He let go of her hand. "Since Arnold and I are in somewhat the same boat, I think we'll be doing a lot of jogging and lifting weights. Maybe I can teach him the value of physical exercise in overcoming sexual frustration."

"Just so you don't cite yourself as a personal example."

"For two weeks, I'll be a veritable choirboy," he said. Then he deliberately gave her a long once-over that made her blush. "After that," he said, holding her gaze, "watch out."

FOR THE NEXT WEEK, Ginny felt as if she was living in an athletic club under renovation. Arnold's walls took three coats of paint to achieve the desired sheen.

Whenever Mitch and Arnold weren't painting, they were jogging or lifting weights or jumping rope. On the two rainy days the living-room furniture was pushed against the walls and Arnold's bedspread became a wrestling mat.

The faint manly scent usually found in fitness centers hung continually, disturbingly in the air, mingled with the sharp odor of new paint. Whenever Ginny passed Mitch in the hall or on the stairs—his damp, warm body charged with the energy of his latest workout or painting stint—she hurried past. The slightest hesitation on her part would propel them into each other's arms, and they both knew it.

As for Arnold, if Ginny had imagined that the loss of Angela would transform him into the boy she'd known, she was wrong. That boy, shy and diffident, had disappeared forever. Whereas the old Arnold might have hibernated quietly in his room for hours, the new Arnold attacked his heartbreak aggressively with constant motion and loud music. Ginny couldn't be sure, but she thought he was also trying to grow a beard.

As the tension-filled week drew to a close, Ginny gave up on the frail hope that Angela might reconcile with Arnold and free Ginny from having to make a decision about Mitch's proposal.

The night before Ginny's trip, Mitch didn't leave the dinner table with Arnold. He'd set that pattern at the beginning of the week obviously to avoid being alone with her. She thought the idea was a good one, so when Mitch remained at the table, she picked up her own plate and pushed back her chair.

"I'd like to drive you to the airport in the morning," he said.

She paused and looked at him. "I've already scheduled a cab."

"You could cancel it."

"I think riding to the airport together might be a little rough on both of us, don't you?"

Mitch leaned back in his chair. "Couldn't get much worse for me. And I'd like to talk to you alone before you leave. I—" he glanced down at the table and then returned his gaze to hers "—I'd like to know where your thinking is right now."

"I haven't really—" Ginny began, just as Arnold clattered down the stairs and came back into the kitchen.

"Hey, Mitch, ready for our after-dinner run?" he asked, dancing around like a boxer and throwing shadow punches.

"Sure." Mitch stood. "I was just checking with your mother to see what time I needed to drive her to the airport." He glanced at Ginny. "So, what time do you want to leave?"

Ginny allowed his maneuver to work. Perhaps Mitch was right, and they should discuss their concerns one last time before she left. "About six," she said. "If that's not too early for you."

"I'll be there."


THE NEXT MORNING, Mitch beat Ginny downstairs by several minutes. Arnold slept soundly, and the house was quiet as she walked into the kitchen carrying her luggage and attaché case.

He stood by the window drinking coffee. "Want some?" he asked, hoisting his cup.

"No, thanks." She absorbed the sight of him. Fresh from a shower and shave, neatly buttoned into a soft cotton shirt and twill pants, he looked like the husband any woman would die to have. The early-morning sun combed his hair with light and burnished his golden tan.

She nearly accepted his proposal then and there. The timing was wrong, though. Only a fool would tell a man she'd marry him and then put half a country between them for the next six days. A moment like that needed to be followed by hours of loving. They would have that when she came home.

"I like the expression on your face right now. It gives me hope," he said, setting the coffee mug on the counter and walking toward her.

"We have to leave."

"I know, and if I kiss you, I might never stop." He reached out and traced the line of her cheekbone. "Oh, Ginny," he said, taking a long, shuddering breath. "I'm going to miss you."

She swallowed, trying to dislodge the lump in her throat. "I'll miss you, too."

"I hope so. God, I hope so." He took his hand away and clenched it into a fist. "Let's go," he said, and swung her suitcases off the floor.

"Oh, I almost forgot." Ginny reached in her attaché case. "Here's next week's check."

"I don't want it."

"Don't want it? What do you mean? We have a business arrangement, and you deserve to be paid."

"We do not have a business arrangement anymore, and if this week ends the way I hope it will, we'll have a completely different sort of arrangement. Keep the check."

"I don't feel right about it." Ginny laid the check on the desk. "I'll put it here. A deal's a deal, Mitch. I don't like vague provisions. We made a bargain, and I want us each to keep our side of it. This is my side. And don't tear it up or do anything immature like that."

"Immature, huh?" He glanced at the check once more. "Wouldn't want you to think I'm immature at a time like this. All right, I'll take it."

"Good." Ginny felt relieved. The money underlined their status one last time, and she needed that definition.

Mitch loaded the suitcases in the car and helped her in. After leaving the townhouse, they drove in silence for several blocks.

"I'll miss you," Mitch said again.

"I'll miss you, too." Ginny tried not to imagine what the long days ahead of her would be like without him.

"It would help if you'd tell me how you're thinking these days."

She sighed. "Oh, Mitch, I'm still afraid that if we become a couple Arnold will feel shut out. He's so vulnerable right now, and I hate to give him another problem to contend with."

"I'll make you a promise, Ginny, that if we're married, Arnold will not feel shut out. For one thing, I am a teacher, and I'm trained to help kids feel included. For another, I think Arnold will feel even more secure with two loving parents to count on instead of only one."

Ginny leaned back against the headrest. "I'd love to believe that."

"Then believe it. Don't make this tougher than it is. And another thing, something I never told you. Before I took Arnold camping, we had a discussion about you.''

''What sort of discussion?'' Ginny sat upright again.

''Arnold feels a great sense of responsibility for you. He didn't want to go camping and leave you alone.''

Ginny laughed. ''You're kidding.''

''No, I'm not. He knows how much he means to you, and that's great, but he also wonders how you'll manage without him.''

Ginny felt the painful stab of an unwelcome truth. In her zeal to make Arnold feel loved, perhaps she had taught him that he was indispensable to her happiness. ''You're saying I need to establish more self-sufficiency in Arnold's eyes?''

''Maybe. But knowing how he feels should also shed a different light on your decision about marrying me.''

''What are you saying, that I'm really a burden, and Arnold would be delighted to have you take me off his hands?''

Arnold grinned. ''Oh, Ginny, how you twist things around until they're in the worst possible light. I'm only saying that your fears about Arnold's resenting our relationship may be for nothing.'' He glanced at her. ''I love you to pieces, but you have a talent for looking on the dark side, my wonderful lover.''

''I'm cautious,'' Ginny said, lifting her chin.

''You're sexy as hell, too. That seat belt slides right between your breasts and makes them stand out like beacons.''

Ginny glanced down and flushed. ''I'm not trying to—''

''That's just it. You don't have to try. You just are. I've been in a constant state of arousal for a week.''

Her body reacted immediately, becoming warm and moist in response. "Then you'll be glad when I'm gone."

"No," he said softly. "Never that."

"Do you want me to call home?"

"If you want to talk to Arnold, sure. But don't give me any news, good or bad, over the telephone. I want it face-to-face."

She needed him so much at that moment that she wondered if there was any way she could cancel her trip. But of course she couldn't do that. "I'd be a fool not to marry you."

"Yes, I think you would."

"But I need these last few days to go over everything in my mind."

"And you have them, with my blessing. Just remember those afternoons in my apartment."

"As if I could forget."

"And that Arnold is growing up."

"So I've noticed. Do you think he'll have a beard by the time I get back?"

"Probably, if you define the word loosely."

Ginny chuckled. "And he says he's through with women forever if he can't have Angela. Did you hear him say that? What single-minded passion a thirteen-year-old has."

Mitch braked the car at a red light and turned to her, his gaze intense as he caught her chin in one large hand. "If you think Arnold's single-minded, you ain't seen nothing yet." Then he kissed her, hard, before the light changed to green.

GINNY HAD a sampling of what he meant when she walked into her Denver hotel room that night and found a dozen red roses arranged in a vase on the dresser. The note said simply "Remember," and there was no signature.

The next day she carried the roses on the plane to Rapid City, South Dakota, and told Bettleman, the powerful advertising man from San Francisco, and his assistant that they were from a good friend. Bettleman teased her all day, and that night when Ginny entered her hotel room in Rapid City and found another dozen roses, she realized that if Mitch kept this up perhaps she'd have to abandon some along the way. Carrying seventy-two roses on the last plane home might prove a bit awkward. She also knew what he'd decided to do with the money she'd paid him before she left.

She called home after dinner and got Mitch. "Isn't this a bit much?" she said, not bothering to identify herself.

"No."

His instant recognition and response thrilled her. "I can't remember the last time I got a dozen red roses, let alone two dozen."

"Then it's about time."

"I love you."

"Ditto. More than ever. Can't tell you how much, but it's a lot."

"Arnold's close by, isn't he?" Ginny guessed.

"Uh-huh. Want me to—"

"In a minute." Ginny hated to relinquish the sound of Mitch's voice. "I miss you like crazy."

"Same here. Been getting in a lot of jogging, and weight lifting and other manly endeavors."

"You'll be muscle-bound when I come home."

"Nope. I work on flexibility, too. I feel that's important for...certain activities I enjoy."

"Absolutely," Ginny teased. "This is kind of fun, being able to talk freely when you can't." A devilish impulse took hold of her. "I have a huge bed in this room, and I'm lying on it right now, wishing you were here with me, Mitch."

There was a pause on the other end of the line. "Well, yes, I agree we should plant something in that untended bed. To go with the roses. Just tell me what you want in there and I'll take care of it. I understand some nurseries have their deliveries flown in."

"Very clever, Mitch, but you can't leave."

"Don't test it."

"Mitch, take it easy." Ginny found her game turning around on her and causing her to squirm with unquenched desire. She wished he would fly out to meet her, but that would be a crazy thing to do, considering Arnold's welfare and her business situation.

"So what do you want planted?" Mitch asked in a low voice. "I'll look for something with a stiff stem that won't droop in the heat," he added, chuckling now. "Long-lasting, too. You can't be expected to enjoy something that wilts right away."

"Stop it, Mitch. And don't you dare do anything foolish."

"You started this gardening conversation," he said, laughing. "Don't worry, Ginny. I'll stay right here. How're the people in Rapid City treating you?"

"Okay," she said, relieved and disappointed at the same time. "Except I'm so homesick I could die."

"How's the research going on adhesive tape?"

"I'm learning more than I ever wanted to know. I have the people in the focus groups wrapping packages so I can observe what they like and don't like about different kinds of tape. It's funny how they— but you probably don't want to hear about this, Mitch."

"Oh, but I do."

"Careful. That sounded passionate. Is Arnold still within earshot?"

"He wandered off, but he'll be back. Despite his newfound independence, he misses having you around. He'll want to talk to you."

"And you?"

"Lady, I want to do a hell of a lot more than talk. But quick, while Arnold's gone, let me tell you the news. Angela called. She admitted that the breakup was her parents' idea, brought on when she turned down all those dates with Billy Herman."

"Uh-oh."

"Yeah. The Gastons decided Angela was too young to go steady with one boy when she obviously had other admirers."

"I'll bet Arnold was ready to kill Billy."

"At first, but your son is getting to be quite a guy. He rode over to Billy's and asked him politely but firmly to stop calling his girl."

Ginny caught her breath. "I'll be darned."

"And tomorrow he's going over to talk to Angela's parents and try to convince them to let him see Angela again."

"I can't believe it, Mitch. A year ago he'd have died before trying anything like that." She hesitated. "You know, if the Gastons agree, then we wouldn't have to rush into—"

"I'm afraid we would."

"Why?"

"Because I need you. Because I want you for my wife, as soon as possible. Because it doesn't matter anymore about Angela and Arnold. What matters is that I love you more than anything in the world, and—here comes Arnold. I'll bet he'd like to say hello."

"Mitch, wait. I—" Ginny stopped as she heard the sound of the phone changing hands.

"Hi, Mom," Arnold said. "How's that sticky business of yours going?"

Ginny groaned at his bad joke, but she laughed, too. If Arnold was up to making bad jokes, he was in much better shape than he'd been in when she'd left. "I'm glued to my work," she said.

Arnold chortled. "Pretty good comeback, Mom. Everything okay out there?"

"Fine. How about back there?"

"Fantastic. I might have a surprise for you when you get back. Anyway, I think we'd better get off the phone. I wouldn't want your long-distance bill to be too high."

Ginny knew Arnold wasn't concerned about the bill. Maybe he was expecting Angela to call. Ginny waited for the twinge of envy to pinch her, but nothing happened. She would have to credit that to her love for Mitch. "Okay, I'll say good night," she said. "And by the way, tell Mitch he can spade up the bed and get it ready, but not to plant anything until I get home. I want to supervise."

"Geez, Mom, I can't believe you guys spent long-distance money talking about landscaping. How boring."

"Yeah, well, you know how life deteriorates after a person hits thirty," Ginny said, smiling to herself. "Good night, Arnold."

THE ROSES continued to arrive. The note with the next dozen said, "Gardener ready," and the fourth dozen said, "Bed prepared." Ginny could hardly wait to get home and tell Mitch that she would marry him. The fifth dozen arrived with a tag that read, "Plantings selected," but the last dozen that arrived while she was in Boise, Idaho, said merely, "Come home. I love you."

Ginny wished she were on a plane that night, but she wasn't scheduled to fly out until the following afternoon. A concluding focus group had been scheduled for the next morning. Ginny didn't want to talk about adhesive tape another minute. She didn't care if she never saw anyone wrap a package again, but this was her job and she'd have to finish the tour.

However, the next morning she learned that the facility she'd rented for the group session had been accidentally double-booked, and Bettleman, who also seemed weary of the process, suggested they cancel the session and pay the respondents anyway. Ginny readily agreed, but her enthusiasm waned when she couldn't book an earlier flight back to Seattle.

Bettleman didn't seem to care. He and his assistant scheduled a round of golf and invited Ginny along. She couldn't decide which would be worse, to sit alone at the hotel or accompany Bettleman and his assistant.

She was not happy about either choice. Then inspiration hit. Finding a map of Idaho for sale in the hotel lobby, she studied it for a moment, and then made arrangements with the concierge for a rental car. She hadn't even noticed before, but Cedarville was less than an hour away.

She would spend the day visiting Mitch's school and basking in the praise people would heap on him there. She'd been unsuccessful in coaxing out of him the details of his Teacher of the Year award, but she'd bet others would be glad to give her the information. After notifying her clients that she'd meet them at the airport, Ginny drove off in her rented compact. She was certain Mitch would be surprised when he found out where she'd been today.

## CHAPTER FIFTEEN

GINNY WAS HALFWAY to Cedarville when she remembered that it was Saturday. She might have had some chance of the high school being open during the week, especially if the school was registering students for fall, but on a weekend, she'd be lucky to find a janitor.

On second thought, maybe a janitor was exactly what she needed. Ginny pictured some kindly fellow brimming with tales about that fine young man, Coach Adamson. Maybe too, she'd discover some gossip about Mitch, how he was jilted by the lovely English teacher, after which he'd left town with a broken heart, according to rumor. She wondered if Mitch would be angry with her for playing detective, but he had himself to blame, she reasoned. If he hadn't been so closemouthed and modest about everything, she wouldn't feel this urge to find out more about him.

After turning off the main highway toward Cedarville, Ginny stopped at a roadside fruit stand for a basket of cherries and paid extra for chilled ones. She ate them as she continued the last few miles along the two-lane road. Orchards and farmhouses eventually gave way to a small community marked with a sign that read Cedarville, Founded 1852, Pop. 5,376, Good Friends and Neighbors.

At a corner gas station she got directions to the high school and was warned that nobody would be around on a Saturday. She found the two-story brick building and sure enough, the place was deserted. Not a single car was parked in the dusty lot except her rental. Out on the football field a couple of kids about ten years old tossed a football back and forth, but she didn't think they'd be able to tell her much about a high school coach who'd left over three years ago.

She gazed at the school, home of the Cedarville Bulldogs according to a wooden marquee that also wished everyone a Happy Summer Vacation. Some detective she was, renting a car and driving into the countryside to sit in front of a vacant building where her lover had once taught. Maybe Mitch had been bored here, she thought. Perhaps the rural atmosphere hadn't given him enough challenge, but he'd hesitated to say that and appear snobbish.

A crow cawed from one of the tall cedars lining the side of the school grounds. The crow and the boys far out on the football field made the only sounds on this quiet Saturday as Ginny sat in the car feeling more and more foolish for impulsively driving all the way out here. Now that she'd seen Cedarville, with its single business street, she had trouble imagining Mitch staying for long. With his talent and energy he'd probably decided to move on. No mystery.

Still, she'd love to find someone who'd known him, or of him, to make the trip marginally worthwhile. She was hungry enough to justify buying lunch in a café she'd passed in town. Maybe the waitress would be a woman who'd lived in Cedarville all her life and remembered the young, blond coach who'd been so well-liked. Switching on the ignition, Ginny backed out of the parking lot and headed for the business center of town.

She parked diagonally between two pickup trucks on the street in front of the café. When she stepped out of the car wearing heels and a lavender silk suit, she realized from the stares of passersby how conspicuous she was. Apparently, nobody in Cedarville dressed that way, at least not on Saturdays.

Ignoring the curious glances, Ginny deposited coins in the meter and walked into the café. She noticed a teenager carrying an order to one of the tables, and an older woman working behind the counter. She chose to sit at the counter, gathering more strange looks as she hoisted herself, slim skirt and all, onto a vinyl-covered revolving stool.

She ordered an egg salad sandwich and iced tea and waited for an opportunity to speak with the woman who wore a large white apron and a hairnet over her gray curls. Unfortunately, Ginny had arrived close to noon—the peak of the lunch-time rush. The woman seldom paused in her constant roaming back and forth as she refilled coffee cups, took orders and deposited plates, silverware and glasses in front of the customers. Ginny noticed she was the only woman seated at the counter.

She dawdled over her egg salad and ate the entire bag of potato chips that came with it. When the last crumbs were gone, she slowly drank her tea. At last her patience paid off, and only two men remained at the far end of the counter. Ginny drained iced tea from her glass, having watched the woman refill others from a large pitcher. When the woman approached with the pitcher, Ginny smiled and extended her glass.

"Pardon me," she said as the woman started to turn away after pouring the tea. "Have you lived in Cedarville long?"

The woman glanced back, looking surprised. "Why do you want to know?"

"I just wondered if you remembered a friend of mine who used to live here. He was a wrestling coach at Cedarville High School."

"Nope. Just moved here last month."

"Oh." Ginny looked down at her plate and felt even more foolish. She probably would have been better off with the teenaged girl. She glanced back at the café tables and noticed the young waitress was, in fact, watching her.

The girl broke eye contact to deliver her order, but then she walked over to the counter. "You mean Mr. Adamson?"

"Yes." Ginny smiled. "Did you know him?"

The girl looked wary. "Not exactly."

"Maybe you weren't in high school when he—"

"Oh, I was there all right. I was a freshman."

Ginny was puzzled by the girl's reaction. She'd expected bubbling enthusiasm. Ginny started to ask something else when one of the men from the end of the counter walked over.

"Lurline, I think we'd best not be talking about Coach Adamson," he said, glancing at the young waitress.

"I just wondered what the lady wanted," the girl said. "I didn't mean any harm, Mr. Jacobs."

"I know, but let's just leave it alone, okay?" The man repositioned a baseball cap on his head.

The girl glanced at Ginny and shrugged. "Okay. I got tables to clear, anyway." She left.

Ginny realized that her mouth was open, and she closed it. "Leave what alone?" she asked.

The man, Jacobs, fished a toothpick out of his breast pocket and stuck it in his mouth before leaning one hand on the counter. His belly hung over the silver buckle of his wide belt. "You're not from around here, are you?"

"No. I'm from Seattle. I was in Boise on business and I decided to drive down here to see where my... friend used to teach."

The man studied her while he shifted the toothpick to the opposite corner of his mouth. "That's right. Bob Taylor said Adamson was in Seattle. Met him at some symphony thing."

*The symphony.* But Mitch hadn't introduced her to anyone from Cedarville. Dread uncoiled in Ginny's stomach. Something was very wrong. Her first instinct was to leave the café, yet she couldn't walk away from this. Her future, and Arnold's, might depend on what this man had to say. She spoke with difficulty. "What was it you wanted Lurline to leave alone?"

"Let's just say Adamson wasn't real popular here in Cedarville."

Ginny gasped. "I thought he was named teacher of the year."

"Yeah, well, that was before." The man's toothpick wiggled as he talked.

"Before what?" Ginny's heart beat faster.

"Look, it's best not to drag it all up again, like I told Lurline." The man pushed himself away from the counter and fished in his back pocket for his wallet as he walked toward the cash register. "Only thing that bothers me is Bob Taylor said Adamson was teaching again. He shouldn't be working with kids. Not after what happened."

A cold chill washed over Ginny. This conversation had the quality of a bad dream. Soon she'd wake up in her hotel room and get ready to direct the focus group, as planned. She watched Jacobs amble out of the café and down the street. What on earth could he have been talking about? What awful thing was he implying about Mitch?

With trembling hands Ginny paid for her lunch and walked out the door of the café into bright sunshine. She longed to get in the rental car and leave this place at once, but she couldn't, not with such horrible implications hanging in the air. The man had said he didn't think Mitch should be working with kids, but he was. He was teaching, and coaching, and most of all, *taking care of Arnold.* Ginny had to know what the man had meant. She'd find the principal, what was his name? Grant? Gridley? Something beginning with a *G.* Anyway, someone could tell her.

"Excuse me," she heard a voice say.

Ginny turned as two women who looked to be in their sixties approached her.

"My name's Bernice Staley," said the woman closest to Ginny. "And this here's Maybeth Duggins," she added, gesturing toward her companion. "We overheard Mac Jacobs talking to you in the café, and we think he should have told you the truth about Mitch Adamson. Mac doesn't care as long as the man's no longer in Cedarville."

"But he could be doing the same thing somewhere else," the other woman said. "You should know."

"Know what?" Ginny's frustration brought the words out with such force that the women backed up a step. "I'm sorry. This is very upsetting. Please tell me."

"Well." The first woman adjusted her glasses and glanced at her companion. "He stood trial for molesting a young boy, someone on his wrestling team."

Ginny felt dizzy. Molesting. A young boy. Mitch. Not Mitch. Not the man who was taking care of Arnold. He wouldn't. No.

"He wasn't convicted," the woman continued, and Ginny struggled to listen, although the words seemed to run together. "But lots of us knew how chummy he was with those boys. Giving them rides home, teaching them to drive."

*Teaching them to drive.* Ginny felt as if she might pass out.

"We just thought you should know," the second woman said. "I mean, if he is working with children, he should be watched. Like they always say, where there's smoke, there's fire. And he sure was chummy with those boys."

"I have to go," Ginny said, stumbling backward.

"Otherwise, he seemed real nice," the first woman called after her as Ginny hurried toward her car. "But you never know, do you?"

Ginny didn't remember much of the drive back to Boise. She tried to tell herself that it was all a mistake. Just because someone was accused, didn't mean they were guilty. Mitch hadn't been convicted, the woman had said, which wasn't saying quite the same thing as "he was found innocent." The two women believed him guilty. So did Mac Jacobs, and maybe Lurline, the young waitress. Of course he couldn't be guilty of such a thing. Couldn't be. But if he wasn't guilty—and this was the part that surged around and around in her brain, making her throat ache with the urge to scream her outrage—if he wasn't guilty, *why hadn't he told her about it?*

GINNY ENTERED the waiting area of the Seattle-Tacoma International Airport with pains gripping her stomach and her head pounding. No matter how innocent Mitch was—and she had to believe he was innocent or risk losing her mind—he'd deliberately deceived her. To make love to her, to ask her to spend her life with him, and not reveal something so important, branded him a liar in her eyes. Not only that, she'd trusted him with the most precious person in her life, her son, and he'd not trusted her enough to tell her his secret.

She'd mashed all the roses into every available wastebasket in her hotel room before she'd checked out, so when she saw Mitch and Arnold, and Mitch held one single red rose, she nearly burst into hysterical laughter. Mitch's glowing smile faded as she came closer and he could see her expression. Arnold seemed puzzled.

Ginny gave all her attention to Arnold as they drove back home, but she couldn't help sneaking glances at Mitch. Each time she did, her heart cracked a little more as she thought of his deception. How could he have made such beautiful love to her, when every moment, by not telling her, he was lying, lying, lying?

"So I had this long talk with Angela's folks," Arnold said. "Mom, are you listening?"

Ginny snapped her focus back to him and turned toward the back seat. "Of course. You talked to Angela's parents. What did you say to them?"

"Well, I explained that we're friends, not just boyfriend and girlfriend. We might even be each other's *best* friend, and we need each other's support when we start high school."

"Sounds like a good argument," Ginny said, managing a smile.

"Mom, you look funny. Are you sure you're okay?"

"I'm fine. I had something at lunch that must have disagreed with me." The hysterical laughter threatened to erupt again, and she gazed out the side window until the urge passed. She'd left the rose on the seat between her and Mitch. He kept his eyes on the road, as if afraid to look at her and confirm that disaster awaited once they were alone. He must think that she'd decided against the marriage because of Arnold, when in fact Mitch had been the agent of his own doom. Their doom. She could almost hate him for that.

"Your stomach's upset?" Arnold asked.

"Yes," Ginny replied, telling the truth.

"Then maybe you won't want the chicken dinner we have cooking at home." Arnold didn't sound terribly disappointed.

Ginny glanced over her shoulder into the back seat to check his expression. He looked almost eager for her to decline the dinner. "I may not be up to it," she said. "But I appreciate the trouble you took to have something ready." She remembered the last homecoming, with flowers and bubble bath and champagne. With luck they hadn't staged a repeat performance, which would make her confrontation with Mitch even more painful.

"Well, we didn't go all out, like the other time," Arnold said, answering her unspoken question. "Just that one rose. And I'm supposed to go over to Angela's tonight. They invited me for dinner, too, but I said I couldn't."

Ginny grabbed the opportunity of getting Arnold out of the house. If he left right away, the agony of postponement could be ended soon. She reached over the back seat and patted his denim-covered knee. "Thanks, but you don't have to stay home on my account. I may not eat dinner, so it would be silly for you to hang around. Why don't you go over there, instead?"

"You really wouldn't care?"

"Of course not." From the corner of her eye, she saw Mitch's jaw tighten. "Once school starts, you two won't have as much spare time to spend together, so you might as well take advantage of the rest of the summer."

"Yeah, that's what *her* mother says, too. She's worried about our grades."

"Should I be worried about your grades?"

"Heck, no! Angela and I will study together. We'll get terrific grades."

"Hmm. We'll have to see how that goes." Ginny's whole body ached with a dull, heavy pain. In a few hours, the entire responsibility for Arnold would be all hers again. Apparently she was a lousy judge of character.

As they reached the townhouse and pulled into the driveway, Ginny saw the wooden, hand-lettered sign stuck into a freshly turned flower bed near the garage. The sign read, Empty. Grief pushed upward from her chest and threatened to break through in a sob. She coughed instead and wiped her brimming eyes. *Empty*. How fitting. Empty was exactly how she felt.

"Did you see the sign, Mom?" Arnold asked, jostling her shoulder with one hand. "Mitch put it there. Pretty funny, huh?"

Ginny managed to nod.

"Boy, Mom, you look terrible. I bet you caught the flu or something on that trip."

Ginny didn't reply. Once they were in the garage, she opened the car door before Mitch turned off the engine. Fumbling with her keys, she hurried through the kitchen and upstairs to her room, where she splashed cold water on her face until she'd temporarily staved off her tears.

"Mom?"

She reached for a towel and blotted her face before turning to find Arnold standing in her bedroom.

"You okay?"

She dredged up a smile. "I'll be fine, once I get some rest," she said. "You go on to Angela's. I'll probably be in great shape by the time you get back."

"If you're sure," he said, already backing toward the door. "But if you need anything, I'll be glad to stay."

She felt a rush of love, and tears threatened again. She dabbed at her face with the towel, as if still drying off. "Thanks, but I'll be fine," she said, her voice heavy with emotion.

"Okay. Maybe Mitch could go out and buy you some of that soup you like, the fancy chicken stuff from the gourmet section." Arnold kept backing away.

"We'll see." Ginny waved him on his way. She didn't know how much longer she could keep her emotions in check, and Arnold didn't need to see her break down. He'd have enough to deal with later.

"Bye," Arnold said. "Take care of yourself." Then he bounded down the stairs. She walked to the window and watched him ride off on his bike. The Gastons would bring him back later that evening, as they had in the past, with his bike in the back of their pickup truck. By that time, Mitch would be gone.

A thump sounded behind her, and she turned. Mitch stood there with her suitcases at his feet, the rose dangling from one hand.

"Thank you," she said inanely. Even at times like this, her manners popped out, perfect as ever.

He tossed the rose on her bed. "I assume you trashed the rest?"

"Yes."

His face contorted with pain. "I don't get it. I don't get any of it. What happened?" His last question came out in a wail of despair.

"I took a side trip today." Her knees shook and she sat on the bed, careful to stay far away from the limp rose. She looked into his face. She wanted to see him squirm. "The last focus group session didn't work out this morning, and I had time on my hands, so I rented a car and drove out into the country."

His eyes widened as he began to understand what she was saying.

"It was a perfect day for a drive. I loved the orchards. I even stopped for some fresh cherries at a stand along the way. I imagine you know the place. You may have stopped there yourself a few times."

Mitch closed his eyes and swayed slightly.

"I found the school, but nobody was there on a Saturday. I was hungry, though, and I decided to have a sandwich in the café on the main business strip. Egg salad. Very good, too. I—"

"Stop it," he said through clenched teeth. His eyes were still squeezed shut, as if he couldn't bear to open them.

"Stop what, Mitch? I'm only telling you about my day. I asked a couple of people if they knew you, and pretty soon Mac something-or-other started hinting that everything wasn't—" she almost choked on the word that came out "—rosy concerning Mitch Adamson," she finished.

"Mac Jacobs."

"That's the one. Anyway, then two helpful women followed me out of the café. They remembered you, Mitch. They remembered you very well, and wanted to tell me all that they remembered."

His wounded gaze focused on her. "Who? Who were they?"

"I don't remember. Bernice somebody and the other one's last name was Duggins. What difference does it make?"

His laugh boomed out, strident and harsh. "Just my luck, you'd run into those two dried-up old biddies. I can imagine what they said about me. So then what? Did you bother to call my principal? Did you even discuss this with Jack Granger?"

"No."

"No?" He stared at her in disbelief. "You took the word of those two old crones and left it at that? You can't possibly believe that I—"

"That you were guilty?" Ginny gazed at him. The fight seeped out of her, leaving her trembling with exhaustion. "No, I can't allow myself to consider that."

"Can't allow yourself." He stepped forward. "What kind of answer is that? Ginny—"

She held up her hand. "Don't touch me."

"I did not do anything wrong." He threw the words at her, but his hands remained clenched at his sides.

"Didn't you?"

"I was found *innocent.*"

"And I believe in your innocence. I have to. But what about deceiving *me,* Mitch? Do you think it's all right to take a job caring for a woman's child, and later on make love to that woman and ask her to marry you, all without telling her that you were once on trial for sexually molesting a child?" Ginny's voice rose a notch. "Do you think that's all right, Mr. Mitch Adamson?"

"Ginny, don't cry."

"I'll cry if I want to, dammit! You have no right to tell me what to do. You have no rights to anything around here anymore. You lied to me!"

"No. I just didn't tell you everything."

"Same difference!" She swiped at her face with both hands. "I *asked* you why you left Cedarville, and you said for personal reasons."

"That's true."

"Ha! They ran you out of town, that's why."

"No, they didn't." Mitch's gaze grew hard. "I still had a job. Granger told me I was welcome to stay, but I didn't think that would be fair to the kids. The gossip would have diluted my attempts to teach them anything. They deserved a classroom that didn't remind them of supermarket tabloids."

"How noble."

"All right." He pointed a finger at her. "You've had your say. You've branded me a liar for not telling you about my past right away. But be honest, Ginny, would you have hired me in the first place if I'd told you about the trial?"

"I'm not sure." But she was. She wouldn't have hired him, no matter what wonderful things Jack Granger had said about him.

"You wouldn't have. I can see it in your face."

"I didn't know you then. Maybe I wouldn't have, but that doesn't excuse your not telling me eventually, especially after we—" She looked away, unable to think of Mitch's betrayal and his lovemaking at the same time.

"Oh? And what about that? What if I'd walked out of the bedroom that first afternoon, caught you looking through the yearbooks and announced that I'd been on trial for molesting one of those young wrestlers in that cozy little team picture? Would you have been kind and understanding?"

"I deserved a chance to try."

"Of course you can say that now, but how would you have reacted then? You haven't been in my shoes, Ginny. You don't know what it's like to have friends, even your own family, start treating you like a leper. You know why I couldn't take Arnold to the orthodontist, that time you thought I had a date? I had my weekly counseling appointment, that's why. I'm in counseling, Ginny, so I can learn to deal with the rejection from this thing."

"Another evasion," she accused.

"Oh, right. You think I should have told you I was in counseling. That was before we made love, don't forget, and long before you worked up the courage to tell me you loved me. You've been skittish all along, and now you think I should have given you all the reason in the world to bolt on me? I'm a fool, all right, but not quite that much of one."

"You gave me no credit, Mitch," she said, her voice choked. "You just made this big assumption that I wouldn't understand, that I couldn't deal with this. That's not fair."

"Maybe not, but after you've been kicked in the teeth a few times, you learn to duck, just in case." His expression darkened and he laughed. "I was so naive I thought that when I was found innocent everything would go back to normal. What a joke. The shame doesn't go away, Ginny. It's like tomato sauce on a white shirt. So when I came to Seattle, I threw away the shirt."

"That's fine," Ginny said, trembling. "And I can understand it. Until now. You said you loved me. You accepted my love. You wanted me to be your wife, and I wanted to be." She stood. "I was ready to come home and say yes, Mitch, and if I hadn't taken that trip, I would have said yes, all without knowing something I had every right to know, before I made such a huge decision. I feel tricked. Tricked and manipulated."

"I planned to tell you."

"When? At the altar?"

"After you said you'd marry me."

"That's too late! Don't you see?"

"No, I don't see!" he shouted back. "I needed that sense of commitment before I bared my soul. I've tried it the other way and been ripped to shreds. I wanted at least a fighting chance this time!"

"You couldn't trust me. You couldn't trust me enough to be truthful. I can't accept that, Mitch."

He grew still. "Can't or won't?"

"Both, I guess. I keep thinking about how I almost agreed to marry you, without knowing, and how you'd planned it all that way. You say you would have told me once I committed myself to you, but I don't know that. I only know that you didn't tell me soon enough to save what we had together."

His eyes became dull and his shoulders drooped. "That's it, then. You want me to leave."

"Yes. Before Arnold comes back. I don't want to put him through the painful process of your moving out."

"And what will you tell him? How will you explain all this?"

"I'll just say you and I had a disagreement. I won't describe the nature of it. That's for you to tell, or not, as you choose."

Mitch swallowed. "I'll tell him about Cedarville. I'll talk to him after wrestling on Monday, unless you plan to pull him out of the program?"

"No. It's over after next week, anyway, and I'm sure he wants to show off for Angela in the last match."

"He's going to be very upset. All this time you've worried about how he'll react to things. What about now?"

"I'm doing this the best I know how. I'm protecting him, too, from someone who could lie to him, to us."

*"I didn't lie."*

"By your definition."

"Ginny, Arnold will not understand this."

"He'll be okay," she said, praying that would be true. "He has Angela, and, as always, he has me. He's always been able to count on me."

Mitch nodded. "I'll be out in an hour," he said, and left the room.

## CHAPTER SIXTEEN

GINNY CLOSED her bedroom door behind Mitch. Then she returned to the bed, picked up the rose and carried it into the bathroom. She took her manicure scissors out of a vanity drawer and stood over the toilet while she cut the stem into little pieces and shredded the blossom. The petals floated on the surface of the water until she reached for the chrome handle and flushed them away. The noise helped drown out the sound of Mitch banging drawers and closet doors as he packed.

She put away her scissors and stared at herself in the mirror. She couldn't look this way when Arnold came home. Unscrewing the cap on her cleansing cream, she smoothed a layer on her face, but the cream kept getting diluted with her tears. She tried to dab at the constant stream from her eyes and got cleansing cream in one eye. She couldn't seem to control her sobs, so she turned on the faucets full blast so Mitch wouldn't hear, and splashed the cleansing cream from her face and out of her eyes. Leaving the water running, she grabbed her largest bath towel and buried her face in it as she sank to the cold tile of the floor.

EVENTUALLY GINNY RAN out of tears. Everything in her body, and especially her heart, ached with grief. She grasped the edge of the vanity and pulled herself upright without looking in the large mirror. She turned off the roaring faucets and listened, her head down. Nothing. She walked to the bedroom door, a distance that seemed longer than before, and quietly turned the knob to open the door a crack. Still nothing.

She waited, barely breathing, for noise from some other part of the house that would tell her he was still there. When absolute silence greeted her, she crept out the door and down the stairs. Pushing back a small part of the living-room curtain, she peeked out to the street. The Toyota, that dented, potato-like thing she'd hated so when it had first arrived, was gone.

The remaining air went out of her lungs and she sagged against the wall beside the window. That was it. Gone. She prowled through the dining room, looking for evidence of Mitch and found nothing. Even the three table settings that had been laid out for dinner had been put away.

The kitchen still smelled of roasting chicken, but the oven was off and the counters clean. Ginny opened the refrigerator and found several foil-wrapped packages, still slightly warm. She took out every one, dumped them into the garbage and carried the garbage bag out to the container in the garage. She couldn't have eaten that food if she'd been starving.

An envelope on the desk caught her eye. Her name was on the outside in Mitch's handwriting. She hoped to God he hadn't written her a note. The last thing in the world she needed right now was some sentimental garbage about how he'd always care about her.

She opened the envelope and peeked inside. He hadn't written a note. Instead, he'd written a check, for the same amount she'd given him before she'd left on her trip. Ginny ripped the check and the envelope into such tiny pieces that they scattered on the floor and she had to spend extra minutes scooping them all up.

At last, satisfied that the first floor contained no further traces of Mitch's presence, she climbed the stairs once more. She marveled that he'd moved out so quickly, although she had no realistic idea how long she'd stayed on the bathroom floor. Perhaps she'd been there longer than she thought.

The door to Mitch's room—the guest room, she amended to herself—stood open. Taking a deep breath, she looked in, and saw at once why he'd been able to leave so easily. He'd left his weight bench and weights. A note was taped to the padded seat, and she moved forward to read it.

Once inside the room, she wished she hadn't entered. It still smelled of Mitch, of his after-shave, and that special masculine scent that she'd come to recognize whenever she held him close. He'd stripped the bed and piled his sheets in the corner of the room. Ginny's throat tightened, and she quickly read the note on the weight bench so she could leave the room.

The note was to Arnold, as she'd expected, and told him that the weights and bench now belonged to him. Ginny stared at the polished aluminum apparatus and wondered how she'd be able to tolerate such a strong reminder of Mitch. She could have it delivered to him and buy Arnold a new weight bench and weights, but Arnold probably wouldn't want that.

As a deluge of tears threatened again, she hurried over to the pile of sheets and scooped them up in her arms. The scent of Mitch and the touch of his sheets, even if she hadn't made love to him in this particular bed, wrenched new sobs from her throat. Running back downstairs, stumbling and almost falling in the process, she threw the sheets, blanket and bedspread into the washer, dumped in soap and turned the machine on. She flung the washer lid down with a clang. "Now, go away!" she cried. "I want all of you out of here. Every last thing!" Then she raced back upstairs, as if trying to outrun her emotions, and stripped down for a shower.

By the time the Gaston's pickup pulled up in front of the house at about ten o'clock, Ginny was reclining with her feet up on the sofa while she watched the news on television. Eye drops and cold compresses had erased the evidence of crying from her face, and she had brewed herself a cup of herbal tea. She'd had two cups, and was still waiting for the relaxing effects to work.

The garage door went up as Arnold put away his bike, and then he used his key to come into the kitchen. "I'm home, you guys," he called.

Ginny's heart constricted. He wouldn't be able to call that particular greeting anymore. "I'm in here," she called back.

Arnold appeared in the arched doorway into the living room. His face was flushed with happiness. "Hi! You're looking better. Are you feeling better?"

"Some," she lied. "Thanks."

"That's good. Where's Mitch?"

Ginny swung her feet off the couch and using the remote control, shut the television off. "Come over here and sit down, Arnold," she said, patting the cushion beside her.

"Why?" he looked wary. "What's the matter? Is it something about Mitch?"

"Well . . . yes."

Panic showed in Arnold's dark eyes. "What? What about him?"

"He . . . he won't be living here anymore."

"How come?" Arnold's voice cracked. "The summer's not over yet. I thought he didn't have to do anything until school started."

"That's the way we had it set up originally, but Mitch and I had a—a slight disagreement and decided to end the arrangement now."

"You did *what?*" Arnold croaked.

"I think you and I can manage for the rest of the summer. I won't have any more trips until after school starts." She tried to keep her tone even, her gaze steady, but Arnold's distress was beginning to stir the demons of despair she thought she'd conquered. Her lower lip quivered and she pressed it tight to her upper lip.

"Why, Mom?" Arnold wailed. "What do you mean, a disagreement?"

"I'd rather Mitch told you about that."

"Mitch? You mean it was his idea to leave?"

"Well, not exactly, but I don't think I should be the one to discuss it with you."

"So, you just let him leave?" Arnold thrust out his chin with its few bits of stubble. "How'm I supposed to discuss it with him, huh?"

"I'm sure you didn't want him to leave, Arnold, but it was inevitable, after all, and a few days doesn't matter, really."

"It wasn't inevitable, dammit! Lately, I've been thinking that—"

"Arnold, watch your language." She didn't want him to go into what he'd been thinking lately. If he'd

caught the affectionate vibrations between her and
Mitch, she didn't want to know about it.

"Why? What're you gonna do to me if I don't?
You've already done the worst thing you could. You
let Mitch leave. You even let him leave without saying
goodbye to me." Arnold's grown-up veneer dissolved
a little more with each second, until he looked heart-
breakingly like the little boy of eight who had demanded why his father had gone, also without saying
goodbye.

Ginny knew that if he started to cry, he'd hate her
even more for witnessing his tears. "As I'm trying to
tell you, it's not like that," she said. "I'm sure he'll
talk to you about this on Monday, after wrestling
practice."

"Wrestling practice? Who wants to go to some stupid old wrestling practice? Who wants to be around
somebody who'll just walk out on a guy?" His body
hunched together, as if every part of it hurt.

"But the last meet is coming up. I thought you'd
want us to take Angela and—"

"Screw the meet! Screw everything!" Arnold bolted
past her and bounded up the stairs. The impact of his
door meeting the frame vibrated the whole house.

Ginny sat, dazed by the violence of Arnold's reaction. She shouldn't be surprised, not after the way
Arnold had changed over the summer. A tear slid
down her cheek. Arnold might have looked eight years
old just now, but he hadn't acted it. Before this summer, whenever he'd been troubled, he'd retreated into
a book, or played his clarinet, or written poetry.

Only now did she realize she hadn't heard him
practice his clarinet once all summer. Classical music
had disappeared from his life, except for that one trip

to the symphony, an experience that Ginny had been reluctant to repeat once she understood how little Mitch enjoyed it.

Mitch. The tears dripped faster now. She clenched both hands and longed for something to hit. He'd moved into her house and her heart with such ease, all because he'd kept the truth hidden. She must have known, somehow. All along he'd seemed too good to be true. Thank God she'd driven to Cedarville and uncovered his secret before it was too late, before she'd brought Arnold in on their marriage plans.

If Arnold had reacted this strongly to the news of Mitch's leaving, no telling what he'd have done if the news had come later, when he was looking forward to having Mitch as a father. Ginny shuddered at the thought of the damage that would have done. She only prayed that too much damage hadn't been done already.

She blamed herself. She should have questioned Mitch more closely about his reasons for leaving Cedarville before she ever hired him. She'd meant to do that, but Arnold's eagerness and Maggie's explanation of a failed love affair had edged her off the track. Then, too, his statement about envious parents had hit a nerve.

Mostly, however, she'd wanted to believe in Mitch, more so as each day went by and Arnold's happiness increased. And recently, her happiness had increased, too. She couldn't think about that—about the loving—or she'd start screaming right there in the middle of her living room. He was gone. Arnold would have to get used to the fact. So would she.

GINNY DIDN'T SEE MUCH of Arnold on Sunday. He biked over to Angela's as soon as Ginny allowed him to phone and make sure he was welcome. She spent the day going over her notes from the focus group tour. She concentrated very hard on those notes, because whenever she didn't, despair took over.

To her surprise, Arnold showed up for dinner and she ordered pizza, which they ate in front of the television, something she'd never allowed before because she'd worried about staining her carpet and the expensive upholstery on the sofa and chairs. It just didn't seem important enough to worry about anymore.

After dinner, Arnold spent the evening in his room talking on the phone to Angela. Then, before he went to bed, he came into her bedroom where she'd immersed herself in her notes again and announced that he'd go to wrestling practice the next morning.

Ginny concluded that either Angela had convinced him to do it, or he'd found the weight set and the message telling him that it was his. She was glad Arnold had decided to go. She wanted Mitch to tell Arnold the whole story, so that Arnold could understand that she wasn't quite the villain he thought her to be.

At the gym the next morning, she averted her gaze from the dented, brown Toyota in the parking lot. She made arrangements with Arnold to pick him up outside the gym after practice. She didn't want to run the risk of seeing Mitch. Once Arnold got out of the Volvo, Ginny put the car in reverse and sped out of the parking lot. She didn't know if Mitch would see Arnold and try to come after her, but she wasn't taking any chances.

Ginny didn't realize she'd been crying on the way to
the office until she glanced in the rearview mirror and
noticed her smeared makeup. At a stoplight she used
a tissue to wipe the half-moons of mascara from under her eyes but she wasn't completely successful.
She'd have to stop at the rest room on her floor and do
a complete repair before she went in to face Claudia
and Maggie.

When she pushed open the door of the rest room,
no one was there, and she was thankful for that small
piece of luck. She rummaged in her attaché case and
took out her cosmetics bag. She hated to look at herself in the uncompromising glare of the fluorescent
lights, but she had no choice. As she dabbed cleansing cream under her eyes, the door creaked open, and
Maggie walked in.

Ginny glanced at her with a guilty smile. "Hi."

"I hope it's allergies that are making you look like
that," Maggie said gently.

"I wish." Ginny grabbed a tissue from the dispenser and wiped the mascara from under her eyes.
Quick. She had to do everything fast, before she
started crying again.

"What happened, honey?" Maggie stepped up beside her and met Ginny's gaze in the mirror. "I
thought you'd be floating on air this morning."

Ginny turned toward Maggie and opened her mouth
to begin the story, but a sob came out, instead. Silently Maggie opened her arms and Ginny went into
their comforting haven. She cried on Maggie's shoulder while Maggie patted her back and murmured
words of consolation.

When the tears slowed, Ginny disengaged herself
and turned away, fumbling for another tissue. "Great,

just great," she said, embarrassed. "I've ruined your suit jacket and any chance of repairing this face."

"I don't give a damn about the suit jacket. As for your face, we can use the allergy excuse if anyone asks. Now blow your nose and tell Aunt Maggie what happened."

Ginny obediently blew her nose and glanced in the mirror as she threw the tissue away. "Lord."

"He's probably listening, too," Maggie said, leaning against the counter. "So shoot."

With only a couple of pauses to blow her nose again, Ginny told Maggie about her trip to Cedarville and the final scene with Mitch. "And that's that," she said. "Except Arnold has four days of wrestling left. I dropped him at the gym this morning and I'll have to pick him up again, but with luck I can snatch him and go, without running into Mitch."

"Wow." Maggie looked stunned, a condition Ginny seldom saw in her friend. "I can't believe it. I just can't believe it."

"I know what you mean," Ginny said. "When I woke up this morning, I was sure I'd dreamed the whole thing."

Maggie shook her head. "So what did happen? He wasn't convicted, so what's the real story?"

"I don't know. I guess his having hidden something so important from me was all I could think about."

"But certainly you don't think he's guilty."

"No." Ginny pushed the swinging lid on the metal trash container and threw her wad of tissues inside. "When the women first told me outside the café, I had a rush of fear for Arnold's safety, but eventually I realized Mitch would never molest anyone. It's something I'm sure of."

"Interesting." Maggie tapped her chin. "You know nothing about it except that he was accused and found innocent, yet you're sure he didn't do it. Juries and judges make mistakes, you know."

"Well, they didn't this time." Ginny straightened. "I know this guy. I've lived with him for weeks. He's filled with compassion—he hates the idea of the strong preying on the weak. That's one reason he agreed to help Arnold. And besides that, his sexual desires are perfectly normal. He's simply not a child molester, and that's that."

"My goodness, you sound as if you still care about him."

"Even if that were true, I can't afford the luxury," Ginny said, turning away to run water in the sink. "After not being honest with me about his past, I don't know if I can ever trust him again."

"That's pretty harsh."

"It's the way I feel."

"Ginny, use your marketing skills," Maggie coaxed. "You earn your living by putting yourself in other people's shoes and probing their motivations. Can you imagine how someone feels who's been falsely accused of a terrible crime? What has that done to his level of trust?"

Ginny whirled. "He should have known he could trust me!"

"How was he to know? He's been betrayed, big-time, and those fears don't disappear overnight. He didn't want to lose you, Ginny, and he was afraid he would. To be honest, I don't know how you would have reacted if he'd told you, say, a month ago. Even if you believed he was innocent, you might have worried about how Arnold would take the news. You might have sent Mitch away to protect Arnold from having to deal with such harsh realities."

Ginny turned off the faucet and pulled a paper towel from the dispenser. "I'd like to think I wouldn't have reacted that way, that I'm a fair person who gives everyone a chance."

"I'd like to believe that about you, too, but I also know how you worry about Arnold's psychological health. Consider the elaborate measures you've taken to make sure Arnold didn't know you were sleeping with Mitch."

"That's not the same thing." Ginny dampened the paper towel in the sink and began sponging her ravaged face.

"Not exactly, but—" Maggie stopped and threw up her hands "—oh, well. I guess it's your business."

Ginny put down the towel and turned to her. "Maggie, are you upset with me?"

"No, sweetie. I just realized that I've meddled in this thing far too much as it is."

"Hey, you've been terrific. I don't know what I'd have done without you."

"You'd have some privacy in the bathroom, for one thing. I should admit that I followed you in here this morning. You looked terrible, and I don't remember your ever sneaking in here before coming into the office, so I had to find out what was wrong."

"And I appreciate that." Ginny reached out to give her a hug.

"And now—be honest—you want me to butt out."

Ginny sighed. "To tell you the truth, Maggie, I don't know what I want."

"Well, stay in here awhile and recuperate," Maggie said, patting her arm. "Maybe it'll come to you. In the meantime, I'll hold down the fort at the office until you feel ready to face the world."

"Think I could live in here, instead?"

Maggie glanced around. "Nah. No view and no cooking facilities. And those lights make you look a hundred years old."

Ginny laughed. "Thanks."

"They make me look a hundred and ten," Maggie said, peering at herself. "Which is why I'm leaving. 'Bye."

After Maggie left, Ginny turned back to the mirror, a smile still on her lips. Gradually the smile disappeared. Yesterday she'd believed Mitch had had no right not to tell her his secret. Today she wasn't so sure.

She repaired her makeup as best she could and left the rest room. The morning was busy, as it always was after a trip, with notes and videos to coordinate into a presentation to the client. Ginny barely got started before a glance at her watch told her she'd have to leave and pick up Arnold. Her throat tightened at the prospect of returning to the gym, but she had no choice. Three more days and the wrestling program would be over, she told herself as she drove through the midday traffic.

She parked where she'd told Arnold she'd be waiting. Boys came out of the double doors and headed for other cars, but Arnold wasn't among them. Finally, her Volvo was the only car left in the parking lot except for Mitch's Toyota. She realized that Mitch and Arnold must be having their heart-to-heart talk. With luck they wouldn't come out together.

The waiting seemed endless, but at last the door swung open and Ginny started the car. She'd be prepared for a fast getaway. Mitch came out, glanced around and saw her car. Arnold wasn't with him.

Confused, Ginny turned off the ignition and got out of the car. She didn't want to talk to Mitch, but someone had to tell her where Arnold was. She walked across the parking lot and he waited by his car, his expression blank.

"Where's Arnold?" she called, not wanting to prolong the contact.

"Arnold?" Mitch looked surprised. "I thought you kept him home."

"I dropped him here this morning," Ginny said, as her stomach began to knot. "He was at practice."

"He wasn't at practice."

"Of course he was. You probably just—"

"I didn't just anything! I haven't seen him."

A wave of dizziness swept over her. Ever since Arnold's birth, this had been her worst nightmare, that he might someday simply disappear. Mitch was telling her that Arnold hadn't been at practice, although she'd dropped him off there. But she hadn't seen him go through the door. She'd been in too big a hurry to get away, in case Mitch might run after her. She hadn't watched him until he was safely inside the building. And now he was missing.

# CHAPTER SEVENTEEN

"WE'LL FIND HIM," Mitch said, opening his car door and throwing his gym bag inside. "Get in."

She did, leaving the Volvo unlocked, not even caring if someone stole it. She wanted Mitch to drive. She was shaking so much she'd be a menace on the road.

"We'll start with your place," he said. "In case he decided he didn't want to face me, after all, and walked home."

"That's fifteen miles," Ginny protested. She'd noticed Mitch's use of the phrase "your place." He'd moved out both mentally and physically.

"Fifteen miles isn't such an impossible distance to him anymore, not with all the jogging and weight training he's done."

"I guess not." Ginny still wasn't used to Arnold's mushrooming self-sufficiency. But self-sufficiency also put him in greater danger. Madmen prowled the streets. She read about them in the newspapers, heard about them on television. They looked for kids who wandered around alone, kids who might be confused about things and not thinking straight, kids who'd lower their guard when confronted with a gesture of kindness from a stranger.

"He probably just went home, Ginny. Don't jump to the worst conclusions. You're pale as a ghost."

"It's just all this stuff you hear, about missing kids. The faces on milk cartons," she said, tensing her jaw to keep her teeth from chattering.

"Yeah, but Arnold's not going to be one of those. He's at home now, kicking back, listening to his stereo as loud as it can go and thinking he played a neat trick on you."

"I'll put him on restriction for a year if that's what he's done."

Mitch was silent for a moment. "How did he take it on Saturday?" he asked finally.

"He...um..." Ginny swallowed and forced her attention back to Saturday night. "He was upset. At first he didn't want to go to wrestling practice, but last night he said he'd go, after all. That's why you're probably right. He changed his mind again and walked home, just like you said. And he wanted to punish me by making me wait and wonder where he was."

"So he's ticked off."

"Pretty much. And hurt. He couldn't understand why you'd left so abruptly, and I didn't think it was my place to—"

"You said that Saturday night."

"Right."

"I've got to talk to him, though," Mitch said. "Poor kid. He must think I'm a louse. I had my speech all figured out for today, and when he didn't show, I kicked myself for not insisting on seeing him yesterday."

"I wish you had, too, now."

"Stan told me that Arnold spent most of the day over there with Angela. Stan thought Arnold was acting like something was wrong."

"Did you tell Stan what happened?" Ginny asked.

"Yeah. Well, I'd intended to, anyway. That's why I asked him out for coffee last night."

"You told him about Cedarville?"

"Yep."

"Why?"

"I'm through hiding, Ginny. I decided that yesterday, with the help of Jan, my counselor. This week I'll talk to my principal at Westwood and tell him."

"But he might fire you!"

Mitch shrugged. "If he does, he does. Stan didn't seem to think he would, and I'm ready to risk it."

"You're either very brave or very foolhardy."

He glanced at her. "Or else I finally understand how it has to be. Enough damage has already been done, and I'm not running away from this anymore."

Emotion swelled within her. This was the real Mitch, the one she'd fallen in love with, the one she'd thought had been a fantasy.

Mitch stopped at a red light. "Come on, damn you, change," he muttered. Then he hit the steering wheel with his open palm. "Why didn't I talk to Arnold yesterday?"

"Because we didn't know this would happen," Ginny said. "I wish I'd done a few things differently, too."

He glanced at her, a silent question in his eyes.

"Now we have to find him," she said, meeting his gaze.

"We'll find him."

Arnold wasn't at the townhouse. Ginny raced upstairs to search for clues that he'd been there and found his wrestling gear tossed in a corner and his gym bag gone.

"Anything?" Mitch asked, standing in the doorway.

Ginny held up the wrestling trunks. "Either he took something else in his gym bag this morning, or he's been home, dropped this off and repacked." She gazed around the room. Something else was missing.

"The Mariners poster is gone," Mitch said. He walked over to Arnold's tape deck and examined the cassettes strewn on the floor. "And some of his favorite tapes aren't here, either."

"He's run away from home," Ginny said, fighting her panic.

"Where would he go?"

"I don't know. Gerry's parents are in Arizona, but they're not well, and he's always felt constrained around them. He barely knows his grandfather in South Carolina." Ginny battled against the hysteria that threatened to rob her of her reasoning power. "I don't know, Mitch. I don't know. I wish—"

"We'll ask Angela," Mitch said, taking charge again. "We know he talked to her a lot yesterday. Maybe this is what they talked about. I've been around a few of these teen romances, and he wouldn't leave, if that's what he's done, without telling her goodbye. That's a whole drama in itself."

"You're probably right." Relief and gratitude for Mitch's clear thinking poured through her. "Mitch, I—"

"Let's go," he said, turning away and starting down the stairs.

Just as well he didn't let her finish, she thought as she left Arnold's room. She was vulnerable now, not thinking straight. She might say or do something impulsive that she'd regret later.

As Ginny walked beside Mitch up the walkway to
the Gaston's sprawling two-story house, she stepped
over a football and around the protruding nubby
wheel of a mountain bike lying on the grass beside the
walk. Ginny could see why Arnold liked coming over
here. The grass, trampled down by running feet and
bike tires, beckoned for more games to be played,
more races to be won, more wrestling matches to be
staged.

Mitch rang the bell and Angela answered the door.
She tried to look surprised to see them, but Ginny
didn't believe her act. The girl invited them inside and
asked if they'd like to sit down.

"We'll just be a minute," Mitch said. "Thanks,
anyway."

"Dad's at school going over a curriculum change
and Mom's at the store," Angela offered in another
show of cooperation. "Did you want to talk to them
about something?"

"No, actually we wanted to talk to you," Mitch
said, glancing around the comfortable living room.
"Are the boys gone, too?"

"Yeah. Swimming at the Y," Angela said. "There's
just me," she said with a smile a little too bright to be
sincere.

Ginny listened intently, wondering if by some lucky
chance Arnold had taken a long time with his goodbyes and was hiding upstairs. At this point she didn't
give a damn about unchaperoned behavior or Angela's knowledge of erotic literature. She didn't care
what they might have been doing upstairs, if she only
could see Arnold and know that he was safe.

"Arnold didn't show up at wrestling practice this morning," Mitch said. "He's not at home, either. Have you seen him?"

"Yesterday," Angela said, fooling with her long, dark curls. "Why?"

Ginny wasn't up to playing games. "Angela, he's missing. We're really worried. If you know where he is, or might be, for God's sake, tell me."

Angela's nonchalance disappeared and she glared at Ginny. "Why? You didn't care about him before. Why are you so worried about him now?"

A wave of hot anger washed over Ginny. She longed to grab the girl and shake the information out of her. Instead, she forced herself to speak calmly. "There are a lot of things you don't know, Angela. Is Arnold upstairs?" Ginny started in that direction.

"He's not here."

Ginny paused. "Then where is he?" she asked, her voice rising in spite of herself. She'd put a lot of hope into his being in this house, which would have made him disobedient but not reckless. But he wasn't here. "Where is he?" she asked again, more forcefully.

Angela glanced away without answering.

"Look," Mitch said, stepping toward Angela. "You may not believe this, but we both love Arnold very much, and we're worried sick about him. If you don't tell us where he is, we'll call the police. We'll also drive all over town looking for him. We'll recruit all the people we know to drive around looking for him. We'll do whatever it takes until he's found."

"And you'll probably tell my parents, too," Angela said, her tone sarcastic.

"You're darn right we will," Mitch said. "We're not fooling around, Angela. This is for real. Arnold's missing, and anything could happen to him while he's wandering around on his own.''

She tossed her head. "Arnold's a lot more grown-up than you think. He can take care of himself.''

"No, he can't," Mitch said, his voice betraying emotion for the first time. "And if my influence has given him the false impression that he can, I'll blame myself if anything happens to him.''

"You should," Angela said, her expression filled with scorn. "You're the one who didn't want to stay around when he needed you. You're the one who threw him away like so much garbage. You keep saying you love him. I don't think so, not the way you've treated him.''

Mitch paled. "I do love him, Angela," he said, his voice hoarse.

"Oh, yeah? Then how come you just left?''

Mitch glanced at Ginny. "That's a long story. I planned to talk to him about it today, but he didn't give me the chance." Mitch seemed to be speaking with difficulty. "Believe me, Angela, that kid has become one of the most important people in my life. If anything happens to Arnold, I . . ." He stopped talking, obviously unable to finish the sentence.

Ginny's eyes filled as she watched Mitch struggle to regain control of his emotions. If she'd ever doubted his devotion to Arnold, she couldn't now. Ginny felt something heavy lift from her heart. She wasn't alone. If she chose, she never had to be alone again.

Angela stood completely still, her eyes wide as she stared at Mitch. Then she swallowed. "Arnold will kill me if I tell you where he is." She glanced at her watch.

"Why did you do that?" Ginny asked, wild for any clues.

"Do what?"

"You looked at your watch. What difference does the time make?"

Angela looked like a cornered animal. "I—"

"Does Arnold have a ticket on something like a bus or an airplane?" Ginny persisted.

Angela shrank back. "I promised," she wailed. "He doesn't want you to find him. He thinks—" She stopped abruptly.

"He thinks what?" Ginny pleaded. "Please, Angela."

Her glance darted from Mitch to Ginny. "Arnold thinks it's his fault that Mitch left," she said, speaking fast. "He thinks Mitch got fed up with having to be around him all the time that week you were gone, so after you got back Mitch cut out. I tried to tell him that might not be right, but he kept saying if it wasn't right, then why hadn't Mitch told him goodbye?"

"Oh, God," Mitch groaned.

"That wasn't right," Ginny said, her breathing uneven. "And it's my fault if he got that impression."

"He also thinks you two want to be together and he's in the way."

Ginny shut her eyes. *Oh, Arnold.* "He's not in the way for anything," she said. "Mitch and I want him around. We're a family, the three of us," she added, knowing how right those words felt. One glance at Mitch's face told her how happy he was to hear what she was saying. Now if only she could get Arnold back, she'd try to rebuild the family they'd almost become. "Please give me a chance to talk to him, Angela."

The girl studied them both. "You guys sound like you mean it," she ventured.

"Please tell us," Mitch said, moving toward Ginny and putting a protective arm around her shoulder.

Angela took a deep breath. "Okay. But if Arnold wants to break up with me over this—"

"He won't," Ginny promised. "He left with the wrong impression, and now we've told you the way things are. If you could talk to him, wouldn't you want to try to talk him out of leaving?"

"Yeah. Well, I did, but he was so upset, and then I got really mad at you guys and decided it would serve you right."

"Where is he?" Ginny asked.

"At the Greyhound bus station. The bus leaves in twenty minutes."

Mitch grabbed Ginny's arm and pulled her out onto the porch and down the steps. She flung open the car door while Mitch ran around to his side. The Toyota squealed away from the curb while Mitch was still closing his door. "Watch for cops," he instructed, careening the car around a corner.

"They'd probably help us get there."

"Yeah, but I don't want to take time out to explain. I wonder where the bus is going?"

"We didn't think to ask." Ginny gripped the armrest as Mitch took another corner at top speed.

"Doesn't matter. We'll make it."

"Yes."

"Did you mean what you said back there?"

"Yes."

"I love you."

"I love you, too. Now drive, Mitch." Ginny knew she should be frightened. Mitch was negotiating the hilly streets of Seattle like a maniac. Somehow she knew they wouldn't crash. She trusted Mitch to get them there in one piece before the bus pulled out. She trusted him with her life.

When they reached the station, a hulking silver bus sat growling and belching foul-smelling exhaust as people filed into it. Ginny's stomach churned when she saw the destination in digital letters across the front. Arnold had intended to go to New York, as far away as he could get on land transportation.

Mitch double-parked the Toyota and he and Ginny raced toward the line of passengers. Arnold wasn't there. "He's already on," Mitch said, and shouldered in front of the next passenger. "Excuse me."

"Hey, buddy," the man complained. "Wait in line."

"I can't," Mitch called over his shoulder and dashed up the steps of the bus.

Ginny waited, twisting her hands together as she scanned the darkened window. She couldn't see Arnold or Mitch. She tried to subdue the thought that another bus, the one with Arnold on it, might have left minutes ago. She had to believe that Arnold was on this bus, and that Mitch would convince him to get off. Passengers continued to file past her. A few gave her a curious glance.

Then Arnold appeared in the doorway of the bus, and time seemed to stop. Ginny caught her breath at the sight of this handsome self-assured young man. He wasn't through growing yet; his arms and legs were still a little too long for the rest of his body, but his resolute expression belonged to the adult he was becoming, not the child he'd been. For the first time in her life, Ginny saw him not as her son, but as another human being struggling for his place in life. She felt a loosening around her heart, and knew she was beginning to let him go.

The moment ended, and the world started turning again as he hopped down the steps, followed by Mitch. Ginny cried out and ran forward. She hugged Arnold's resisting body, not caring whether he'd hug back or be embarrassed or pull away, which eventually he did. She had to convince herself he was really there, all sixty-nine inches of him.

"Mom, geez," he said, ducking his head so his red face wouldn't show.

"New York, Arnold! What on earth would you have done in New York?" She was crying, too, and knew he'd hate that. Tough.

"Could we talk about this someplace else?" Arnold asked, glancing nervously around.

"Sure, we'll..." She hesitated and looked around, too, trying to find Mitch. The bus doors folded shut and the driver revved the engine. "Where is he?"

"Who, Mitch?"

"Of course, Mitch. He was right behind you, and now I don't see him."

Arnold's dark eyes sparkled. "I don't know. Maybe he decided to go to New York instead of me."

"What?" Ginny nearly fainted.

"Just kidding, Mom. Geez. He's getting my refund. He'll be here in a minute. Mitch wouldn't go anywhere. He told me you guys are getting married."

Ginny put her hand over her thumping heart. So Mitch had told him and Arnold had apparently accepted the news as positive, or he wouldn't be standing here. Flooded with relief, she decided she could afford to scold Arnold. He might be growing up, but he wasn't grown. "Listen, that wasn't funny at all.

And as for this trip you almost took, young man, it's time that you and I had a serious talk about—"

"Everyone ready?" Mitch appeared and handed Arnold some money. "There's your refund."

"Mitch, do you know what this young man just did? When I didn't see you right away, he told me you'd probably gone on the bus instead of him."

"Pretty good, huh, Mitch?" Arnold said with a grin. "I really had her going."

"No, not pretty good," Mitch said, putting his arm around Arnold. "You have just given your mother the scare of her life, and we'll talk about that in a minute, but adding a stupid joke on top of it isn't very respectful."

"Oh." Arnold glanced at Mitch. Then he looked at his mother. "So you two are going to be ganging up on me from now on, is that it?"

Ginny gazed at Mitch. He smiled. "Yes," she said, putting her whole heart into a return smile. "That's exactly how it will be. And Arnold, you're going to love it."

## EPILOGUE

GINNY OPENED the front door of the townhouse to discover a clean-cut young man, about nineteen or twenty years old, standing on her front stoop protected from the light drizzle by her porch overhang.

"Mrs. Adamson?" he asked.

"Yes." Ginny still enjoyed hearing her new name, even after two months of marriage, so she smiled, even though she suspected this was a sales call about to interrupt her Saturday morning.

"Is...is Coach...I mean, Mr. Adamson here?"

Ginny revised her evaluation. "You must have taken the summer wrestling class," she said, although he looked too old and she didn't remember him at all.

"No, ma'am. Is he here?"

"Yes. I'll get him." Ginny backed away from the door, leaving it open but stopping short of inviting the young man in. He'd used the word *coach* to refer to Mitch. Mitch's only coaching so far in Seattle had taken place this past summer. That left only one possibility. This person was from Cedarville.

Ginny walked into the dining room, where Mitch and Arnold hovered over their work stations. They'd covered the cherry dining table with newspapers and had the parts for a three-foot model of a battleship spread out. The room smelled of glue and paint thinner. The project had been set up for two weeks, and

Ginny figured on at least two or three more. They ate all meals in the kitchen or in the living room in front of the television.

"Mitch," she said.

"Just a sec." He finished putting a tiny plastic part in place with tweezers before he looked up. "What, my love? I heard the doorbell. If it's the Girl Scouts, I like the kind with peanut butter in the middle."

"No way," Arnold said, concentrating on a delicate stripe he was painting on the hull. "Get mints, Mom."

"It isn't the Girl Scouts. It's a young man. He wants to see you. I think...I think he's from Cedarville." She hated the change in Mitch's expression. He'd looked so happy and relaxed working on the model with Arnold, but now his expression closed down, and his gray eyes took on a tough glint.

"Granger must have given out my address." Mitch put down the tweezers and stood. "What does he look like?" he asked in a muted voice.

"Sandy hair, cut short. About average height. Oh, and there's a dimple in his chin. He looks sort of like Michael Douglas with short hair."

Mitch gazed at her, but didn't seem to see her. "Jeff," he said.

"Hey," Arnold said. "Isn't that the name of the guy who—"

"Keep your voice down," Ginny warned. "He's right on the front porch and I left the door open."

"I could care less if he hears me." Arnold got to his feet and started toward the living room. "Because I'm gonna punch his lights out."

"Arnold, wait." Mitch caught his arm.

"Come on, Mitch." Arnold tried to pull away. "I know you can't do it, and Mom isn't up to the job, but I can. Let me flatten the son-of-a—"

"No." Mitch tightened his grip, which still could subdue Arnold, although the boy had put on extra pounds and muscle, as well as another inch in height, just since the wedding. "I'll talk to him."

"I wanna be there, just in case he tries anything funny," Arnold said.

"Okay. Why don't you both come in and meet him?" he said, glancing at Ginny.

"I may not be able to control my temper, either, Mitch," she said.

"And you know how she gets when she's mad," Arnold said with a chuckle.

The tension eased a little in Mitch's expression. "Now I'm starting to feel a little sorry for Jeff," he said with a small smile.

"Hah." Arnold glared in the direction of the front door. "That'll be the day. No way will I ever feel sorry for that sucker."

"Let's go," Mitch said. "After all this time, he may have taken off, anyway."

Jeff hadn't left. When the three of them trooped into the living room Jeff remained standing outside the open front door, his hands in the pockets of his denim jacket, his expression anxious.

"Come in, Jeff," Mitch said, walking forward. "How are you?" he asked, extending his hand after he closed the door.

"F-fine." Jeff blushed bright red as he accepted the handshake, but ended it quickly.

"Jeff Knowland, this is my wife Ginny and my son, Arnold."

Not inclined to shake this boy's hand, Ginny nodded and Arnold followed suit. She'd noticed how Arnold had straightened with pride when Mitch had
introduced him as "my son."

"Have a seat," Mitch said, gesturing toward the
sofa and two chairs.

"That's all right," Jeff said, shifting his weight. "I
was wondering if we could . . . if we could talk alone
somewhere?"

"Why?"

"This is sort of personal."

"Well, Jeff, I'll tell you." Mitch folded his arms and
gazed at the young man. "What happened back in
Cedarville invaded me personally, and I'm not too
worried about whether you'd be uncomfortable talking about something personal in front of these two
people. Besides, they're witnesses, something I didn't
have three years ago."

Ginny barely heard Arnold's muttered "way to go,
Mitch." She felt the same way. This kid barely deserved an audience with Mitch, let alone a private one.

Jeff blushed again. "Okay. Yeah, you're right.
You're doing a lot, just letting me in the front door."

"That's for sure," Arnold mumbled.

"Speaking of which, how did you find me?" Mitch
asked.

"Mr. Granger gave me the address. He said he'd call
you." Jeff paused. "I guess he didn't."

"He might have tried," Mitch said. "We're all
pretty busy."

Jeff glanced at Arnold. "You sure are a lucky kid,"
he said.

"What d'ya mean?" Arnold asked, looking startled.

"You've got what I wanted, Coach Adamson for a father."

"A father?" Arnold croaked. "You practically ruin the guy's life, and you say you wanted him for a father?"

"Yeah." Jeff shoved his hands back into his pockets and gazed at Mitch. "Yeah, I did. That's what I'm here to tell you, Coach. After you left I started doing drugs, and finally I was so bad, I landed in a rehab program and they put me in counseling."

"That's good," Mitch said.

Jeff shrugged. "It's better, anyway. I'm clean now, but I had to face up to what I'd done. I thought I'd lied about the...you know...because I hated you. My counselor helped me figure out that I didn't hate you at all. I, um—" he paused and looked down at the floor "—I guess I...loved you so much I couldn't stand for the other kids to have anything from you, any attention. So I fixed it so none of us could have you around." He glanced up again. "In a stupid way, that was easier than sharing you."

Mitch swallowed. "I see."

"The truth is, you were the best thing to come along in my whole screwed-up life, and I had to screw that up, too." Jeff's eyes glistened.

Ginny's resolve to distance herself from this kid who'd hurt Mitch began to melt. She knew how it felt to lose Mitch, but she'd been lucky enough to repair the relationship. Jeff hadn't. She glanced at Arnold. The set of his jaw didn't seem quite so tight. He'd almost lost Mitch, too, although through no fault of his own. Still, he had to appreciate the privilege of being on the inside when Jeff was so clearly on the outside.

Mitch took a deep breath. "So, what do you want from me now, Jeff?"

"Just the chance to tell you I'm sorry, although I know that doesn't make up for anything. I should probably find every kid who had you as a teacher or a coach, or would have had if you'd stayed in Cedarville, and tell all of them I'm sorry, too. You should see the guy they got to replace you. A real nerd. I guess they were playing it safe, but the guy's a total zero. No personality."

"You weren't the only one to blame," Mitch said. "The parents didn't support me the way I thought they would."

"Yeah, 'cause they were all jealous, that's why. Kids listened to you more than to their own parents, so the parents got mad. They were glad to find something wrong with you. At least some of them were."

Ginny remembered her early jealousies of Arnold's hero worship. When Mitch had said that envy had been part of the reason he'd left Cedarville, he'd been telling her the truth. He simply hadn't been ready to tell her all of it.

Jeff glanced around the room. "I guess that's all, then. I feel better seeing you in this nice place, with a family and all, and I'm glad you're teaching again. Mr. Granger told me you didn't for a while."

"That's right."

"You should always teach. You were..." Jeff hesitated and looked up at the ceiling. Then he swiped at his eyes with the back of his hand. "You were the best teacher I ever had," he said quickly, and turned toward the door.

"Jeff."

He turned back. His eyes were wet. "Yeah?"

"Keep in touch. Tell me how you're doing."

"You mean that?" Jeff's lower lip quivered.

"I mean that."

Jeff pressed his lips together. Then he gave a quick nod and bolted for the door.

Mitch stood there staring at the closed door for a long time after Jeff left. Finally, he turned back to Ginny and Arnold, and his eyes were damp, too. Ginny moved forward and discovered that Arnold was coming with her. The two of them enveloped Mitch in a three-way hug.

The moment lasted about ten seconds before Arnold started to tickle Mitch, and Ginny tickled Arnold to defend Mitch, and the three of them ended up on the floor in a mock wrestling match that left them all laughing and gasping for breath.

"Hey, what time is it, anyway?" Arnold said, extricating himself from the pileup.

"Noon, I think," Ginny said, resting with her head on Mitch's stomach. "You hungry?"

"Nope. But I'm due over at Angela's in fifteen minutes. See you guys."

"It's raining," Ginny protested. "If you ride your bike over there you'll get soaked."

"I'll wear my rain stuff, that jacket and pants thing. Besides, I like riding in the rain."

"It's dangerous."

"Danger is my middle name."

"Arnold, for heaven's sake," Ginny protested, running out of motherly objections. "You were just over there last night. And what about Billy Herman? He called again. Did you call him back?"

"Yeah. We might go to the movies tomorrow. Did I tell you he might go out for wrestling?"

"No," Ginny said. "That's interesting."

"Yeah. And next year I might go out for football."

"Arnold, you will n—" Ginny couldn't say any more because Mitch had his hand over her mouth.

"That sounds interesting, too," Mitch said, keeping his hand over Ginny's mouth while she tried unsuccessfully to bite him.

Arnold laughed. "She doesn't want me to," he said, gazing at his struggling mother.

"Whatever gave you that idea?" Mitch said.

Ginny stopped fighting and Mitch removed his hand. "I won't go to a single game," she vowed, frowning up at Arnold.

"I might not even do it, Mom. But it sure is fun to see you get all riled up."

"Arnold, so help me—"

"Gotta go," Arnold said. "I'll be late."

"But Arnold," Ginny protested. "You're going to the movies tomorrow. Mitch and I never see you anymore."

"Aw, don't give me that," Arnold said, grinning down at her. "When I leave you guys can play lovey-dovey. Don't complain."

Ginny blushed. "Arnold!"

"Well, it's true," he said, his grin teasing her. "Disgusting, but true."

"Okay," Mitch said. "We'll concede that point, but what about Angela's parents? Don't they deserve some time alone, too?"

"Are you kidding? They've been married forever. If they didn't have kids around all the time, they'd be bored to death."

Mitch laughed, which caused Ginny's head to bob up and down. "I'll mention that to Stan next time I see him."

"And I bet he'll tell you it's true," Arnold maintained, heading out of the room. "So long, love-birds."

Ginny lay on the floor listening to Mitch's steady breathing and the sounds of Arnold getting his bike out of the garage. "I don't like it when he rides in the rain."

"I know, but he's done it lots of times before. Seattle kids have to learn to ride bikes in the rain. He'll be okay."

"I don't want him to play football."

"I know that, too. My guess is he won't. He loves the band too much, and he couldn't play at halftime if he joined football. He just likes to see you react."

Ginny sighed. "Which I do, right on cue." She was silent for a moment. "Do you think he feels shut out of our relationship?" she asked finally.

"No. I think he has the hots for Angela, and leaving us alone is a wonderful excuse to see her all the time."

"Don't say things like that," she said, pinching him in the ribs.

He caught her hand. "I thought you always wanted the truth, the whole truth, and nothing but the truth from me."

"I do, but you don't have to be so blunt. I'm not ready for my son to have 'the hots' for anyone."

"Are you ready for *me* to have the hots for someone?" he asked, bringing her hand up to stroke her palm against his cheek.

She smiled. "Only if it's someone I know."

"I think you know her." He slid his arm under her shoulders. Then with his wrestler's agility, he rolled over to brace himself above her before she realized what was happening. "I think you know her quite well," he said, his gray eyes warm as he gazed down at her.

She realized what he had in mind. "Mitch . . . here? On the rug?"

"Any objections?"

"None," she said, abandoning herself to his kiss. Within moments he'd erased any doubts from her mind. This was definitely the perfect use of the cherished living room rug.

® *Harlequin* ®

# JANELLE TAYLOR

## *Valley* of *Fire*

**HARLEQUIN IS PROUD TO PRESENT *VALLEY
OF FIRE* BY JANELLE TAYLOR—AUTHOR OF
TWENTY-TWO BOOKS, INCLUDING SIX *NEW
YORK TIMES* BESTSELLERS**

VALLEY OF FIRE—the warm and passionate story of
Kathy Alexander, a famous romance author, and
Steven Winngate, entrepreneur and owner of the
magazine that intended to expose the real Kathy
"Brandy" Alexander to her fans.

Don't miss VALLEY OF FIRE, available in May.

# FREE GIFT OFFER

To receive your free gift, send us the specified number of proofs-of-purchase from any specially marked Free Gift Offer Harlequin or Silhouette book with the Free Gift Certificate properly completed, plus a check or money order (do not send cash) to cover postage and handling payable to Harlequin/Silhouette Free Gift Promotion Offer. We will send you the specified gift.

## FREE GIFT CERTIFICATE

| ITEM | A. GOLD TONE EARRINGS | B. GOLD TONE BRACELET | C. GOLD TONE NECKLACE |
|---|---|---|---|
| # of proofs-of-purchase required | 3 | 6 | 9 |
| Postage and Handling | $1.75 | $2.25 | $2.75 |
| Check one | ☐ | ☐ | ☐ |

Name: _____

Address: _____

City: _____ State: _____ Zip Code: _____

Mail this certificate, specified number of proofs-of-purchase and a check or money order for postage and handling to: HARLEQUIN/SILHOUETTE FREE GIFT OFFER 1992, P.O. Box 9057, Buffalo, NY 14269-9057. Requests must be received by July 31, 1992.

PLUS—Every time you submit a completed certificate with the correct number of proofs-of-purchase, you are automatically entered in our MILLION DOLLAR SWEEPSTAKES! No purchase or obligation necessary to enter. See below for alternate means of entry and how to obtain complete sweepstakes rules.

### MILLION DOLLAR SWEEPSTAKES
#### NO PURCHASE OR OBLIGATION NECESSARY TO ENTER

To enter, hand-print (mechanical reproductions are not acceptable) your name and address on a 3" × 5" card and mail to Million Dollar Sweepstakes 6097, c/o either P.O. Box 9056, Buffalo, NY 14269-9056 or P.O. Box 621, Fort Erie, Ontario L2A 5X3. Limit: one entry per envelope. Entries must be sent via 1st-class mail. For eligibility, entries must be received no later than March 31, 1994. No liability is assumed for printing errors, lost, late or misdirected entries.

Sweepstakes is open to persons 18 years of age or older. All applicable laws and regulations apply. Sweepstakes offer void wherever prohibited by law. Prizewinners will be determined no later than May 1994. Chances of winning are determined by the number of entries distributed and received. For a copy of the Official Rules governing this sweepstakes offer, send a self-addressed, stamped envelope (WA residents need not affix return postage) to: Million Dollar Sweepstakes Rules, P.O. Box 4733, Blair, NE 68009.

HS1U

## ONE PROOF-OF-PURCHASE
To collect your fabulous FREE GIFT you must include the necessary FREE GIFT proofs-of-purchase with a properly completed offer certificate.

(See center insert for details)